THE MEDAL: BOOK

DANIEL McQUEEN—
pay the bitter price of being a prodigal son.
With his father's head resting in a hangman's
noose and his own rebellious heart true to the
woman he has grown to cherish, he must de-
cide whom he will betray.

KATE BUFKIN—Indomitable innkeeper and guardi-
an angel to her half-mad brother, she was a
match for any man. She saw something in
McQueen that made her love him—something
that McQueen himself was only beginning to
realize existed. But someone else had plans to
possess and vanquish her.

MAJOR JOSIAH MEEKS—The one-eyed widow
maker. A sadistic soldier of the Crown whose
ruthless plan, if successful, will crush the Pennsylvania and New Jersey patriots, and damn
Dan McQueen for all time as freedom's assassin.

SISTER HOPE-DEFERRED-MAKETH-THE-HEART-
SICK—One of the gentle Daughters of Phoebe,
a cheerful spinster whose piety was exceeded
only by her love of intrigue and passion for
liberty. Her barn held secrets that Major Meeks
would kill for.

COLONEL NATHANIEL WOODBINE—The gentleman soldier who made up in ambition what
he lacked in height. He hungered for the favors
of his business partner, Kate, and for a place in
history. And he was not a man whose desires
went long denied.

★ THE MEDAL ★
Book I

GUNS
OF
LIBERTY

Kerry Newcomb

BANTAM BOOKS
NEW YORK · TORONTO · LONDON · SYDNEY · AUCKLAND

GUNS OF LIBERTY
A Bantam Domain Book / February 1991

ISBN 0-553-28812-1

Published simultaneously in the United States and Canada

PRINTED IN THE UNITED STATES OF AMERICA

OPM   0 9 8 7 6 5 4 3 2 1

For Patty, Amy Rose, and P. J.

Prologue

April 29, 1775

"Eight.
"Nine.
"Ten!"
Daniel McQueen pivoted on his left foot. His right
arm came up, and when it was extended he reflexively
squeezed the trigger. The dueling pistol thundered in
his fist. Twenty paces away, Jacques Flambeau simultaneously turned and fired. Daniel flinched as a bullet
fanned the air inches from his cheek. The gunshots
were deafening within the confines of the abandoned
barn. A pair of owls roosting in the weather-rotted roof
beams fluttered upward through the remains of the
roof and lost themselves against the sunlit Canadian
sky.
Flambeau staggered backward as the .50-caliber
ball struck him in the side. The French Canadian
slammed against a stall gate, pulled himself erect, and
stumbled toward the Highlander.

Daniel lowered his pistol as a trail of acrid-smelling powder smoke curled from the barrel to dissipate in the still air. Molten golden beams of sunlight filtered through the cracks in the barn's battered walls and transformed motes of dust into spinning stars.

A man of thirty-four, Daniel McQueen had not only cultivated all the skills necessary for survival in the wilds, he also had an eye for pretty ladies, a thirst for strong drink, and a habit of finding trouble. This time trouble was a jealous French Canadian sea captain by the name of Jacques Flambeau. Daniel hadn't wanted this duel. But what had begun as an afternoon's dalliance with a pretty lass had become an ugly affair of honor between the captain and Daniel.

As echoes faded into distant thunder, Flambeau stumbled, faltered another couple of steps, and dropped his dueling pistol. The weapon thudded on the hard-packed earth. The dying man dragged his steps through straw and mud. His windburned features contorted in pain.

"*Mon Dieu*," Flambeau gasped. Blood trickled from the corner of his mouth. A crimson stain spread across the front of his mustard-colored, brocaded waistcoat. "Valerie...I am killed," the French Canadian managed to say. "Oh—to see once more...."

He groaned and sank to his knees, his eyes rolled back in his head, and he fell forward. The dead man hit hard enough to crack his nose. By then, however, of course, Flambeau was beyond pain.

Daniel glanced toward the other two men in the barn: Jacques Flambeau's older brothers. They had tried and failed to talk Jacques out of the confrontation. Justin and Sevier Flambeau were hardened types who'd made their fortunes as voyageurs and outfitters. They feared no man alive, least of all this dark-eyed Scotsman, no matter how strapping his build.

Daniel walked across to the man he had killed. He knelt and placed his big hand upon Flambeau's blood-soaked chest and sighed in sad resignation. "I wanted none of this," he said, loud enough for Justin and Sevier to hear.

"Then you should not have come to this barn, monsieur," Sevier, the eldest, replied. He hooked his thumbs in the broad leather belt circling his ample middle.

"And have your brother brand me a coward? Honor is the one possession a poor man clings to. It makes him the equal of any king." Daniel drew back and, with his hand moist and shiny with blood, started toward the entrance to the barn. Justin Flambeau, a round-faced, muscular man a few years younger than Daniel, moved to block the duelist's escape. Daniel did not slow his pace but continued through the barn until he and the voyageur stood a few feet apart. Daniel came from brawny stock, mountain folk who'd fought to hold their land and beliefs for hundreds of years.

"You are in my way," Daniel said. The voyageur's hand curled around the hilt of a long knife sheathed at his waist. Daniel noted the movement and tensed. It fell to Sevier to defuse the situation. The eldest Flambeau spoke up.

"Mon frére, we too know the meaning of honor, oui? This is not the time or the place."

Justin reluctantly stepped aside, permitting Daniel to pass unimpeded. Daniel emerged into the sun-drenched morning and found that his horse was where he had left it, the animal's reins tied to a red oak. Opposite the animal another three horses were tethered to a wagon wheel that had been buried up to the hub in the soft earth. A gig drawn by a single mare blocked the wheel-rutted road that led from the abandoned farm to the outskirts of Montreal, with its brick two-

and three-storied homes and shops that stood sun-washed and peaceful-looking along the majestic St. Lawrence River.

Valerie Rulonne sat within the gig, a carriage just large enough for two. Her face was powdered and slightly rouged, her hair immaculately coiffed, and she wore a gown of pale blue brocade appropriately laced and ruffled. Daniel would never forget the look of horror in her eyes as he walked across the overgrown farmyard where children might have once played or tended to their chores. There were no children now, only adults whose tragic escapades had bloodied the sunrise.

Valerie Rulonne was indeed surprised that Daniel had survived the duel, for Jacques Flambeau was noted as a crack shot and an expert hunter. Surprise quickly turned to black rage, and her lip curled back in a menacing and most unladylike snarl. She gave the lines a savage tug and tried to turn the gig back on the road toward town, but Daniel hurried over and caught the mare by the bridle to prevent the woman's escape.

"How dare you, monsieur! Unhand my horse this instant."

She grabbed for the whip at her side and lashed her former lover unmercifully on his shoulders and raised forearms. Daniel endured her blows in silence. He stepped closer to her and with a well-timed move wrested the whip from her grasp and threw it to the ground. Then, with his right hand still moist and crimson, he held her and smeared the blood of Jacques Flambeau across her powdered face. Valerie struggled to free herself from him. Daniel released his hold as she doubled over and retched, spewing her hastily eaten breakfast over her gown and her buttoned shoes.

"Miserable bastard."

Daniel ran his clean hand through his unruly red mane and windburned features and winced as the welts on his forearms rubbed against the tattered remnants of his shirtsleeve. He gingerly examined his flesh wounds. She'd peeled his arms and shoulders well enough. Now they each had something to remember the other by.

"His blood is on my hands and your heart, lass. Time will tell which is easier to wash clean," Daniel told her. He retrieved the whip and tossed it onto the floor of the gig as Valerie buried her face in her hands and sobbed out of anger, sorrow, and frustration. Daniel left her to her grief. He was anxious to quit this place before someone else attempted to peel his hide or put a bullet in him.

Sevier and Justin watched him from the remains of the doorway of the dilapidated structure. Clouds scudding across the face of the sun placed the brothers in shadow while Daniel remained in sunlight. They watched him without speaking, but their sullen, brooding faces betrayed their thoughts. Both men were loath to allow their brother's killer to simply ride away. And yet they were bound by a strict code of conduct to allow just that. However, once the Scotsman reached the city, he was fair game. They knew it and so did Daniel McQueen.

Mounting his bay gelding, he rounded the carriage and pointed his horse toward Montreal. He slapped his tricorn hat against the rump of his gelding and the animal broke into a brisk gallop, carrying its rider past the overgrown pasture, the remnants of a fire-gutted farmhouse, and on into the city.

Time had little meaning in Lower Montreal: The traffic of hard men and loose women among the bawdy houses and taverns and brothels rarely let up, day or night. Ships rode at anchor alongside sturdy piers.

Wagonloads of pelts were drawn up to overflowing warehouses. Voyageurs invaded these darkened streets to blow off steam in wanton celebration. Rivermen and seafarers called Lower Montreal their home for as long as they lingered in port and coins jingled in their pockets. It was a place of few questions: A man was whomever he claimed to be and from wherever he chose to be. Lower Montreal was a good place to hide. Everyone was passing through and bound for hard times, adventure, perhaps even riches in the wild Americas.

Daniel Christopher McQueen struggled to sleep in his room above the Cock's Crow Tavern. He had drunk himself into a stupor and still saw Jacques Flambeau's face—so totally surprised when confronted with his own mortality. Daniel was still dressed in the same boots, black breeches, and torn linsey-woolsey white shirt he'd worn at the barn. He sat in bed with his long legs outstretched upon the covers and a couple of down pillows tucked behind him. He stared sullenly at the empty bottle at the foot of the bed, blaming it for his lack of sleep. He hadn't even been able to work up a decent case of dizziness to blot out the face of the man he had killed.

"The damn fool," Daniel muttered to the silent room. "I aimed for his shoulder. Not my fault he stepped in front of my bullet." His voice was filled with suppressed anger.

This excursion into Canada had proved disastrous. Henchmen from the Hudson Bay Company had robbed his traps, destroyed his equipment, and been his ruin. Now this damn duel.... At least his food and lodgings were paid for here at the Cock's Crow. But he had no illusions. The generosity of the man he was waiting for always carried a high price.

Still, Daniel had no place else in the city to go,

and he was curious. So, for now, the Cock's Crow would do. The bedroom's furnishings were austere, consisting of a bed, an end table built of maple, and a single high-backed chair near the door. A white china pitcher and a basin, both chipped, had been left on the end table. Music played on fife and concertina drifted up through the floorboards along with the rowdy noises of the customers below.

Daniel listened to the gravelly voices raised in a voyageur's song but found no joy in the revelry. He had no desire to join them, not tonight with a man's death and the high cost of honor weighing upon his conscience.

The rasp of a sliding wooden latch alerted him. *The devil is at the door*, he mused grimly, and lifted a brace of pistols from the end table. These were balanced weapons, of plain, simple Pennsylvanian construction, rifled and deadly accurate despite their shortened barrels. He called them his "Quakers" because the guns could be counted on to keep the peace, turning his enemies into "friends."

The oaken door creaked on its iron hinges and swung back to reveal a tall, spare figure feebly outlined against the dimly lit hall. He was draped in a deep brown cloak that swept to the floor, and his features were shadowed by a flat-brimmed hat that he tilted back from his forehead as he entered the room. He was not a handsome man: His features were sharply drawn and dominated by a beakish nose. A patch covered his left eye. His cheeks were sunken, his neck scrawny. The man's long arms ended in broad bony hands.

Daniel knew him in an instant, for their paths had crossed and recrossed since the French and Indian War.

"Major Josiah Meeks." Daniel kept his pistols trained on the British officer, a fact that did not escape Meeks's attention. "You were just a powder flash away from losing your other eye."

"Still on edge," Meeks purred. "Primed and ready to explode. I like that, yes. I have always liked you, Danny McQueen."

"Sure you have. And pigs have wings," Daniel said. Perhaps they shared a mutual respect for one another's fighting ability, but affection—hardly.

"Now you wound me." Meeks closed the door and dragged the high-backed chair over toward the bed. "Here I have paid your room and board for these many days. Well, no matter, at last I have arrived. And you did me the kindness of waiting. It has been a long time since Braddock's Road. You were but a lad of thirteen then—but man enough, it is true. And then, there was that trouble with Ottawa and Pontiac. We are indeed old comrades in arms." Meeks leaned forward and placed long fingers on his knobby knees. The Englishman, at forty, might look in need of a good meal, but Daniel had fought side by side with the man and knew there was uncommon strength in his hungry frame.

"I heard you had returned to London," Daniel said.

"I never remain in one place for long. I follow the sound of battle. The smell of blood and powder smoke lured me as surely as the siren's song did Ulysses. What do you follow, my friend?" Meeks removed a clay pipe from his pocket, filled it, and lit the contents of the bowl with the candle on the end table.

"I am not your friend." Daniel lowered the pistols to the bed and kept them within easy reach on the quilt.

"Ah, the bitterness of the prodigal son," the major said dryly. "You abandoned your father, but not the guilt, dear fellow. You have my sympathy."

Daniel's dark gray eyes flashed with anger. The

major was treading precarious ground now. Daniel's father, Brian Farley McQueen, had fled to the colonies after the defeat of the Jacobite uprising in Scotland. Of noble birth in his native land, Brian McQueen was reduced to a humble station in life. Relying on his talent with iron and forge, he opened a blacksmith shop on the outskirts of Boston. There Brian McQueen made a new life for himself. There he became a widower, losing his faithful wife to pneumonia, and there he raised his son, Daniel, and taught him to master the forge and the molten eye of fired metal. But Daniel was a headstrong lad born with a wanderlust. Twice he'd run away, the last time eleven years ago.

That was on the night of their quarrel, when Daniel, bitter over a lost love, had left to seek his fortune in the wild interior of the continent. After more than a decade of fighting, trapping, and living by his wits, those old arguments and resentments seemed petty now. Deep within, he yearned to see his father once again. Yet pride, and his own failure and a sense of being beyond his father's forgiveness, had prevented his return to Massachusetts.

"Damn it, Major. The hell with your sympathy. Why did you send for me? And leave my father out of it." Daniel climbed off the bed and stood, swaying slightly, in the middle of the floor.

"If only I could," Meeks said.

"What does that mean? Enough of your game, I say."

"Where do your loyalties lie, Danny boy—with the crown or with these treasonous rebels?"

"With myself." Daniel glowered. "My father—"

"Rots aboard a prison ship in Boston Harbor. He had turned his forge into an armory for rebels and was arrested only a couple of days before the incident at Lexington."

Meeks accurately read the puzzled expression on Daniel's face and as succinctly as possible gave an account of the skirmishes at Lexington and Concord only ten days past. Daniel listened, incredulous that the patriots, as they called themselves, had taken up arms against British troops. He felt a stirring of pride in his heart, but that was quickly supplanted by concern for his father. Major Josiah Meeks wouldn't have gone to the trouble of tracking him down just to give him news of his father.

"What of my father?"

"Brian Farley McQueen will hang for his seditious activities," Meeks replied with a smile. "Unless, of course, he is pardoned for his misdeeds. You, my capable young friend, can win that pardon for him. And a pouch of gold for yourself."

"How?" Daniel asked, his eyes narrowing.

"Come with me." The major headed for the door. He didn't bother to wait and see if Daniel would follow. The officer knew his man. Daniel hastily donned his greatcoat and pocketed his pistols. He had the distinct impression he was heading into more trouble than he had ever known.

Daniel and the British major darted from the doorway of the Cock's Crow and out into the settling mist. A few quick steps across the lantern-lit alley and they reached the stable that serviced the boarders at the tavern. They waited in the doorway of the stable to allow their eyes to adjust to the gloomy interior. The hairs rose on the back of Daniel's neck and his hand dropped to his coat pocket and closed around his gun.

"It will be dawn in a few hours. We can be well on our way by then," Meeks said.

"We haven't finished talking." Daniel glanced aside.

He stiffened, sensing a movement in the hidden reaches of the nearest stall.

"And you won't," a third party interjected. A person, unseen, spoke from the stall to the left of the doorway. Daniel recognized the voice in an instant. It could only belong to Justin Flambeau.

Movement up ahead! Then another voice....

"You in the cloak, this is none of your business. Leave us." Sevier Flambeau materialized out of the shadowy interior of the stable and stepped into the pallid glare seeping through the open doorway. He blocked their path and brandished a dueling pistol that wavered from Daniel to the major.

"I am an officer in service to His Majesty—" Meeks began.

"Go now and live!" Sevier interrupted, shifting his stance.

Meeks turned toward Daniel. "I don't suppose you can reimburse me for your tavern bill."

"Not a shilling."

"Then you must needs pay me in service." Meeks sighed. "Sorry, lads, you cannot have him. Not yet, anyway."

"You heard the major," Daniel said. "Best you stand aside and let us see to our horses."

The voyageur spat in the dirt at his feet and squared his bulky shoulders. He held his pistol level. His face, like his brother Justin's, was round, and florid from too much drink. He was the eldest and knew he should have had more sense. Then again, his hands were still dirty from his brother's freshly dug grave.

"Stand aside, is it, mon ami? Then make me."

"As you say," Daniel replied. There was a muffled explosion and fire spewed from his coat. A fraction of a second later the toe of Sevier's right boot exploded in bits of leather and blood. Sevier howled and fired.

Daniel was already in motion. He dropped and hurled himself into the shadow patch to his left and crashed into Justin as the other voyageur lunged forward with his knife. Daniel knocked Justin off his feet and scrambled atop the voyageur. He caught the man's wrist, twisted until Justin dropped his knife. Then Daniel dragged him to his feet and flung the voyageur against the stable wall. Justin gasped for breath and charged forward.

It was Josiah Meeks who halted the voyageur in his tracks. The major stepped out of the shadows, his cloak billowing like the wings of a great bat as he swung an arm's length of timber. The wood cracked in half across Justin's skull and dropped him in his tracks.

Sevier moaned and cursed and rolled in the darkened aisle; he cradled his bloodied foot that was now absent a few toes. "I will kill you. One day, I swear—"

Daniel swung a well-placed kick and rendered the man unconscious.

"Bravo," the British major said with a callous laugh. "A well-placed blow often speaks more eloquently than a timely retort."

Daniel was anxious to quit this city before he met any more of Sevier Flambeau's relatives. He hurriedly saddled his horse and led the animal out of its stall. The bay shied and was difficult to handle, made skittish by the fight and the smell of blood.

Justin groaned. Sevier began to mumble something, though neither man opened his eyes. That suited Daniel just fine. He ruefully examined his singed, blackened pocket and patted it once again to make sure all the embers were extinguished. Then he walked his horse out into the alley. It was a hell of a time to leave, so misty and dark and chillingly damp. Why was Meeks in so much of a hurry? He mounted, and a moment later the British major emerged from the stable and swung astride his own gray steed.

Daniel walked his bay a few steps forward to corner Josiah Meeks against the wall of the stable.

"What is this?" Meeks asked, frowning.

"An answer to my question, Englishman. How do I save my father from the hangman's noose?"

"Ah. Simple. A life for a life. You must kill a man."

"Who?"

Meeks smiled, but there was little humor in his single, baleful eye. "George Washington."

Chapter One

May 10, 1775

"Stand and deliver, or die in your tracks!" the tallest of the three highwaymen exclaimed. The black hood he wore muffled his voice; the black cloak concealed his long-limbed frame. Two more hooded figures, one to either side, held their saddle pistols at the ready.

"It would be a shame to splatter that pretty face and yellow hair o'yours all over the hickories," a small, thickset thief added.

The third highwayman, a slim, red-eyed ruffian, sat silent, allowing his two companions to speak while his unwavering gaze swept the young woman's pretty form from her slender white ankles at the hem of her cotton dress to her rounded hips and bosom. Curls the color of autumn meadows, yellow-gold in the waning of the year, poked out from beneath the tricorn hat she wore. Kate Bufkin was as fetching as moonlight on the Delaware River.

Young Kate endured the rascal's lascivious appraisal and refused to be frightened into submission, though she was alone, twenty-two miles out from Philadelphia along the Trenton Road. Five miles ahead lay home and hearth, the safety of the inn she ran with her brother. It was noon and she'd been traveling since sunup, driving her four-wheeled wagon along the heavily rutted road. She was tired and thirsty. Her back ached; her homespun cotton dress was no longer blue but gritty with dust. And the eight large crates of Irish Brown Reds in the wagon had kept up a continuous complaint, squawking and flapping their wings every time the wagon jolted.

In short, Miss Kate Bufkin was in no mood to be trifled with—especially by the likes of these highwaymen.

"You'll be stepping off that chicken wagon, there's a good miss." The small, thickset man brought himself around to the side of the wagon.

The third man broke his silence. He did not intend to share the favors of such a comely tavern wench with anyone. "Back off, Chaney," he warned, closing in on the other side, leaving only their leader to obstruct her passage.

Kate gathered the lines in her left hand, caught up the whip in her right. With a flick of her wrist she laid open Chaney's shoulder, then lashed out at the hooded man to her right and caught him along the neck.

He yelped and fired his gun. The sudden explosion startled the team. The mares bolted forward as the leader of the three highwaymen, his black cloak flapping, made a mad dash out of harm's way. He raised his pistol and fired. Kate flinched, sucked in a lungful of powder smoke, and wondered how the man could have missed.

She did not intend to give him another chance. She cracked her whip across the rumps of her mares and urged them to even greater effort. In a matter of seconds she had raced past the thieves. The wagon lurched to one side, clipped a tree trunk someone had only partly dragged out of the road. The chickens renewed their protests at such ill treatment.

The highwaymen brought their horses under control and gave chase. Another pistol shot sounded as Kate glanced over her shoulder and saw the highwaymen a couple of hundred feet back. They'd easily catch her; she was pulling too great a load. She gave a momentary thought to lightening the wagon. But there was no time. Besides, she was loath to part with any of her property without a fight.

Kate reached under the bench seat and brought the blunderbuss secreted there up beside her on the bench seat.

The Trenton Road followed the Delaware River as it wound through the hills. Kate could just glimpse the sun-dappled water. The land was heavily forested, garbed in the green foliage of spring. She sped past maple and hickory, white oak and ash, whose leafy limbs stretched above the road to form a ceiling of intersecting branches. The wagon careened through a patchwork of sunlight and shadow as it approached the covered bridge across Half Mile Creek. It was downhill here, and the wagon made good speed. But it was small comfort to Kate. The incline beyond the bridge might prove her undoing; it would surely dissipate her lead. Still, Kate vowed that blood would flow before such brigands laid a hand on her.

Several white-tailed deer dashed from the forest's edge and cleared the road as the wagon rushed by. Two boys near the covered bridge paused to lean upon their fishing poles and watch the oncoming wagon as it sped downhill toward them. Kate could not risk the lives of innocents in making her stand at the creek.

Her next choice became Indian Head Rock at the top of the next hill. Here the road was bordered by cherry trees to one side and on the other a boulder twice as large as the wagon. The massive gray stone resembled the profile of an Indian, silently guarding the road.

At the rock, then, she would make her stand. Such a course was well clear of the youngsters at the bridge. Even now the lads began to wave until the guns of the highwaymen barked their warning of death in the afternoon. The youths dropped their rods and pails and dove for the creek bed at the sound of the guns. In their haste they left a line of freshly caught perch to die along the road.

The wagon rumbled onto the bridge; the iron-rimmed wheels made a tremendous clatter as they rolled over the weathered planks. The interior of the covered bridge offered a momentary respite from the sun. It might have been nice to pause awhile and enjoy the moment had there not been a trio of armed men trying to kill her.

The horses started to slacken their pace, but Kate cracked her whip and stung the rumps of her frightened team.

As the wagon cleared the bridge Kate spied movement out of the corner of her eye. She glanced up and gasped to see a shadow shape detach from the edge of the roof. A rawboned, red-haired man in black trousers and boots, a linsey-woolsey shirt, and buckskin jacket came crashing down on the wagon bed.

Daniel McQueen missed the bench seat and toppled onto the chicken cages. He crushed one cage and nearly ruined two others. Kate switched the lines to one hand and grabbed for the blunderbuss beside her on the seat. Daniel saw her swing the barrel toward him and kicked out as she squeezed the trigger. The weapon peppered the air with its load of round shot and nails.

"By my oath!" Daniel shouted through a flurry of red feathers. "I'm here to help you, lass."

Kate, already off balance, dropped the gun and lost her hold on the lines as the wheels struck another rut and jolted her off the seat. She landed atop her unexpected passenger. Cages cracked beneath them. Chickens scratched and pecked their way to freedom and beat their wings against the air. They rose in an ungainly semblance of flight and landed in the bed of the careening freight wagon.

Daniel rolled off the crates and landed against a keg of ale and another of rum. He had to brush Kate's skirt from his face and in the process caught a momentary peek at her creamy white ankles and shapely calves before she righted herself into a more dignified position.

Daniel gallantly excused himself and scrambled over the remaining chickens in an effort to catch the lines. He missed by inches. One of the roosters stabbed its beak through the bars of the cage and nipped his belly as Daniel clambered toward the bench seat. He yelped and dove out of one harm's way into another. The mares were racing full out and making good progress up the hill despite the wagon's heavy load. But the lines were dragging along the ground beneath the singletree.

A man would have to be crazy to try for them.

Daniel scrambled over the siding, managed to balance on the crossbar, and with one hand on the wagon seat lowered himself to within reach of the lines. He'd have to take care to avoid the hooves of the mare closest to him. For a moment he thought he might lose his purchase.

Chips of rock and muddy debris spattered his

arms and stung his cheeks like a swarm of hornets. He timed his effort and tried for the lines, missed, and almost lost his forearm to a flashing hoof. He tried again and caught the lines on the fly and leaped back up onto the seat, kicked the brake, and hauled back with all his might just as the wagon reached the top of the rise near Indian Head Rock. The wheels skidded in the dirt and the wagon shuddered and angled sideways.

Kate had only just regained her balance when the horses dug in their heels. She flew forward, and only by the grace of God and the strength of Daniel's outstretched arm did she avoid a nasty tumble onto the skittish mares.

"What are you trying to do?" she exclaimed, straightening upright and trying to salvage a scrap of her dignity.

"To save your life," Daniel replied.

"You could have fooled me, sir!"

The Scotsman ignored her insult and hopped down to the road, drawing his pistols from his waistband. He walked alongside the wagon.

"Hold the team," he said.

"Why?"

"They might bolt again. You've raised them tenderhearted."

Kate, speechless at such effrontery, simply stared. Before she could think of a suitable reply, the man was past her and standing at the rear of the wagon. Down below, the highwaymen emerged from the shadowy interior of the covered bridge and climbed the rise.

Daniel leveled the pistol in his right hand and fired. Kate shielded her eyes and watched with amazement as two of the brigands pitched from horseback— *two with one shot!*

The redheaded stranger turned toward her, smiled wanly, and shrugged. "I use a heavy load," he explained.

The last of the highwaymen, the tall, thin one who had ordered her to stand, waited by his fallen companions. It was obvious he wanted no part of a solitary attack. Nor was the man on the hill willing to come under the highwayman's gun. It was a standoff.

Daniel ambled back to the wagon and climbed up alongside the young woman. He tucked the "Quakers" away and gestured toward the road ahead.

"He'll not be bothering us again," he said. Kate continued to stare at him. "Well, surely you'll not refuse hospitality to such an orphan soul as myself, especially after all I have done."

"Hospitality, is it? After you cost me two crates of chickens with your clumsiness?" She drew herself up as if to continue her caustic response. Then, with mercurial swiftness, her anger dissipated. The icy hardness in her blue eyes melted, and she flicked the lines and started the mares forward. She liked boldness in a man, and this one seemed as bold as they came.

"Well, my 'homeless' pup, do you have a name? For I am Kate Bufkin, and I'll not be riding with a stranger."

Daniel told her his name—the truth—and gave a shallow account of how he came to be along the Trenton Road—a lie. But there was music in his voice and laughter in his eyes, and though Kate believed little of his self-account, oddly, she didn't care. The recent danger was quickly left behind and as quickly forgotten as the miles rolled effortlessly past.

"You impossibly stupid oafs," Major Josiah Meeks exclaimed from astride his gray stallion. He removed his hood and shrugged the cape back off his shoulders as his single eye bore into the men sprawled in the dust of the Trenton Road.

"I was supposed to die first," portly William Chaney said with his face in the dirt. Blood caked where the whip bit his shoulder.

"Black liar," the slender one said, groaning and knuckling the grit from his bloodshot eyes. His neck burned like fire. Kate's whip had left a scarlet welt below his jaw, a gift of pain for him to remember her by—and Black Tolbert most certainly would. He was a thin-skinned, vengeful young man, capable of bearing a grudge for a lifetime if that was how long it took to see things righted to his satisfaction.

"You've got no call to say that," Chaney protested. "We agreed. I was to die first. You were supposed to wait until McQueen's second shot. Wasn't that so, Major Meeks?"

"Get out of the dirt!" Meeks said, his gaunt features livid with anger. "They're gone." He couldn't remember who was supposed to "die" first, nor did he care.

For a tuppence he would have ridden off and left both of his associates where they lay. But Will Chaney, though dumb as a plow, was ruthless in a fight, and Black Tolbert, the whoremonger, was a keen and deadly marksman with rifle or pistol.

Meeks shaded his eye and studied the settling dust up by Indian Head Rock. Well—no matter, he decided. Despite its clumsy beginnings, his plan had achieved a successful outcome. Daniel McQueen was on his way to the Hound and Hare Inn.

Chapter Two

The Hound and Hare Inn was set back about fifty feet off the Trenton Road and in the middle of a semicircular cobblestone drive that allowed a carriage or horseman easy passage back onto the tree-lined thoroughfare.

The inn itself was built of white oak planks and held together with nails forged from melted-down horseshoes. It stood two stories, with eight large windows across the front and back and four to either end. The structure ran ninety-five feet by twenty and offered four comfortable rooms upstairs for guests. Kate Bufkin and her brother, Loyal, each had a small bedroom off the tavern and winter kitchen that dominated the ground floor.

Daniel McQueen noted that part of the second story and the gable roof showed fire damage; the timbers were broken and some of the upstairs windows were blackened by fire. Kate noticed how he studied the place.

"By rights it should have burnt to the ground,"

she said. "But a winter storm came up. It was a veritable deluge. I've never seen the like. Loyal, my brother, said it was a miracle. It put out the fire, though not until Mama collapsed with a lungful of smoke. She never recovered. Pneumonia took her, the last week in February."

"I'm sorry," Daniel said, and meant it. He had lost a parent and was on the verge of losing another if he couldn't figure some way out of his predicament.

The building needed work; so much the better. He turned his attention to the courtyard in front of the inn. It was surrounded by a low wall built of native stone, and several tables had been set out in the sunlight. A massive keg was turned on its side and balanced on the wall. He caught the faint but distinct aroma of hard cider. A number of apple trees shaded the courtyard and dotted the grounds surrounding the inn, which faced in an easterly direction.

A couple of horses were tied to one of the rings set in the courtyard wall, and two men were seated at one of the tables. A pewter pitcher and two mugs stood upon the tabletop between them. Kate tensed on seeing the pair.

A third man, who bore some resemblance to Kate, waved as she drove the freight wagon into the drive and swung past the courtyard and around the north side of the inn, where a barn had been erected back in the trees.

"We can unload through the back door," Kate said.

"We?" Daniel's eyebrows arched.

"If you're going to stay awhile, you'll have to earn your keep."

"Now, lass, I never said I was staying."

"You will," Kate replied, eyes twinkling. "You told me on the way here you were in hopes of finding employment. Maybe we can use you. Besides, you've yet to taste one of my apple pies."

This is turning out to be easier than I had hoped, Daniel thought as he rounded the wagon to help Kate. She climbed down without his assistance. She was a headstrong lass. But why was she in a hurry to secure the services of a man she hardly knew? Daniel began to have misgivings about all this. He had a feeling he had stepped into trouble. A few moments later, and he knew it for a fact.

A big, strapping, corn-fed young man of nineteen rounded the corner of the inn. He stood a head taller than Daniel and looked to carry an extra thirty pounds, much of it on his heavily muscled chest and shoulders. His brown hair was already thinning from his broad expanse of forehead, where the skin was sunburned and peeling. His arms swung loosely at his side. He wore nut brown pants tucked into his black boots and a coarsely woven cotton shirt and brown coat. His tricorn hat was faded and worn from sunlight and rain.

"Afternoon, Miss Kate, I've been waiting for you."

"And draining my stock of hard cider or I miss my guess, Henk Schraner. So what brings you from farm and field?"

"Father's out front with poor Loyal," Henk said. "My brothers are back. They came in last night from their yondering. Now they can help with the farm and I can help you, like I said...." As Henk spoke he eyed the rough-looking newcomer who had accompanied Kate Bufkin on the wagon. Henk made no attempt to hide his jealousy.

"There's many a robber on the road these days," he added.

"Aye, and here's one who did for me when I was

accosted at Indian Rock by three highwaymen. Killed two of the brigands, he did."

"Oh?" Henk's eyes widened, yet still he was suspicious. He resented this stranger all the more. "Then I'll offer you my hand," the farmer's son said. He outstretched a work-hardened hand.

Daniel had seen country hams smaller than the palm outstretched to him. He clasped Henk's hand. Instantly the fingers tightened in a bone-crushing grip. Henk smiled. Daniel smiled. Their knuckles turned red, then white with loss of blood. Daniel might have had to yield, for the youth possessed uncommon strength. It was Kate, though, who unwittingly ended the contest.

"I've hired Daniel McQueen to help Loyal and me repair the upstairs rooms."

"What?" Henk turned to her, momentarily losing his concentration.

Daniel jerked his hand free and began flexing the abused appendage. At the same time he, too, swung around to face Kate Bufkin. By heaven, this lass offered one surprise after another. A hireling now, and in a pretty girl's employ. Daniel would have been flattered; however, he had the distinct impression he was being used to block Henk's ardent attempt to remain at the inn. The hulking youth was obviously smitten.

Henk's brows furrowed into a frown that seemed to crease his forehead all the way up to his receding scalp line. "Hired?" he repeated the word as if mulling over its true meaning. Then he nodded, accepting what he had heard. Looking at Daniel, he said, "How long do you plan on staying?" Suppressed rage made the words seem leaden and flat as he spoke them.

"As long as it takes," Daniel replied, refusing to be cowed or bullied into abandoning his newly gained position of Hound and Hare's jack-of-all-trades. Daniel was ashamed of his duplicity, but he had to remember that, at least for now, there seemed no other way to save his own father's life.

"'As long as it takes,' say you. We'll see." Henk spun on his mud-caked heels and walked around the house. A round-bellied, balding man in his mid-forties appeared at the corner of the tavern. He waved to Kate, then stepped aside as Henk barreled past him. The older man seemed perplexed and hurried after the younger man, who lost no time in mounting his horse and galloping off down the Trenton Road.

"Papa Schraner. . . . Perhaps he will talk sense and reason to his son."

"I warrant he'll need to be a foot taller and a hundred pounds heavier," Daniel observed dryly. "And speaking of talking sense, you—" His gray eyes narrowed. Kate would hear none of his protest. She nudged a precipitously balanced barrel of nails. The load toppled from the wagon into Daniel's hastily outstretched arms.

Kate Bufkin had put him to work.

Chapter Three

"Let us pray," Loyal Bufkin began. He was seated at one end of a long board table crowded with food. There was a platter of round bread, another of cheese, and a wooden tray of roasted chickens—those that had been injured in the melee earlier in the day. The chickens were bordered on one side by a platter of boiled potatoes and on the other by a fire-blackened, deep pan of apple pan dowdy sweetened with molasses, its juices bubbling up through the broken crust.

"Lord, we ask this blessing upon our home and take this food to the nourishment of our bodies. We give Thee thanks and praise...." Loyal glanced up, his gaze darting from Daniel on his left to Kate on his right. "What was that?"

Loyal was a man of medium height. He was fair-skinned like his sister. His once attractive features were marred by a flattened nose and flared nostrils. When he spoke, his voice carried the dry, nasal huskiness of a man given to breathing through his mouth. He stood and placed his fists on the oaken table and stared off across the empty tavern as if he were hearing war drums emanating from behind the walnut bar, where the inn's supply of libations were neatly arranged in bottle, keg and jug.

The inn's only paying residents were a joiner and a parson, and both of them had retired upstairs to the only two serviceable rooms. The tavern itself had six long tables and benches and a number of high-backed chairs arranged about the fireplace. The walls were decorated with a series of paintings depicting incidents from the Old Testament: David and Goliath, Daniel in the lion's den, and Solomon rendering judgment. The whale-oil lanterns burning directly overhead illuminated the immediate area. The rest of the room was awash in dancing shadows.

Daniel lowered his pewter mug of Dutch beer and looked over at Kate. He had worked alongside Loyal all afternoon. The man had hardly spoken, offering only a friendly greeting and a comment about the weather, that it had been a cool spring but he was expecting a warm summer. Yet there was a haunted cast to the man's features; though he was roughly the same age as Daniel, he moved like a much older man. His gestures were deliberate and measured, as if requiring a momentary rumination before committing himself to action. Daniel had known such men before, veterans of battle who carried the horror inside. Such men often sought the solitude of the howling wilderness or lived among their own kind yet isolated, eventually going mad.

"I heard nothing," Daniel told him.

"Have you no ears?" Loyal stood, knocking the chair over. He circled the table and hurried to one of the shuttered windows in the front of the tavern. He peered through a firing port and studied the moonlit courtyard.

"Come to dinner, brother Loyal." Kate's soft voice reached across the empty room.

Loyal glanced around at his sister. Her gentle, reasoning tone cut through the heart of his panic and brought him back to reality. His vision cleared; his bunched and worried features relaxed. He placed a hand upon the strong, solid walls alongside him and, just to be sure, cocked an eye toward a water barrel he kept filled to the brim to guard against the flaming arrows of an Indian attack should one occur, a remote possibility at best. This was settled, civilized country now, and the dangers here originated among white men, not red.

"We used to live in the north country, near Fort Detroit," Kate recounted. "During the Ottawa uprising, our farm was burned. My father and Loyal were captured by Chief Pontiac. Loyal saw my father tortured to death. Then the Ottawa stripped my brother naked and set him free. They intended to hunt him for amusement. But he escaped them and hid until the rebellion was crushed. I was only five, but I still remember the way he looked when he stumbled into Fort Detroit, more dead than alive."

Kate's voice drifted off as Loyal straightened his chair and took his place at the head of the table.

"A fine meal, sister," Loyal commented. "I'm in your debt, McQueen. If it weren't for the presence of an unattached male visitor I'd be slopping hard bread and porridge."

Kate blushed. "How you talk so."

"It's true." After good-naturedly defending his statement, Loyal threw back his head and laughed heartily. Only when he had filled his plate did he grow serious. "So Kate has taken you on, eh? What talents have you—can you work with wood?"

"I'm no stranger to it. And smithing was the trade

of my father." Daniel paused. The way he had said it made it sound as if his father were dead. That made him sick at heart and brought to the fore just why he had come to the Hound and Hare and why he must continue to stay until Meeks said differently.

"Is your father deceased?" Kate asked.

"I hear he's in a poor way," Daniel said.

"Then shouldn't you attend him?"

"I can help him more right where I am." Daniel noted the look of confusion on the girl's face. "What I mean is—my father has...well, we quarreled. And I have not seen him for a long time."

"That seems hardly reason enough."

"Sister!" Loyal interrupted. "It is Mr. McQueen's affair and none of ours. Pass the butter, please."

Kate fumed in silence. She forced herself to eat, though it was in her nature to belabor a matter. Her mother had once claimed young Kate Bufkin would argue with a fencepost.

She changed her attitude and the subject and tried a different tactic. "You're right. Anyway, if Mr. McQueen leaves I'd have to contend with Henk Schraner all over again."

The fare was as good as Daniel had ever eaten, and he paid Kate Bufkin that very compliment. She might be brash and headstrong, but he liked that in a woman. If he had stumbled onto the Hound and Hare Inn all on his lonesome, he would have counted himself a fortunate man and made the most of the situation. But he was here under pretense, a trickster who had stolen his way in among good people. Such thoughts as these dampened the pleasure to be found in the presence of the comely lass he had "rescued."

The barn was dark and smelled of rotting straw, of leather, and of horses from their stalls at the rear of the structure. Daniel had mounded hay in a stall close to the front door. The barn also housed a forge where the north wall had been extended to contain it. A smaller set of doors opened onto the smithy. Daniel noted that the bellows and furnace were well constructed and adequate to handle such repairs as the inn required.

Brian McQueen's smithy was twice as large as this shop. *Aye, Father would have called this small forge a toy,* Daniel thought. And what would he call his son? Assassin? Traitor? Certainly not a savior, even though the irascible old Highlander would be spared a jig at the end of a British rope due to his son's actions. Brian McQueen wouldn't see it that way, and he'd say as much. A man either did wrong or he did right, but *never just the best one could do at the moment.* There were no shades of gray on his father's palette. The old Scotsman's intractability had erected a wall between them. Yet Daniel loved the man, despite the years and the distance. He would do what he must to save him.

Straw crackled underfoot. Daniel tensed and dropped his hand to one of the "Quakers" at his side. A woman's silhouette appeared in the barn door, backlit by a moon that floated like a pearl in an obsidian sea. Kate Bufkin held up a lantern, its flame turned too low to dispel the shadows. She raised the wick, and the fire within the glass flue blossomed. Daniel's red mane shown between the rails of the stall to her right. The night air carried a chill, and she had wrapped herself in a shawl. The hem of her linsey-woolsey nightshirt fluttered a few inches above the earth. The gusting breeze felt good on her calves.

She stood over him, a folded woolen blanket in hand.

"The nights are cool still."

"I am in your debt, Kate." He stood and spread the blanket over the straw he had mounded for a bed.

"Maybe I wanted to see if you're still here. You might have slipped away and taken my mares."

"Is that what you thought?"

"Maybe." Her lips were upturned in a teasing smile. "I will tell you something, Daniel. My mother was a dutiful widow...for a while. And afterward when we moved to New York and she took a position as a nanny and teacher..." Kate's story trailed off as she realized how much she was revealing to this newcomer. Yet she felt she could trust him. "My mother was not a patient person," the young woman said, lowering her voice. "Neither am I."

Kate started back to the inn. Daniel watched her go, wondering what she had meant. It was too much puzzlement for one night. He stretched out, settled back in the straw, and went to sleep.

It was a familiar dream recalling the past. The years drifted away and Daniel was once again a ten-year-old boy riding his father's broad shoulders as Brian Farley McQueen strolled along the edge of the fairgrounds following a crowd of onlookers toward the finish line of the race. To young Daniel peering over the adults, it seemed most of the townspeople had the same idea. The riders had left half an hour ago, racing toward Boston proper three miles beyond the first low hills. A column of dust in the distance signaled the participating riders were on their way back. Six of the fastest horses in Massachusetts were competing for a fine new carriage that Brian McQueen had been commissioned to build. The race was the highlight of the fair. Young Daniel could feel the tension in the air, and as the horsemen came into view, the boy began to kick his heels against his father's shoulders.

"Easy, lad. I'm no racehorse," Brian said, wincing with every blow. Daniel clutched his father's hair and pointed.

"I see them, Father! The black is in the lead, just like you said she'd be."

"Of course." Brian McQueen grinned. He tried to find a suitable spot for himself among the crowd. Being a man of compact build, he craned his bull neck and raised up on his toes to peer past the shoulders of the men and women blocking his path. Suddenly, the crowd shifted. He saw a gap, made his move, and wormed his way to the fore. He lifted Daniel off his shoulders so as not to anger the crowd behind him.

Daniel cheered for the black mare that had held the lead since the start of the race. The sleek, swift animal was a frequent guest in the stable where Brian McQueen kept his blacksmith shop. Squire Trevane often boarded the animal at the smithy. Trevane was a well-to-do landowner whose estate holdings had been purchased with the profits from his shipping business in Boston.

Trevane knew horses, and the black mare was as fine a specimen of horseflesh as Brian or his son had ever seen. Young Daniel had grown to consider the black mare as much his as the squire's, so he cheered and waved the horse on as if he were its rightful owner.

Even in his dream, Daniel could smell the sweat and the dust and feel the press of the adults around him as the crowd became more animated and surged closer to the finish line. Townsmen and farmers shouted till they were hoarse and pummeled the air with their fists. The ground trembled underfoot. The horses loomed large, their manes flowing and hooves churning the dirt.

"Yes," Daniel shouted. "C'mon, Lady Jane. C'mon." His voice was drowned out by the din of adults. He didn't care. He was certain Lady Jane recognized him in the crowd. He was certain she would win just for him, the boy who groomed her and always brought her treats from the garden.

In a thunder of drumming hooves and a blur of motion, the pack of horses crossed the finish line, the black mare leading by a length. The race concluded in a bedlam of wild cheers and an onrush of people carrying tankards of ale to the riders. Brian McQueen guided his son through the throng and out onto the meadow, where the dust still settled in the wake of the racing steeds. And there the dream unfolded its captured memory. Big, blond-haired Jonah Starbuck, whose stallion had been unable to overtake the black mare, laid the wooden handle of his whip across the nose and neck of his mount. The animal neighed in terror and tried to break free, but Jonah Starbuck held fast the reins and the stallion received blow after blow from its furious owner. Starbuck stood a head taller than any of the men around him, and his mercurial temper and powerful physique had won for him the respect and fear of the townsmen. None approved of his conduct. None made a move to stop the woodsman from punishing the unfortunate beast, until Brian McQueen left his son in the meadow, walked up behind Starbuck, and cried out, "Enough."

The ill-tempered bully fumed and glared at the smaller man standing before him. He allowed the stallion's reins to slip through his fingers.

"Well, blacksmith, is it for you to teach me how to deal with what is mine?" the big man said, hands on his hips.

"It appears someone must," Brian replied calmly.

Starbuck tilted back his head and laughed so hard his belly shook and the brass buckle in his belt bobbed up and down. Then he took the whip by its handle and uncoiled seven feet of braided oxhide. The townsmen and farmers milling about the other horses fell silent.

"Come, little 'teacher,' you've a lesson to learn, by my oath."

Brian advanced on the woodsman. The whip snaked out, caught his ankles, and dropped Brian in his tracks. He rolled over and scrambled to his feet, and Starbuck laid the blacksmith's back open with two quick lashes; Brian groaned and dropped to his knees, fought the tears and the white-hot pain searing his bloody shoulders beneath his tattered shirt. The whip lashed out twice more as Brian whirled about to face his attacker. Streaks of crimson crisscrossed his neck and chest.

"No!" Daniel shouted, and grabbed a rock and hurled it at the woodsman. The stone glanced off Starbuck's knee. The bully groaned as he faced this second threat. He spied the boy, scowled, and cocked his hand; the whip trailed along the grass behind him.

"Insolent whelp," Starbuck growled. "I'll give you a taste of my lash." He advanced on the ten-year-old, momentarily forgetting the blacksmith until the bully heard footsteps and swung about, intending to catch Brian McQueen by the neck. But Daniel's rock had provided the necessary diversion. Bloody but escaping the grasp of the whip, Brian darted inside the big man's guard and wrapped the woodsman in a rib-cracking bear hug. Arms made strong and hard from a life of lifting anvils and loading pig iron and wielding "Thor's" hammer locked at the small of Starbuck's back and tightened.

Jonah Starbuck wriggled and moaned. He tried to pummel the smaller man, but every time the bully lifted his fist, the blacksmith increased the pressure. Breathing became the foremost thing in Starbuck's mind. Daniel watched in awe as Jonah Starbuck's rawboned form seemed to shrink in on itself and—when Brian released his hold—fell limply to the green grass.

Then Brian returned to his son, oblivious of the staring crowd. Blood seeped from his lacerated shoulders. The whip had cut a livid gash along his neck.

"Father, you're hurt," young Daniel said, the voice echoing in his mind now.

Brian placed his hand on his son's shoulder. Even that simple motion caused him to wince. "Doing what must be done can be a painful thing," the blacksmith said. "A righteous act is its own salve."

Daniel looked up at his father and clutched the blacksmith's bloodstained hand, wishing he might bear the pain, not knowing one day he would.

Other dreams followed, one fragment upon the other. Daniel saw himself aboard a careening wagon with a woman at his side whose hair was heather gold. He saw a dark and sinister figure standing in the shadows of a gallows. In that restless sleep he visited the north country and heard the cry of the wolf and the lonely breath of the wind in the lost places. So he passed the night, slipping from one memory to the next.

When he woke at first light he found himself staring into the jaws of death.

Chapter Four

Daniel stared into the blood-smeared black muzzle of a full-grown mastiff. The animal straddled him, placing its bearlike front paws to either side of Daniel's neck. The very size of the dog—two hundred pounds of muscle and bone and a lower jaw showing a row of incisors as it loosed a growl—belied the gentle brown eyes set in its large, wrinkled skull.

Daniel's fingers ceased their surreptitious crawl toward the pistols at his side.

"Easy, my lad. Now, there's a good pup."

Pup? My God, he has a growl like thunder. Daniel calculated his chances of breaking free and didn't like the odds. A mastiff could rip a man's throat out in seconds. This one snarled again. A morsel of meat and brown fur was caught in the corner of its mouth but disappeared when the animal licked the blood and drool from its chops. Muscles rippled beneath its reddish brown coat. This couldn't last forever.

Sweat rolled down Daniel's forehead and followed the creases in his skin down his cheek and around his neck. He tensed, knowing he was going to try to sit up, slowly and in a very unthreatening manner.

The animal bared its fangs. Then again, Daniel decided, the morning was still young. Why ruin it by being torn limb from limb? Besides, the straw was comfortable—yes, a bed fit for a king. Why leave it? *Daniel, you're a coward. Agreed. But I have both arms and legs and intend to keep them.* He settled back onto the blanket and prepared to pass the day here if necessary, when a woman's voice rescued him.

"So you've met Gideon," the mastiff's owner observed. She clapped her hands once. "Gideon, get thee behind me."

Gideon obediently trotted to the doorway and sat on its haunches behind the woman standing there.

The woman herself was short and stout and wore a smoke-gray dress buttoned to the neck and a charcoal-gray apron. A gray habit covered her head, leaving visible only the plain, tanned oval of her face. She carried a keg under one arm, and by the ease with which she handled it, Daniel guessed the keg was empty.

"I don't know you, good pilgrim. I am Hope-Deferred-Maketh-the-Heart-Sick. I was named for my grandmother, who I am told was the consort of a pirate. Yet she became a good Christian before her death. You may call me Sister Hope. For I am one of the Daughters of Phoebe. There are only six of us now. None have come to join our number. And we live beyond Cobb's Hill at the edge of the forest."

"Yes'm." Daniel had heard of religious sects made up solely of women, though he had never before encountered one. He stood and dusted the straw from his trousers and linsey-woolsey shirt. "I'm Daniel McQueen. Kate...uh...Mistress Bufkin has employed me in the restoration of the Hound and Hare."

"A goodly task." Sister Hope noted the man kept the mastiff in his guarded gaze. "Wait in the wagon, Gideon." The mastiff snorted and trotted off toward a two-wheeled cart drawn up before the barn. "And do you not be searching for more of God's creatures to eat. You've broke your fast this morning on that groundhog. That is enough for now." Sister Hope shook her head in despair, as if she had scolded a naughty child and knew very well she had not been heard.

Daniel wrapped his guns in the blanket and piled straw atop them. Then he sauntered toward the door. He felt a good deal better with that hound of hell off his chest.

Sister Hope appraised this rough-looking stranger. "Well, sir, I judge you to have seen your share of violence." She placed her hands on her broad hips and looked up at him. At four feet ten inches, she looked up at most everyone.

"I'm a peaceable man, Sister."

"You're big, though not as strapping as Papa Schraner's youngest boy, Henk. But when the final trumpet sounds I warrant it will find you farther down the path."

"I shall strive to make it so, if only because Henk carries on such a poor conversation. He has all the charm and wit of a press gang."

Sister Hope had a good sense of humor and shared his poor opinion of Henk Schraner. Henk was certainly the sour apple in the barrel.

"Then you know the Schraners, Mr. McQueen."

"Only the son."

"There are more than the one," she told him.

Daniel groaned. Trouble again; a replay of Montreal flipped through his memory.

"Henk has two brothers, Eben and Barnabas," Sister Hope continued. "Half brothers, really, by Jon's first marriage." She patted her apron and started back toward her cart. "I came to leave a barrel of our sweet pickles off for the tavern. And to draw off a keg of cider for Sister Constance. It helps her to sleep at night, the poor old soul, for her joints are aching of late and even our blackberry wine doesn't help. But Kate's hard cider is strong enough to deaden the conscience of a saint." Sister Hope glanced aside and winked.

Daniel found himself warming to the woman. She was plainspoken, like Kate, though not as mercurial in her moods. Sister Hope was slow and steady.

When they reached the cart the woman ordered Daniel to extend his hand toward the mastiff. The dog rumbled deep in its throat and eyed the outstretched limb as if it were a snack.

"Gideon!" Sister Hope angrily covered Daniel's hand with her own. The mastiff nuzzled her hand. When Sister Hope withdrew it, the mastiff continued to lick Daniel's knuckles and its tail curled up and began to wag.

"If only people would learn to accept one another so easily." She rubbed her palms together and brightened. "Well, now, good sir, we have some pewterware that needs some repair. I don't suppose..."

"Aye. Bring it to me," Daniel said. "I'm a fair hand at the forge." He lowered the pickle barrel onto his shoulder and started toward the tavern, across the courtyard, and through the front door. He selected an appropriate spot for the barrel, near the walnut bar where the libations were served if a man cared to stand and wait for service, which seemed in short supply this morning. The upstairs guests had yet to make an appearance and their mounts were in the barn, so it was a safe assumption they were still abed.

Kate had left food on the bar for her guests to help themselves; they had already paid for their night's lodging. A platter of apple fritters, bread, and cheese, and a steaming pot of strong tea to warm them on their way was a courtesy of Kate's own choosing. Still, it did not seem right to make one's guests fend for themselves. What had taken Kate away at such an early hour? And where was she?

Sister Hope seemed to read his mind, for she sighed softly and said, "Her brother, poor soul. He takes to spells. I warrant you find him and you'll find her."

Chapter Five

On the far side of the field behind the tavern, Kate Bufkin added another handful of cow parsley to her basket and decided she had gathered enough to make the beautiful yellow dye she would need for the flax Sister Hope was supposed to bring her today. A hundred yards away, Loyal Bufkin went crazy right out in the middle of a cornfield he'd been weeding with the hoe in preparation for an early summer's harvest. Loyal Bufkin yelled and cursed in a voice that lashed the stillness like a bullwhip. He swung his hoe at a host of unseen enemies arrayed against him, battled his imagined foes to the death. His farm implement was a saber, and with each slash he mowed down the garishly painted Ottawa demons charging out of the impenetrable forest of his mind.

Kate hefted her basket of cow parsley and barberry leaves and found a shady spot beneath a spreading chestnut tree where she could rest and wait out her brother's spell. It wouldn't pass until the corn rows ran red with rivulets of blood before his wild eyes. The land had trembled once to the crash of musket and the tramp of militia, to Ottawa war cries, slashing tomahawks, and clashing swords. But that had been many years ago. The countryside may have been pacified, but the Ottawa still followed a warpath through Loyal's weary mind.

The spell ended as quickly as it began, much to Kate's relief, and Loyal sat down in the furrowed field and caught his breath. Young cornstalks a couple of feet in height had sprouted from the soil, tended with his loving care like everything else in his garden, like the bees he kept and the fruit trees he nurtured.

Kate relaxed, closed her eyes, and listened to the buzzing bees and the wind stirring the branches overhead. She marveled at how she could almost feel the pulse of the earth under her head, and she thought of Daniel McQueen. She had crept out to the barn before daybreak and found him asleep in the straw; she had contemplated waking him but thought better of it. Not that she was afraid of seeming forward. Such ladylike concerns might suit the girls of Philadelphia—not Kate Bufkin, who had an inn to rebuild. But a man needed his rest, and so she watched in silence, appreciating the rise and fall of his muscular chest as he breathed.

Daniel had looked so hard and fierce, even in repose, nothing like the farmers hereabouts. Yet there was also something innocent about him. She could not explain that even to herself.

Kate Bufkin began to hum quietly and she plucked a stalk of sweet clover from the earth and chewed on the root end as she continued to ruminate on the stranger she had brought back to the Hound and Hare. She wondered where his travels had taken him, and what his life had been like, and was there a woman somewhere pining for the sight of him, and were

there...goodness...children and a lonesome bride—
or worse, no bride at all but a fatherless brood of
young whelps.

What were his loyalties? These were dangerous
days. The British were bottled up in Boston, British
and American blood had been spilled at Lexington
and Concord. Representatives from the thirteen colonies were meeting in Philadelphia to pick a commander-
in-chief for an army that was only just being formed.
Could Daniel be counted on to serve the patriot's
cause or would he stand with the Tories? No, surely
not. His kind of man were born rebels, she had seen it
in his eyes.

A shadow fell across Kate, and she noticed she
was no longer alone here near the edge of the meadow.
Sister Hope of the Daughters of Phoebe had found her
out and come to join her. If Hope was here, then—Kate
tried to scramble to her feet, but a veritable avalanche
of dog flesh crashed into her and pinned her to the
ground.

Gideon nipped at her and lapped her neck and
face while Kate struggled to extricate herself from the
overly affectionate dog. Her pleas went unanswered,
because she couldn't help but laugh. Her neck was a
ticklish spot. So Gideon continued to "maul" one of
his favorite victims until Kate produced a morsel of
apple fritter from her apron and tossed it as far away as
she could. Gideon lumbered off after the treat and Kate
seized the opportunity to climb to her feet.

She dusted the dirt and grass from her homespun
dress. Sister Hope inspected the contents of the basket.

"These will do nicely," she said. "I'll have you
know I've brought you enough cloth to curtain every
window."

"You are too kind to me."

"Sister Agnes has sent you some of her pickles. I had your man put them in the tavern."

"Then you met Mr. McQueen?"

"Indeed." Sister Hope's eyebrows arched. "And it is plain to see why you've taken him on."

"For shame, Sister Hope. What on earth are you implying?"

"Me? Not one thing." Her feigned innocence spoke volumes.

"He claims to have some talent with the forge."

"Why, certainly."

"And he can cut wood and carpenter some."

"And isn't bad to look at while he's tending to such things."

"Sister Hope," Kate protested, nervously straightening the folds of her lime-green-colored apron. "Just what kind of person do you think I am?"

"A woman." Sister Hope embraced the younger woman in a motherly fashion. "Don't let these somber colors fool you, my sweet. I once sampled fruits from the forbidden tree. Sin has a sweet nectar. Which is to say, I have the same feelings inside as any woman. Only more of mine are tinged with memories and tamed, while yours are fresh and headstrong and tempting."

"Hope, really, you misjudge me. I am innocent."

"Now, perhaps...but later?" Sister Hope shook her head. "I'll speak no more of it. Just remember, my dear, that it is men who wield all the power. If a woman is to survive she must guard herself and choose when and where to sacrifice that one special gift she has. Do not squander on a simple wayfarer that which can humble even a king." Sister Hope dabbed at her upper lip with a cotton kerchief that she produced from somewhere in her apron.

"I don't think I have ever heard you speak like

this." Kate was perplexed at the woman's remarks. Since the death of Kate's mother, the Daughters of Phoebe had all exhibited maternal concern toward Kate, Sister Hope more than any of them.

"Walk me back to the inn, there's a dear," said Sister Hope. "Gideon!" The mastiff immediately fell into step alongside the women.

"I don't think that is all a woman has," Kate suddenly blurted. "A woman can be strong. Lord knows my mother was, until the fire ruined her lungs. A woman has as much courage as any man."

"My dear one, you only say what I have always said. And yet 'His Lordship' always has his way. Because 'His Lordship' has the power. However, it is given to women the ability to tame that power and from time to time make it do as we wish." Sister Hope clapped her hands together and sighed. "Permit an old woman her observations in the twilight of her life."

"Really, Sister Hope, how you carry on." Kate knew that once Hope got into her "wearier than thou" attitude there was nothing to do but endure it. "I dare say you shall outlive us all."

But Hope-Deferred-Maketh-the-Heart-Sick wasn't hearing it. She eyed Loyal with suspicion as they walked past him. A gentle sort and quiet to a fault, he became quite the opposite when the spells came over him. Hope was never fully at ease when Kate's brother was around, because one never knew when Loyal might slip out of the real world and into the private hell of his own past.

"We'll have sweet corn aplenty come July!" he called out to Hope. He cradled the leaves of a stalk as gently as if he were holding the arms of a child. Sister Hope told him that she and the others of her religious community would be over with their baskets come harvest time. Loyal seemed pleased.

"And your benefactor, has he come through yet?" Sister Hope asked Kate.

"Nathaniel Woodbine is part owner, not my benefactor," the young woman corrected. "As per the agreement he had with my mother, every spare coin we make shall reimburse him for his loan. Eventually the Hound and Hare will belong to Loyal and me free and clear."

"And yet I suspect Mr. Woodbine would prefer you ever in his debt."

"His infatuation was with mother, not me." Kate did not enjoy discussing her mother's affairs. Sister Hope may have turned her life over to the Lord, thought Kate, but she had certainly held on to her lively curiosity about the affairs of others.

As they neared the inn, Kate noticed smoke curling from the chimney by the barn. True to his word, Daniel had fired up the forge. Perhaps hiring him had been a rash act. Still, despite Hopes's words of caution, Kate felt she had made the right choice. As for her own emotions, she would keep them tightly reined. She had no time for romantic dalliances, for there was work aplenty to do. However, the lingering image in her mind was not the day's chores, but a man asleep in the hay in the stillness of the dawn.

Chapter Six

"Daniel McQueen!" Kate called out to the man at the forge. It was hot work, shaping iron, and he had stripped to the waist. Soot and ashes clung to his muscled shoulders. He was busy hammering a strip of glowing metal into a graceful bend and didn't hear her. Kate held a pitcher of cool buttermilk, churned but an hour ago, and set it in the root cellar in its pewter container for safekeeping.

She gingerly approached, uncertain whether she should interrupt his work. Drawing close, she could discern in detail the musculature of his back, and though his movements were fluid and clean, he seemed forged of the same iron that clanged beneath the blows of his mallet. Scars were visible, jagged white lines crisscrossing his back where he'd been "kissed" by a cat-o'-nine-tails. Someone had tried to lay his flesh open. The scar tissue ran more heavily along his right side and over onto his shoulder.

Daniel finished hammering and dipped the latch he'd been fashioning into a nearby barrel of rainwater.

He noticed the woman out of the corner of his eye and turned, startled at first to see her. He did not, however, seem embarrassed by his half-nakedness.

"I brought you some buttermilk." Kate held out a wooden cup, prepared to fill it. Daniel wiped his forearm across his sweat-streaked brow and left a smudge there.

"Thank you most kindly." He reached past the cup, took the pitcher from her.

"I've another—uh—pitcher for Loyal...." Her explanation faded as he tilted the pitcher to his mouth and drank.

Buttermilk sloshed down his jaw and neck and mingled with the perspiration that rolled down his torso. He drank without pause, without seeming to breathe; he didn't stop until he'd drained the contents of the pitcher and set it down with a clank and a sigh of satisfaction.

He glanced at the cup Kate held. "I'm sorry. Were you wanting some?"

"No, I seem to have forgotten I was in a barn and not at table." She dropped the cup into the pitcher. "Obviously, sir, you haven't."

"Ah, fair Kate, you save my life and then insult it." Daniel handed her the pitcher. His red hair was in wild disarray and looked for all the world like the flames leaping in the forge every time he worked the bellows. "But unlike my Highland kinsmen, I have a forgiving nature."

"How fortunate, sir," said Kate, suppressing a smile. At last, her own good nature won out and she laughed. "I'm sorry." She fished in her apron pocket and brought out a chunk of bread wrapped in a cloth and handed it to him. "A peace offering, Daniel McQueen."

"Accepted." Daniel set the bread aside and brought her over to a wooden box already half filled with nails.

He indicated a mold he'd found buried under the remnant of a cart and a box of old horseshoes that contained far more than the tavern was likely to need for its own mounts or those of its patrons. "A trick my father taught me. I made these nails from the cast-off horseshoes. It's saved us a pretty penny, I warrant. My father never bought a nail."

Daniel nodded toward the iron bar he'd been working with. Kate could see it was well on the way to becoming an ornamented latch for one of the bedrooms upstairs.

"Fixing the roof is the most important job, but I was curious to see if I still knew my way around fire and iron." Daniel had used muscles he'd forgotten about. His shoulders ached and his face was raw from the fire, but he felt good.

"And you do." Kate was much impressed by his skill. "But since I can only offer you room and board and a few shillings for your labor, take your rest when you need it." She picked up the pitcher. "Keep you some water from the well here."

"A pretty lass is as refreshing as the coldest, purest drink." He stepped forward and momentarily blocked the young woman's way.

Kate stopped in her tracks and looked straight into his square-jawed face. His eyes were the color of storm clouds, gunmetal gray and tinged with fire and daring. An ember in the forge exploded in a shower of sparks that shot upward behind the Highlander and outlined him in its crimson-orange light.

Neither spoke. Kate could scarcely catch her breath. The forge was nothing compared to the heat emanating between them. They were silent and more than a little wary of one another.

"What are we doing?" Kate asked softly, breaking the stillness of the moment.

"I don't know," Daniel answered. "But maybe I better stop, eh? Your pardon, lass." He stepped aside. "Been a long time since I held these tools, since I've built anything." He ran a hand through his hair and attempted in vain to smooth the unruly locks.

He glanced around the smithy. His mind searched for the right words to say how he felt. For a moment, his contentment overshadowed the real reason he had come to the Hound and Hare. It was good to forget, even for a moment, to set treachery aside and feel part of something again, to feel he belonged. He had been a long time wandering. It was good to pretend, if only for a little while, to be home.

A phaeton rolled into the drive and brought their idyll to an end as they both moved from the shade of the barn. The low-sided, four-wheel carriage was drawn by a matched pair of blaze-faced geldings and driven by a man whom Kate instantly recognized.

Colonel Nathaniel Woodbine of the New York Militia was a man of below-average height and above-average ambition. He stood no taller than Kate, about five feet three. He had sloping shoulders, a thick chest, and his ample girth was firmly encased in a brown frock coat and waistcoat of the same material. His rust-colored breeches and stockings disappeared into shiny black boots. A saber with an ornamented guard dangled from a broad black belt draped across his chest. A white silk ruff was gathered at his Adam's apple by a silver clutch and fanned out beneath his throat. He was fair of skin, victim of constant sunburn; he wore a white wig, as was the custom of the day, denoting his gentlemanly station.

Four dragoons in dark blue coats and pale blue breeches sat their mounts several paces behind their commander. The four quickly dismounted and made a hasty progress into the courtyard. One of the men tugged on a cord and rang a brass bell that had been mounted on a post alongside the entrance in the stone wall.

Moments later Loyal emerged, tankards in hand, and led the way to the cider barrel.

Woodbine stepped down from the phaeton, doffed his tricorn, and opened his arms to embrace the young woman coming toward him.

"Kate Bufkin, there's not a prettier girl in all of the colonies," Woodbine greeted. He placed Kate's arm in his and walked with her toward the barnyard, where Daniel pulled on his shirt and immediately found himself introduced.

"Glad to meet you, my good man," said Colonel Woodbine after learning the redhead's name. "A smith, are you? And a woodsman, by the look of you," he added, eyeing McQueen's buckskin breeches.

"I've trapped some," Daniel conceded. He remained guarded, for he carried a deep-rooted suspicion of men of wealth. And through no fault of Woodbine's, the gentleman reminded Daniel of the father of a girl he had once loved and almost married until that same father discovered his prospective son-in-law's humble origins. A blacksmith's son had no place courting the daughter of Boston's aristocracy.

"A man of few words." Woodbine brushed the road dust from his coat. "I like that." He quickly appraised the Highlander towering over him and did not seem in the least put off by McQueen's size. Woodbine knew there were other powers than sheer brawn, and he wielded them with relish.

He looked at Kate and guided her toward the tavern. "And how do we stand, Mistress Bufkin? Will you be ready to receive Colonel Washington?"

"And whomever else arrives with him," Kate assured him. "Mr. McQueen will repair the pewter. And as you'll see, the downstairs tavern virtually escaped damage.''

Daniel watched them walk arm in arm and felt his temper rise. Jealous? Why? he wondered. He'd scarcely been here a day. What was Kate to him? True, he liked her for her spirit, and he had seen many fine qualities in her from their first meeting. But he was here as an imposter. He had no right to feel anything at all.

Woodbine had spoken of Washington coming to the tavern. So that explained why Meeks wanted him here.

Daniel looked around at the hens scratching in the barnyard dirt for insects. He should go back to work, return to his place at the forge. But Kate and Woodbine had disappeared through the side door of the tavern and something in Daniel, despite his best efforts to the contrary, forced him to follow.

Woodbine stood in the center of the tavern and liked what he saw, from the polished mahogany tables to the cabinets lined with pewterware and china. A Seth Thomas clock commanded the center of the great hearth, and hanging in a place of honor was a portrait of William Penn. Two racks of long-stemmed clay pipes had been set to either side of the Seth Thomas, and a pair of leather and wood trenchers stood at either end of the mantel.

A number of straight-backed chairs as well as benches were arranged about the tables, while several cushioned easy chairs were placed near the box windows overlooking the courtyard. Kate had even acquired a chair that tilted back, allowing a footrest to raise in front, an ideal resting place for a man with the gout. A chess set had been left near one of the box windows. It had been a gift from Woodbine, who noted with satisfaction its place of honor.

"You've done well, Kate," he said, and he took her hand in his and patted it. "I could not have chosen a better partner." His voice took on a purring quality as he stroked her fingers, then bowed and kissed her hand.

The gesture made her uncomfortable.

Kate sensed an implied relationship in Woodbine's manner of speaking. Her mother had been an attractive, lonely widow. Two years ago, in the employ of Nathaniel Woodbine, she had entered into an affair with the well-to-do merchant. Though married and seemingly devoted to his ailing wife, Woodbine had professed love for Ruth Bufkin and to prove his sincerity had purchased the Hound and Hare Inn, a discreet but manageable distance from his offices in Philadelphia and his wife's estate in New York. The fire and Ruth Bufkin's death had changed everything.

Or had it?

Kate felt the constant, steady pressure of Woodbine's fingers enclosing her hand and was loath to draw away and wound the man's pride. He tilted her hand palm upward and, reaching inside his coat, withdrew a silver snuff box and placed it in her hand. It was a finely crafted piece and heavy, worth a goodly sum, to be sure. The lid of the snuff box bore a fine line etching of a meadow and a weeping willow.

"Have our taciturn friend, Mr. McQueen, melt this down into coins," said Woodbine.

"I cannot accept any more of your generosity, Nathaniel," Kate protested.

"I insist."

"But you have given so much...."

"I won't hear another word." Woodbine closed her hand around the silver box. "Your mother was special to me. And in your own way, you, too, have become someone I hold most dear."

The side door opened and Daniel entered the tavern. Woodbine released Kate's hand and stepped back, a look of displeasure on his face. He had little use for hirelings who intruded on his privacy. Yet, in uncharacteristic fashion, he cooled his anger.

"Well, sir, tell me, in these divisive times, which road do you walk—the king's road or the patriots?" The merchant winked at Kate, then stood back, stroking his chin and waiting for an answer.

"My own road," Daniel said.

"That often leads right down the middle," Woodbine said. "And the middle is the worst place to be when the shooting starts. Better to be on one side or the other. But you're a smart lad; you'll make the right choice when the moment comes."

Woodbine bowed toward Kate and once again kissed her hand. He started toward the door, then paused to take an extra tankard from a nearby shelf built into the wall near the door.

"My men appear to be enjoying Loyal's cider. I think I'll join them, for there is none better the length and breadth of the Trenton Road." He stepped out into the courtyard and held out his tankard for Kate's brother to fill.

The dragoons, as hard-looking a group as Daniel had ever seen, stood when Woodbine appeared among them.

"By God, Loyal, you've a gift for this," said the merchant.

Loyal beamed with pride and nodded his thanks. A simple man, he trusted openly. It pleased him that others found merit in the work of his hands.

Kate and Dan also stepped outside.

"You're welcome any time, Colonel Woodbine. You've been good to us, as good as one to his own kin. Isn't that right, Kate?" Loyal said in his rasping voice.

"Like a kind uncle," Kate replied.

Nathaniel Woodbine's eyebrows arched, but he said nothing. He donned his tricorn hat with a flourish and motioned to his men, who quickly drained their tankards and headed out of the courtyard. One of the dragoons, a short, solid man older than Daniel by a decade, paused to scrutinize the Highlander.

Daniel noted the man's attention and returned his stare until the man looked away.

"Corporal, will you join us?" Woodbine said as he made his way toward the phaeton. The militia men mounted their horses.

Daniel glanced down and spied the flash of silver in Kate's hands.

"Handsome work, that. Worth a good deal," he commented dryly.

Kate waved as the phaeton rolled past and then looked down at Woodbine's gift. "Perhaps too much," she mused aloud worriedly.

Nathaniel Woodbine settled back in the padded leather seat of his carriage, guided the geldings from the drive onto the Trenton Road, and pointed the animals toward Philadelphia.

"A kind 'uncle,' is it?" he muttered to himself, and snorted in contempt for the word and all it implied. Kate Bufkin was a blossom waiting to be picked. "We shall see about that."

Chapter Seven

By the twentieth of May, Daniel had repaired all the pewterware and fashioned a wrought-iron lattice-work arch that he fit over the entrance to the court-yard. Now the tavern's patrons would pass beneath black iron vines that intertwined upward from either side and became a hound and hare caught in a tableau of the hunt.

When Daniel had finished, he, Kate, and Loyal stood out in the drive. Kate produced a bottle of the most potent brandy Daniel had ever lifted to his lips. They all drank a toast to Daniel's handiwork. Daniel folded his arms across his chest and beamed with pride and satisfaction. It was indeed quite good. Not perfect, to be sure. He had made a twist here and there in the wrong place and the rabbit was not quite the right proportion in relation to the hound, but by and large, his work was worthy of the man who had been his teacher, Brian McQueen. Daniel gulped his brandy and let the burning liquid chase away the pain of his predicament.

"Tonight I'll fix you anything, Daniel McQueen. A meal the like of you've never tasted," Kate said.

"There's no need."

"It was a grand day when you rode to my sister's rescue on the Trenton Road," Loyal exclaimed, and patted the craftsman on the shoulder.

"Rode...I more or less leaped." Daniel laughed, eager to change the subject. "I'll saddle one of the mares and get the candles. Sister Hope ought to be done with them by now."

"Sister Agnes keeps the bees, and it is she who makes the candles. It is a source of great pride to her," Kate corrected. "But you should rest now. You've spent many an hour before the forge."

"The ride will do me good." Daniel seemed eager to go.

"Perhaps I should show you the way," Kate suggested timidly.

"No!" Daniel snapped, with more force than he had intended. "What I mean is...I know the way—you told me earlier, remember?"

Kate lowered her gaze and blushed. Daniel, who would have liked nothing better than to be alone with her, silently cursed his blundering manner. What was she doing to him? With any other woman he'd know exactly what to say and do, but she had turned him into an oaf, clumsy in word and deed.

"Take whichever horse suits you," Kate told him. Her wounded tone made Daniel feel small inside. She turned from him and headed for the tavern door.

"My sister's a proud one," Loyal said. "It isn't often she lets a person close to her." He glanced at Daniel, who could not meet his stare. "I do believe that's the only thing Kate fears. Poor girl." He smacked his lips after downing his brandy.

"What do you fear, Mr. McQueen?" Loyal added.

Now Daniel looked at him. There was more to Kate's half-mad brother than the Scotsman had initially perceived. Loyal laughed softly as if reading Daniel's thoughts and then stepped beneath the wrought-iron arch. He lifted his eyes to the animal figures rendered by the artisan.

"Hounds and hares," Loyal noted coldly. "The world is reduced to the chase. But which of us is the hound?" His voice grew distant, thoughtful, and then he faced Daniel again. "And which the hare?"

An hour's easy ride from the tavern, Daniel walked his bay the last few yards up a hill ringed by white oaks to where the ashes of a campfire still curled smoke and two men awaited him.

Major Josiah Meeks stretched his gaunt frame and stepped around the remains of the campfire. His brown-brimmed hat and eyepatch gave him the appearance of a swashbuckling rogue. He puffed on his clay pipe and hooked his thumbs in the broad belt circling his waist.

Black Tolbert stood a few paces off to the left. He held a pistol at the ready, cocked and primed and set to bring down the first stranger who entered the clearing. He recognized this incoming rider and held his fire. Still, he was slow to lower his gun. There was no love lost between Daniel McQueen and Black Tolbert.

Daniel dropped a hand to one of the "Quakers" tucked in his belt. Meeks defused the situation by stepping between the two antagonists. The major's brown cloak flapped with each long-legged stride.

"We waited all morning, Danny boy," the major said.

"You said to meet on the tenth day after I arrived at the inn. You didn't say what time of day."

"And you enjoyed keeping us out here while you

played 'bushy park' with a tavern wench." Tolbert slapped his neck, crushing a nettlesome insect. He pulled a leather flask from his pocket, took a couple of swallows of rum, and returned the flask to his forestgreen coat.

The veins in Tolbert's cheeks were like crimson lines drawn upon a war map. In another few years of self-abuse he'd be a dissolute wreck, but today he was an unbalanced and dangerous adversary.

Daniel didn't care a whit. "Consider these discomforts just so much practice for your time in hell."

Black Tolbert grew livid and tried to step around Meeks, who only just managed to restrain his impetuous henchman.

"I've heard enough from both of you," the major complained.

Tolbert turned on him and his anger slowly subsided beneath the officer's withering one-eyed stare.

"You hold the purse strings," Tolbert grumbled. "But I'll brook no more of McQueen's insults." The assassin halfheartedly lowered his weapon, uncocked it, and tucked the gun in his waistband.

Meeks turned his attention to the man on horseback. War was a dark and bloody business. Sometimes it required the skills of such men as Black Tolbert. Josiah Meeks was a private, cynical man who could foresee in the coming conflict a chance for his own advancement and the acquisition of wealth and property. Tolbert would help him on his way.

"Danny boy, I find your attitude disturbing at best."

"My attitude? I'm here, yes? And I've worked my way into the confidence of those who run the Hound and Hare, as you wished." Daniel paused in his litany of accomplishments, and his eyes narrowed, his expression shrewd. "How did you know Washington would be coming there?"

"A little bird told me." Meeks dismissed the impertinent inquiry. "Now, are you certain you can extend your stay? The Continental Congress has yet to name a commander-in-chief. There are other names being discussed. Ward, for one. Even that disreputable traitor, Hancock. If one of them is chosen we shall adapt our plans. Will Chaney has already ingratiated himself to one of Hancock's servants."

"Then you may not need me, after all," Daniel said, a note of relief in his voice. Maybe he could extricate himself from this situation. *And leave other innocent men to die?* His thoughts became gloomy again.

"These rebels would be fools not to choose the Virginian. Colonel Washington is their most capable man." Meeks sauntered back toward the campfire, retrieved a small, barrel-like container called a pin, and poured a measure of hard cider into a silver cup. The cup was a keepsake that seemed to hold special importance for the Englishman, for he had carried it among his belongings for as long as Daniel had known him. "Colonel Washington must die—whoever else the rabble chooses. He is too dangerous. Sooner or later, the continentals would turn to him." Meeks smiled to think of it. What a blow to this burgeoning insurrection, to lose their best man in a single strike. It might even take the heart out of the revolution and send these seditious farmers scurrying back to their fields.

"If that's what you think, then you know nothing of us. Braddock's Road taught you nothing at all," Daniel said.

Back in 1755, General Edward Braddock had led a force into the Ohio country, to punish the French and the Ottawa. The British troops had met with a crushing defeat and the only thing that kept their long retreat from becoming a bloody rout were the colonials, lead by Braddock's aide, young George Washington, who stood and fought the tenacious Indians to a standstill. A big-boned, husky lad of thirteen by the name of Daniel McQueen had fought alongside many a brave man and learned the truth of war.

"Us?" Meeks didn't like the sound of the word. "Have 'you' become an 'us'?"

"I warrant it's that yellow-haired girl," Black Tolbert interjected, drawing close. It was his turn to make Daniel squirm. He could sense the man on horseback stiffen. "Maybe I ought to take up at the tavern, Major Meeks," Tolbert purred. "She gives me any trouble, and I got a sword between my legs that'd keep the wench in her place."

Daniel's foot shot out and clipped the grinning brigand just below the chin. Black Tolbert's head snapped back and his eyes rolled up and showed nothing but white as he toppled over on his backside. He landed in the dirt with a muffled thud.

Meeks sighed, crossed over, and knelt by the unconscious man. He checked to see if Tolbert was still breathing. Reassured, he stood and faced Daniel.

"I do not need this trouble." Meeks pulled the cloak around his bony shoulders. "Just remember your father—"

"I haven't forgotten," Daniel muttered.

"Good, because just for a second I saw something in your eyes I didn't like." The Englishman moved closer. "Know this. If anything goes wrong—your fault, my fault, anybody's fault—your father hangs. You understand, Danny boy?"

Daniel nodded.

"I don't hear you," Meeks repeated ominously.

"I understand," Daniel said coldly.

The major seemed satisfied. "You had better leave before Tolbert comes around. He'll want to kill you for this, of course."

Daniel glanced from the unconscious man sprawled on the ground back to Josiah Meeks. "He'll try."

The horseman turned his mount and rode out of the clearing, down from the knoll and into the woods, pointing the mare west.

A few minutes later, with Black Tolbert revived but groggy, Major Josiah Meeks led the way downhill and off at a canter across the fields in the direction of the Trenton Road. Only when they were out of sight did a shadowy figure detach itself from a hillside overlooking the campsite. This audience of one looked after Meeks and Tolbert for a moment as if undecided which trail to follow. Then, like a hunter after his prey, the horseman swung his mount about and galloped after Daniel McQueen.

Chapter Eight

Gideon stood defiantly at the foot of the steps leading up to the front porch that ran the length of the farmhouse. The mastiff, aroused from its afternoon nap in the warm sunlight by the approaching horseman, moved quickly to defend its territory from the encroachment of a stranger. The animal growled, then loosed such a savage series of barks that Daniel was loath to dismount.

A gray-clad woman cradling a bowl of cornmeal batter appeared on the porch. She looked to be in her mid-thirties. An austere, unattractive woman, she retreated in. Then, gripping her wooden spoon like a war club, she crossed to the edge of the porch and glared out at the intruder. It was plain to see she felt no fear. Gideon could more than handle this stranger.

"What business have you here, sir?" she asked.

To her surprise, Daniel dismounted, squatted in the dirt, and called the mastiff by name. Gideon quieted, then took a hesitant step forward, his blunt nose testing the air for the man's scent. The voice was certainly familiar. Daniel called out again, and this time the huge dog trotted forward and allowed the man to scratch its neck and rub behind its ears.

The woman with the bowl stared in utter disbelief.

"I am Sister Ruth." Gathering her resolve, she moved to block him should he attempt to enter the house. She brandished her wooden stirring spoon like a club. Batter dripped from its "warhead."

"Be well, Sister Ruth. I'm a peaceable man." He held out his arms in a gesture of innocence. However, the flaps of his coat parted to reveal the matched pistols tucked in his belt.

He saw her eyes dart to the weapons and, to set the woman's mind at ease, drew the guns.

She gasped.

He tucked the "Quakers" into his coat pockets, removed the coat, and draped it over his saddle. Wearing only his linsey-woolsey shirt, trousers, and calf-high black boots, he tethered the mare to a porch post. Sister Ruth continued to keep him from the porch and the open doorway.

"Daniel McQueen!" another voice interjected from inside the house. Sister Hope appeared in the doorway. She looked out of breath as she trundled onto the porch. Her round cheeks reddened as she gasped for air, and her homely face brightened, for McQueen's arrival provided her with an excuse to escape her chores. She had ten skeins of woolen yarn waiting to be woven on the loom. It could wait.

"You know him?" Sister Ruth exclaimed.

"I do," Sister Hope replied. "And can you not see Gideon does as well?"

The mastiff had followed McQueen but no longer attempted to intimidate the man. Instead, the animal sat on its haunches and never took its eyes off Sister Hope.

"One can't be too careful," Sister Ruth sniffed, "in these troubled times. See you do not tarry." Like a general abandoning the field of battle to the opposing camp, she retreated from the porch and vanished into the shadowy interior of the stoutly built log house.

Sister Hope-Deferred-Maketh-the-Heart-Sick sighed as the other woman left. Then she stepped down off the porch and extended her hand to the visitor.

"You must excuse Sister Ruth. She is a widow now, but once this was her husband's farm. She invited our community to come and live with her, though she never lets us forget who actually owns the land. Sister Ruth can be a trifle brusque. Sister Eve, our superior, manages to keep her in line." Hope took a moment to stroke Gideon's coat. "Go on, now," she ordered, and the animal trotted off across the meadow.

Rabbits darted across its path, but the animal had learned from sad experience it couldn't catch them. The mastiff continued on into the woods. Daniel marveled at the way an animal of such brute power obeyed the likes of this woman.

"I've come to see Sister Agnes about the beeswax candles for the inn." He was anxious to be on his way. Something had bothered him since leaving Meeks and Tolbert at the clearing. He had a feeling of being followed. Call it a sixth sense or a premonition or merely the result of his experience in the wilderness, but whatever the source, it had never failed him.

"I will take you to her," Sister Hope told him, and started around the corner of the house.

Daniel lingered a moment to check his back trail; he studied the forest through which he had just traveled. He saw nothing, yet felt everything, and with a tightness growing between his shoulder blades, he wondered if the surrounding trees were as innocent as they seemed. He tried to convince himself it was merely his imagination and almost succeeded. But old habits—and the wariness the wild places bred in a man—die hard. Reluctantly he turned his back on the forest's shadowy depths.

Henk Schraner didn't plan on killing Daniel, but sure as God made serpents crawl, Henk intended to see Kate's handyman sweat every time the bastard stepped outside. *Enough near misses,* Henk silently calculated, *and I suspect Mr. McQueen will seek his fortune elsewhere.* The jealous young farmer settled down behind the twin halves of a lightning-split oak, bracing the long-barreled rifle his father had made on the blackened, twisted tree trunk. He kept his vigil about a hundred yards from the front of the farmhouse.

The Daughters of Phoebe were dedicated to lives of simplicity and prayer. Time meant little here on their farm nestled among the rolling hills. Their garden was a neatly ordered plot of ground where rows of corn rose alongside tomatoes, peas, and squash.

A split-rail fence protected the garden from the wandering dairy cows that were free to roam the grassy meadowlands about the farmhouse. The farm itself was like an oasis of cleared ground in a sea of oaks and hickories, birches and elms. The surrounding forest provided the farm its privacy.

Henk, for his part, was grateful for the trees and the undergrowth. Vinces and creepers had already left a green tangle across the shattered tree trunk; the land had begun to reclaim its own. One day he wouldn't be surprised to find the farm buried beneath loops of leafy green ropes. Henk pictured the six spinsters sitting motionless in their rockers on the front porch, their flesh covered by wind-stirred leaves.

Henk chuckled at the thought, sighed, and worked a kink out of his leg. First things first, however. Lifting a spyglass, he observed the chestnut tethered to the porch rail. It was Daniel's gelding. His owner was inside. When he decided to emerge, Henk had a big surprise for him.

Henk dug down in his possibles pack and retrieved a cloth-wrapped chunk of bread and a length of blood sausage. He made his meal there in the quiet of the forest, arm resting on the rifle, which was loaded and primed.

He comforted himself with daydreams of a frightened Daniel McQueen, scampering down the Trenton Road for the safety of Philadelphia. Henk sighed in satisfaction. He wouldn't even wait for Daniel's dust to settle in the courtyard of the Hound and Hare before he came calling on the beautiful Kate Bufkin.

Henk massaged a cramp out of his right calf and settled back against the trunk. He patted the rifle and readjusted his position, easing his buttocks off a sharp stone. Already the wait had unnerved him. His thoughts drifted to the Schraner farm, not an hour's ride from the front porch below. Papa would no doubt be furious that the cows had not been milked or the eggs gathered this morning. Let Eben or Barnabas see to such chores— and high time they did.

Anyway, Henk did not fear the old man's wrath. Lucy Dee Schraner, Henk's mother, a widow who had become Papa Schraner's second wife, could be counted on to temper her husband's anger. She had done so for the past three years of their marriage, turning a blind eye to her son's faults and championing his every cause, no matter how vain. *Dear doting Mum*, Henk mused in the silence of the woods. *Every son should have one.*

Henk grinned at his own cleverness. He inhaled deeply the spring fragrance of the woods where the pungent fragrance of rotting wood vied with the heady aroma of white sweet clover borne on May breezes from nearby meadows. Buzzing bees and rustling leaves heralded a world at peace, in sharp contrast to the violence in the young man's heart.

Sister Agnes worked the straw through a cow horn whose pointed tip had been sheared away, leaving a narrow hole that compressed the straw as it emerged. Every eight to ten inches she tied the length of straw with twine, creating a kind of tough, grassy rope that she could coil into the appropriate shape of a skep, a straw hive, for her bees.

Later she would sew the loops together to hold them in place and create a solid structure. Most interesting of all, Daniel found, was her choice of work spots, for she calmly perched upon a wooden stool ringed by half a dozen skeps whose occupants swarmed around her in a veritable tornado of wickedly buzzing life.

A young woman with round, wide eyes, she glanced up as Sister Hope called her by name and noticed the rough-looking, redheaded stranger who stood at Hope's side.

"This is Agnes's peaceful spot; no one bothers her here," Sister Hope remarked.

Daniel warily watched the swirling cloud of bees and nodded. "I can understand that," he said. It would take a braver man than he to approach the woman through the surrounding swarm. The bees not only filled the air, but landed on the woman's burnoose and on her shoulders. Yet the young woman seemed perfectly at ease.

"Yes, Hope...." Sister Agnes said, continuing her work as she looked away. She smiled at Daniel. "You must be Kate Bufkin's new man. Hope told us all about you."

Daniel sensed the diminutive woman at his side stiffen with embarrassment. "Why, I didn't think she knew 'all.'"

"Mr. McQueen has come for the candles you promised Kate." Sister Hope pointedly ignored their remarks.

"I am told there are no finer beeswax candles in all the colonies."

Daniel's compliment found favor with Sister Agnes; she positively beamed. "Sister Constance taught me the craft. Now the poor dear is ill abed." She paused to reflect, then continued. "You'll find the candles in the barn, yes—two large sacks of candles just inside the door." Sister Agnes hesitated. "I could show you...."

"We'll find them, dear." Sister Hope waved a pudgy hand toward the tall-roofed structure erected for the livestock. The shed, like an afterthought, was attached to the back wall. Both structures were showing their age, and Daniel made a mental note that he would find time to reshingle the worst spots for these good souls.

"God bless you, good sir," Sister Agnes called out as Sister Hope led Daniel away.

He glanced back and waved but offered no reply. Christian admonishments left him uncomfortable and at a loss for words, even more so considering the grim reason for his presence in the farm country of Pennsylvania.

Sister Hope was unaware of his inner conflict and chattered on about the founding of the farm community, and how six women of various walks of life had been called by the Holy Spirit to live communal lives of simplicity, prayer, and celibacy.

The farm itself held no greater surprise for Daniel than when he pulled open the wide, heavy barn door. Daylight streamed into the dusty interior to reveal a most unusual stockpile of supplies, especially for a place devoted to peace.

In place of hay bales and pitchforks, barrels of black gunpowder were stacked tall as a man, lethal Pennsylvania rifles, the pride of the colony's gunsmiths, were arranged in neatly ordered racks. There were crates too of lead shot and a basket of crudely honed knives and tomahawks, their blades somewhat irregular in length and hardly razor sharp. They were wicked-looking all the same. Indeed, the barn was a veritable armory. Daniel could see the wisdom here. What British officer would suspect the Daughters of Phoebe of engaging in seditious acts?

"There—" Sister Hope pointed to the trim sacks of beeswax candles hanging from a post at the end of a row of stacked rifles. "Help yourself." She was amused at his expression of surprise.

Daniel slowly, almost reverently, made his way among the rifles, powder, and shot. Hoisting the sacks from the peg, he then draped them both over his shoulder. By the time he had returned to the front doors he noticed a small flock of sheep drifting back toward the farmhouse from across the meadow.

The animals were flanked on either side by women in gray, one large-boned, an Amazon without headdress, the other as slight as a will-o'-the-wisp. Each of the two women held a stout, seven-foot-long crook.

Daniel stood in the barn entrance and watched as the larger of the two shepherds left the flock and hurried on toward the barn.

"That's Sister Mercy with the flock. She's a child

compared to the rest of us and quiet as a church mouse. And here is Eve." Sister Hope gestured toward the other daughter, who covered the ground with long strides, lifting her coarse gray skirt above her ankles for greater speed. Sister Eve's auburn braids slapped her shoulders like thick ropes and her cheeks reddened as she all but ran the few remaining yards, digging her shepherd's staff into the soft earth with every other step. Suspicion glittered in her narrowed eyes as she confronted the man. Sister Hope quickly made the introductions, hoping to defuse Sister Eve's obvious displeasure.

But Sister Eve hardly heard the woman's words. She gripped the crook like a quarterstaff and appeared ready to attack him.

"Good afternoon, Sister Eve. I'm hoping you'll not crack my skull for an armful of beeswax candles," Daniel said. "I came here as a friend." He nervously eyed the tight grip she kept on the cudgel. He flashed his most winning smile, one he'd used without success on a she-bear north of Hudson Bay.

"Peace be with you," Sister Eve replied, keeping a firm hold on the shepherd's crook. It was carved of hickory wood, thick enough to crack a man's skull and long enough to give her ample reach. "Sister Hope, you know better than to bring a stranger to the barn."

"He is no stranger," Hope protested.

"And do you speak for him?"

"Kate does," Sister Hope replied.

"I speak for myself," Daniel interjected.

Neither woman paid him any mind. Sister Eve was a formidable presence. Her voice carried the ring of authority that immediately clued Daniel as to whose word was law among the Daughters of Phoebe. After another few moments' debate, Sister Eve returned her attention to the man in front of her.

"You have discovered our secret," Sister Eve began. "I will not ask where your loyalties lie; truth or deceit would sound the same." Sister Eve sighed and shook her head.

"Freedom has a high price," Sister Hope added. "If Washington's named our commanding general, he'll require an army. And an army needs weapons." She folded her arms across her ample bosom, a smug look on her face. Using the barn for an armory had been Hope's idea. What better hiding place? Who would ever suspect this community of women of aiding and abetting a revolution? She wasn't worried about the well-mannered Scotsman. Hope trusted her instincts.

"Come, now, Sister Eve," Hope continued. Mr. McQueen here is Highland born. His people were fighting the English long before us. It would take a bold deceiver to go against his own history."

"I dance to no man's pipe." Daniel crooked a thumb toward the barn door. "None of that concerns me."

"It will." Sister Eve leaned forward on the shepherd's crook, and her gaze bore into McQueen. "Comes a time, you'll have to choose whether to make your stand among tyrants or free men."

Daniel started to quip that perhaps the representatives meeting in Philadelphia needed an ardent rebel like Sister Eve to fan the flames of insurrection whenever things started to cool. "Sister Eve, you're a regular firebrand, I'll say that." Maybe the seeds of rebellions might find fertile soil and take root in him, but not now—not with Meeks breathing down his neck.

"Indeed, if we must trust you," Sister Eve said in a resigned tone, "we might as well feed you." She started toward the farmhouse, her guarded attitude yielding to an innate sense of Christian hospitality.

"My thanks to you, good Sister. I don't wish to be

any trouble," Daniel said with all the humility he could muster.

"I think, good sir, you already are," Sister Eve retorted, cautiously good-natured.

A rifle shot cracked and a geyser of dirt erupted a yard in front of Daniel.

The two women froze, stunned that Sister Eve's jest had proved out most accurately.

Daniel on the other hand, was a blur of motion. He'd dropped candles and was running toward his gelding, covering the distance with surprising speed for a man his size. He reached the horse and vaulted into the saddle as Sister Ruth emerged from the front door.

This time she carried a broom, a small improvement over her bowl and spoon.

"Inside!" Daniel roared at her. She gasped and did as she was told, followed by Sister Eve and Sister Hope. He spun the bay and galloped off toward the line of trees, where a filmy banner of powder smoke revealed the rifleman's location. A second shot followed a minute after the first. But Daniel was riding low over the neck of his horse, reins in one hand and a pistol in the other. He held the flintlock outstretched like a lance and rode right into the sights of his assailant. Distance was meaningless; the forest grew larger in his vision, became more defined, oaks and hickory, a tangle of bramble and berry bushes...and at last, the lightning-blasted remains of a tree masked by a cloud of powder smoke.

McQueen grabbed for his other pistol and leaped from the horse. The bay went crashing into the clearing. He darted among the afternoon shadows, choosing his steps, avoiding twigs and brittle branches, ever moving, ever searching. And the forest matched him quiet for quiet. He skirted his assailant's hiding place, approached it from the side only to find the site abandoned.

The horse foraged in a patch of sunlight about twenty yards away. Daniel slowly turned, studied every bush, every trick of sunlight filtering through the branches overhead. It had to be Tolbert. Black must have followed him from the hilltop. But where the devil was the bastard now?

A rifle fired somewhere off to his left, back toward the wheel-rutted trail Daniel had taken to the farm. A man's shriek of terror followed by a howl of pain reverberated in the woods, then came a most familiar guttural growl. Finally there was the sound of a galloping horse.

Daniel wasn't the only hunter in the woods this day.

He found Gideon lying in the middle of the wagon trail, and for a moment Daniel thought the dog had been shot. But the mastiff stood as Daniel emerged from the timber, and after an initial warning snarl, the animal picked up its spoils of war and trotted toward Daniel's outstretched hand. The mastiff squatted in front of Daniel. Gideon's jaws were firmly clamped around a bloody swath of cloth, possibly the seat of someone's pants, and a buckskin shot bag whose contents—gun patches and rifle balls—the dog had already emptied in the middle of the trail.

Daniel knelt and scratched the dog's fierce head and, shoving a pistol in his belt, managed to wrest the shot bag from Gideon. He stood and examined the bag. Its rawhide fastenings and the pouch itself had been ripped apart. He lifted the buckskin flap and found what he'd been looking for on the flap's underside. Crude letters had been burned into the hide, and Daniel read them aloud.

"H. S." He glanced up at the fresh tracks left on

the trail and said the first name that came to mind: "Henk Schraner."

Gideon growled deep in his throat. Daniel looked at the dog but kept the pouch. "Sorry, boy. I think I ought to return this. Personally."

Chapter Nine

It was dark by the time Daniel unsaddled his horse in the barn of the Hound and Hare. He had returned with the candles and a belly full of Sister Ruth's cooking. Her skill with pork and biscuits and honey cakes more than made up for her lack of humor. Though he had not met Sister Constance, who was infirm and resting in her bedroom—and young Sister Mercy, a mere girl, had been much too shy to engage him in much conversation—Sisters Eve, Agnes, and the irrepressible Sister Hope had been excellent company. After a little prompting, they had been only too eager to tell him all about the Schraners, how Jon Schraner, whom everybody called Papa, lost his first wife to a weak heart and a brutal winter, how three years ago he met and married Henk's mother and gave the lad a father and a family name. The Schraners were deeply committed to the patriot cause. They sounded like good people, and Daniel hoped to avoid a confrontation with them. He was loath to fight any of them or spill innocent blood for the likes of Henk Schraner.

"This killer has a conscience," he muttered. He gave the mare an armful of fresh hay. Riding up to the inn he'd seen several horses tethered in front, and he was curious as to their owners.

He shouldered the heavy sacks of beeswax candles and made his way out from the barn, where he paused to breathe in the cool night air and listened to the music from a concertina that drifted through the shuttered windows of the tavern. He could hear men singing a merry song whose tune, though familiar, now supported a wholly different set of decidedly patriotic lyrics, ridiculing King George's anatomy and lauding the actions of the minutemen at Lexington and Concord.

No doubt Kate is leading them, he thought, smiling. Her rebel's zeal was equal of any orator in Philadelphia. And she could certainly hold her own with the likes of Sister Eve. He wondered if she knew of the arms stored by the Daughters of Phoebe.

An owl glided effortlessly overhead, soaring below the roof of the barn and on past the hog pen and the chicken house. A moment later the owl suddenly dropped like a rock and landed on the edge of the garden near the corn. Some nocturnal animal shrieked in mortal terror, the cry cut short as the owl rose into the air, clutching its feebly struggling prey in its powerful talons.

Daniel shivered. Death was a swift, indiscriminate hunter, and a man must play out his drama, never knowing which was the final act and which deed the summation of a life.

"Daniel."

Daniel whirled around. His right hand dropped to his pistol before he realized it was Kate Bufkin who had called him by name. Even then he hesitated, suspecting that somehow his thoughts had conjured her and she was no more real than a trick of moonlight.

"I was worried," Kate continued; her words proved she was no figment of his mind.

She moved closer to him, and he wrinkled his nose, catching the fine scent of her. She smelled of wildflowers, sweet and pure as spring itself. She was simply attired in an indigo summer dress and a cream-colored apron; her long hair was gathered beneath a lace cap.

"Did you lose your way?" Her earlier displeasure appeared to have vanished. Had she truly been worried that he was lost or that he had taken off for parts unknown?

"Only at the dinner table." Daniel patted the candle sacks. "The good Daughters of Phoebe insisted I break bread with them. They were starved for news of the north country, of the colonies and Canada. I told them what I knew, and as they were still hungry, I lied about the rest. I fear they now believe I drove back the Ottawa singlehandedly."

"One so brave deserves a reward," Kate said, her blue eyes full of promise.

Now, this is more like it. Daniel had no intention of being a gentleman, not if she offered him the opportunity to be otherwise. "What did you have in mind?" he asked, confident of her unspoken invitation.

"Come and have a glass of Madeira," she said, knowing full well that was not what he expected to hear. Kate had planned it that way.

Daniel entered the tavern and found himself immediately engulfed in lamplight and noise. He half expected the men to cease their singing at the sight of a stranger. They noticed him, to be sure, but the ale had flowed too freely and one young man played with exuberance on his concertina and there was singing to be done and tankards to be drained and bold lies to be bandied back and forth until they rang with the clarity of truth.

"A Redcoat came to Lexington.
He came to Concord, too.
We turned him back
This Lobsterback
And left him black and blue.

So went the song, each bold declaration building on the one before until it sounded as if the revolution were already won and the British scurrying homeward, glad to have escaped with their lives. Daniel knew only too well the fallacy of such an illusion. His own father, and his father's father, had tasted cold British steel at Culloden when the flower of Highland manhood had died before the British muskets in a final, desperate bid for victory. No, the Scottish had experienced Britain's tenacity firsthand. And yet, listening to these men awakened the ancient warlike stirrings of his own race. They had all been immigrants searching for freedom, and they had found it on these wild shores. Now the British had come to stamp out the fires of liberty. It was the same old war, only a new battlefield.

Daniel struggled to suppress the kinship he felt for men such as these and headed for the nearest empty table. Kate brought him the promised glass of Madeira, a playful smile on her lips as she set the bottle on the table and sat across from him.

"No one plays a finer tune then Tim Pepperidge. You could join them." She nodded toward the good-natured rebels gathered about the fireplace. Pepperidge, the concertina player, danced a jig as he played his song, and another man, a merchant newly returned from the Caribbean, produced a hornpipe and added his talents to the merry tune. The rest appeared to be farmers, save for a soldier who had stopped at the inn for the night.

"Come dance, pretty Kate, and let your brother tend the bottles," the soldier called out. He cut a rather dashing figure in the red and blue uniform of the Virginia Militia and approached Daniel's table. He caught Kate by the arm and tugged her toward the music makers.

The woman gestured helplessly toward Daniel and allowed herself to be led away.

"In the morning I'll be off for Philadelphia, and there's a cold and lonely ride. Surely you've a dance or a melancholy ballad to warm a soldier on his way," the militiaman chided.

"Cold indeed," Kate told him. "Tomorrow will be a warm and gentle spring day, on my oath, Lieutenant Crowe."

She perched upon the table and then, after whispering instructions to young Pepperidge, began to sing a ballad of such tender and melancholy air that it tugged the heartstrings of every man around her and tears sprang to their eyes. She sang a Scottish song, of Highland evenings and a wee bonnie lass whose lover had gone to war and never returned. Kate sang of a lass who would take her father's pistol and sword and search the long hills for her love.

"And ere she searches still," Kate Bufkin sang, "beneath the blue sky, among the flowers that bloom where brave men fell, she searches on and ever on."

Daniel was in no mood for sad songs and the Madeira soured in his mouth. He felt an awkward jealousy at the way the lieutenant carried on over Kate. Daniel shoved clear of the table and made his way to the bar, where Loyal waited with a leather jack of ale.

Moisture streaked Loyal's features. He dabbed at the battered remnant of his nose with a coarse scarf he kept tucked in his waistcoat pocket.

Two men watched Daniel from the far end of the bar. They looked a few years younger than Daniel, but from their rugged features it seemed they had traveled hard country in their time. They kept their rifles handy, and though wearing homespun farm clothes, their powder horns and shot bags bore Huron markings.

Daniel nodded to them, then fixed his weary gaze on the drink before him. He slid the wineglass toward Loyal and went for the ale. It was a bitter, bracing drink.

"Why is it men always sing before going to war?" Daniel asked.

Loyal shrugged. He didn't like to think of such things. He had seen the horror of war and smelled the stench of violence and breathed it all in until it seemed he was doomed to replay those memories over and over in his sleep. The screams of the scalped and dying ever haunted him, though now and then Loyal did have his moments of peace.

Tonight, for example, Loyal was the soul of propriety, a congenial host. Daniel had noticed when customers were about and the tavern filled with life, Kate's brother seemed happier and more in control of himself. It wouldn't do to have him driving off the paying guests, saber in hand and slashing at the shadows of imaginary savages.

Daniel tugged Henk's shot pouch from his belt and dropped it on the bar in front of him. He'd have given anything to see the look on Henk's face when Gideon came charging out of the woods like some hellhound loosed upon an unsuspecting world. Considering such a scene tempered his anger toward his assailant. Henk would rue his actions this day, no doubt every time he sat. Daniel chuckled softly and, turning, placed his back against the bar and watched Kate. Now, here was a pleasant subject. She was a rare lass with a voice and a smile to arouse desire in any man.

As if in answer to his thoughts, Kate glanced up from the circle of men and met his gaze. When their eyes locked it was as if a bridge of fire were built between them.

He tried to catch his breath. He couldn't pull his eyes away. Indeed, in that moment, he was lost. His life had become even more complicated than before. He was being swept along by events beyond his control. A solitary man, Daniel found he could love this woman, he could walk that bridge of fire to reach a woman like Kate. Looking across the room into the depths of her blue eyes—hot as a summer sky—Daniel wondered if he'd just received an invitation to try.

Then a cold steel point dug a tiny hole in his shirt just below his ribs.

"Outside," said one of the two men who had been standing at the bar sharing a bottle of rum.

Both men had approached him. The one with the knife was a stocky, sunburned man whose features were partly hidden beneath a thick beard the color of freshly turned earth. His companion was a few years older and carried an extra thirty pounds on his thickly muscled frame. He was clean-shaven. Above his right eye, he bore a nasty white ridge of scar tissue that trailed into his receding hairline. The two men bore a resemblance to one another in the close set of their eyes beneath their brooding brows.

"Outside," the smaller man repeated, and pressed home his demand with the point of the knife.

Daniel shrugged, turned back to the bar, and placed

his elbows to either side of his tankard. "Are you Eben or Barnabas?" he asked, playing a hunch.

"Eben," said the man with the knife, unabashedly perplexed at the Highlander's cool behavior.

"Then you must be Barnabas Schraner." Daniel glanced toward the larger brother, then drained his tankard and set it on the bar top with a resounding bang. He wiped the back of his hand across his mouth and sighed in satisfaction.

Barnabas crossed around and stood on the other side of Daniel. He reached out and took the bloodied shot pouch in his hairy hand.

"Maybe my brother has not made himself clear." Barnabas kept his voice low.

Loyal was staring at them and seemed concerned, though he couldn't tell for sure if there was actually any trouble. The three men appeared to be having a friendly, private conversation.

The knife in Daniel's side was anything but friendly. And he'd about had enough of it.

"Eben here is downright eloquent, but I see no point in following you lads out into the barnyard."

"Why is that?" Eben kept a firm grip on the hilt of his knife. This Scotsman was certainly a cold one. Most men would have crumbled at the first kiss of steel.

"Because we'd be alone, away from the fire, and you'd jab me once too often with that pig sticker. Then I'd have to kill you." Daniel's voice turned icy as he spoke. "Both of you."

He looked at Barnabas, who stared back into Daniel's gray eyes and saw something he didn't like. Beneath the creases of a rough and friendly smile lay something silent and deadly. A man comes upon a sleeping wolverine, he ought to have sense not to wake the beast.

"Put the knife away, Eben."

"But Barnabas—"

"Eben!"

"Yeah." The man to Daniel's left sheathed the knife. Eben scratched at his beard and motioned for Loyal to bring him a tankard of ale.

"This be brother Henk's," Barnabas said, examining the shot pouch. His homely face was marked with curiosity. "What have you done to him?"

"Kept him from shooting me. I had paid a visit to the good Daughters of Phoebe. Henk fired on me from the woods. I don't know why. Maybe he resents the way I've come to work here. Anyway, I made for him, but Gideon chased your brother off before I could catch up to him. What would you have done?"

Barnabas wiped a film of sweat from his scarred forehead. He pursed his lips and grumbled in disgust. This was all bad, and nothing to be done. "The same as you."

Eben said nothing. He listened and drank from the tankard Loyal had left for him. He kept a wary eye on Daniel. He didn't fully trust Kate's hired man. The man was too much a stranger. But Eben had to respect the cool detachment with which the man had handled himself. When Daniel glanced in his direction Eben caught a glimpse of what his brother had seen, the hard and ruthless edge to the man that the wilderness had honed.

"Henk's a mighty jealous lad." Eben looked over his shoulder at Kate.

"I'll find Henk and read him from the book," Barnabas said, shoving clear of the bar. He looked up at Daniel, who stood a head taller than either Schraner brother. "He will not trouble you again." Barnabas took the remains of the pouch and tucked it in his belt. He nodded a farewell to Daniel. "Come along,

Eben, no telling what Henk's up to or what devilment he's planning. We better find him."

The younger brother grumbled in reply. He had a deep thirst and stared forlornly at the tankard he'd just emptied. At last, grudgingly, he retrieved their long rifles from where they'd left them at the other end of the bar. Loyal cautioned him to be on the watch for Ottawas, though such Indian trouble was well in the past. Eben said he would, humoring the poor soul.

"Big doins in Springtown come the first of June," Barnabas mentioned aloud as an aside to the Highlander. "We'll light us a liberty tree like in Boston and hang King George from it, by heaven." He hooked a thumb in his brown frock coat and winked. "Raise us a militia that night, I'll warrant. And raise a cup of grog and maybe a lady's skirt, too, upon my oath." His eyebrows raised, and there was devilment in his expression where menace had reigned supreme.

He clapped Daniel on the shoulder. "Kate told us you were a man of many talents. We'll need them if we are to have our freedom."

Many talents? If he only knew, thought Daniel. The Schraners had left but a few moments ago. Eben had even apologized for jabbing Daniel with the knife. And Barnabas had once more promised to control his half brother. The Schraners had proved themselves to be fair, honest men.

"Honest," now that's a word one could hardly apply to you, Daniel silently told the reflection staring at him from the surface of the ale, the face of a pretender, a liar, one of Josiah Meeks's murderous crew.

Daniel lashed out at the leather jack and slapped it the length of the bar in a shower of ale. It bounced onto the floor and clattered to a stop against the leg of a table over against the far wall.

The music stopped.

The singing stopped.

Kate and the soldier, the merchants, and travelers turned toward the man at the bar. No one spoke. Indeed, no one knew what to say at such an awkward moment.

His sudden violent outburst had caught them off guard.

Daniel turned, pointedly avoiding Kate's surprised stare. He didn't want to see anyone—and, embarrassed, he didn't want to be seen. Daniel looked neither right nor left but beat a hasty retreat from the tavern, defeated by his own lack of control and his brooding guilt.

Chapter Ten

Midnight.

Old Scratch coming, Beelzebub himself. I know him firsthand, close as a brother. His face is the color of fresh-spilled blood, like at hog-slaughtering time. That red. I never see his hands or any of the rest of his body. Just his face, and it keeps getting larger and larger until it fills everything and everywhere I look.

Loyal screamed.

The face seemed to melt; like a wax mask, it molded itself, became human, became the war-painted visage of an Ottawa warrior.

Get thee back. You'll not take me. Where is my saber? Bring me a rifle. Someone bring me a rifle. For heaven's sake, the savages are in the stockade. Turn them back. Oh sweet Jesus, the babies with their heads cracked open against the rocks. Murdering savages. Father, there's too many of them. Run. Run. Keep away, you red devils. Let my father go. If you've come for steel, then here be you. Taste it. Father, the flames all around you. I'll save you. I swear it. But there's too many of them. I don't want to die. Not like that, not burned and blind and screaming. No. Run, I have to live. Shut my ears to the screaming. Forgive me, Father. Forgive me. Ahhhhhhhhhh!

Saber in hand, Loyal crashed through his shuttered window and landed barefoot in the barnyard, where he slipped and fell to his knees in the mud. He managed to stand and then charged into the heart of a driving thunderstorm.

Forgive me, Father. I won't run. Not this time. I'll come to you. I'll feed them a length of steel. Don't die. Father. Don't die!

Lightning flashed bright and searing hot as if loosed from hell. Thunder shook the barn. Daniel sat upright in his bedroll in the hayloft, where he had moved to be more secure. The lower stalls were simply too vulnerable. A few days earlier Kate had offered him one of the upstairs rooms, but Daniel preferred the privacy of the barn and the freedom it provided to come and go should the need arise.

Then beneath the rumbling storm came Loyal's hoarse cry. Daniel crawled across the loft and peered through the loading window, and by the storm's lurid light he saw Kate's brother slashing at the rain. The poor man shouted, but his words were rendered unintelligible by the angry downpour. Daniel didn't need to hear; he knew the spell was on the man. The demons that lurked in Loyal's mind had risen up and taken hold. There was nothing to do for it but try to keep the man from injuring himself.

Daniel pulled off his shirt—no sense in getting it soaked or torn—and pulled on his boots and headed for the ladder. His eyes had grown accustomed to the dark, and he had no problem making his way down to the straw-littered floor. He hurried to the barn doors, unbolted them, and opened one just enough to slip through.

Cold rain struck his naked torso, and he gasped. Now, where the hell was Loyal? Daniel called the man by name as he walked toward the inn. Had the earth opened and swallowed the deluded soul and left Daniel to wander lonely in the rain? The chickens in their pens, the hogs huddled in their shed, and the cow beneath its shed roof stall across the barnyard...all the animals were smart enough to seek shelter.

"Appears I'm the only fool." Daniel wiped the rain from his face. He cleared his vision enough to see Kate emerging from the side of the inn.

She held a brass and glass lantern before her, and the fire within cast a baleful red glow like the eye of a demon. She had heard her brother and had come to find him in the night.

Daniel called out to her. She hurried toward him. A few steps out into the downpour, and her shawl and dressing gown were plastered to the young woman's lithe form.

She shouted something, lifted the hem of her dressing gown, and began to run toward him.

It took Daniel a few seconds to realize Kate was trying to warn him. *Against what?* he thought.

Then he heard the splash of a footstep behind him and turned on his heels as Loyal Bufkin swung his saber in a vicious arc.

Kate screamed.

Daniel slipped in the mud and went down, a mishap that saved his life. A yard of cold, curved steel cut the empty air and left a sickening whisper of death in its wake.

Loyal, his face contorted in a mask of rage,

loosed an animal-like cry and stabbed at the fallen man.

Daniel rolled out of the path of the blade. The weapon sank several inches into the mud. Daniel kicked Loyal and knocked him aside. Loyal stumbled to his right, dragging his saber free. He slashed at the rain-choked wind and cursed aloud as if beset by savages. Then his gaze focused on Daniel and he attacked.

The Highlander ducked inside the blade's path and tried to pin the smaller man's arms. Loyal reeked of rum. He must have downed a keg by himself, Daniel thought. The liquor had loosed his demons.

Loyal's madness had endowed him with remarkable strength. He broke Daniel's hold and clipped him in the chin with the saber's brass hilt.

Daniel tried to catch Loyal's outstretched arm, but the deranged man worked free and delivered another blow to Daniel's jaw. He staggered back against the split-rail fence. Blood seeped from his puffed lip. The rain washed the blood from his mouth and down his neck and belly. Daniel sensed rather than saw Loyal's next move, and he darted to his left.

The sword blade cleaved the top rail and caught in the one below.

Daniel launched himself at the madman and drove him backward into the mud, knocking the wind out of him. Loyal's eyes rolled back in his head, his mouth formed a silent "O," and he curled on his side and gasped for breath. He groaned, his features contorted with pain, and he dug his feet into the mud.

Kate cautiously approached the men through the rain. She stifled an outcry as Daniel rose from the mud. He doubled over, with his hands on his knees, and sucked in a lungful of air, all the while keeping a watchful eye on Loyal Bufkin.

Kate knelt by her brother and, cradling his head in her lap, wiped the mud from his face. She wrinkled her nose, recognizing the smell of strong drink on his breath.

"He'll be all right," Daniel managed to say in a hoarse voice. "Appears he's drunk his share of rum this night."

"He knows better." Kate shook her head in resignation. "It makes the spells so much worse."

"Kate..." Loyal said in a weak voice.

He blinked, wiped the rain from his eyes, and looked from his sister to Daniel. His brows furrowed as he struggled to understand how he happened to be lying on his back in the rain. Daniel retrieved the saber from the fence, just to be on the safe side. But he need not have worried, for the terrible hallucinations appeared to have left the poor soul. Loyal recognized them both now.

"What happened?" Loyal covered his face with his hands. "Oh, God. Not again. How long, oh Lord... how long?" He closed his eyes, unable to endure the look on Kate's face. "I had such a thirst, Kate. I couldn't hold it off—not a moment longer." His head sank back against her breast, and he lost consciousness, his hand dropped into a mud puddle.

Daniel left the saber for Kate to bring and knelt by her side. Reaching down, he lifted Loyal in his arms and started toward the inn. Kate followed, carrying her brother's saber, with which he had fought the treacherous creations of his tormented mind.

They left Loyal asleep in his bed. Kate fastened the shutters across his window and assured Daniel that her brother would no doubt sleep through the night. She had seen him like this often enough to read the nature of his spells.

Daniel returned to the tavern room, which was

quiet now, lit only by a single lantern and the glowing coals mounded in the fireplace. He added a log to the hearth and stoked the coals with an iron poker until the ruby red embers split open and released their imprisoned flames to feed upon the fresh supply of timber. Kate entered the room; she carried a heavy gray cloak draped over her folded arms. It was patched in places and tattered around the edges but still thick and warm to the touch.

"You'll catch your death," she said.

"I've been trying to for years," he replied, shivering.

She handed him the cloak. "Loyal was going to use this to wrap the scarecrow in the garden." Kate stood back as he swung the cloak around his brawny frame, hiding the bronzelike torso she found most appealing now that the emergency was passed.

"It suits me," Daniel said with a grin. "Perhaps I should spend my days in the cornfield to show my gratitude."

"You aren't made of straw," the young woman teased.

Thunder rumbled in the distance like some far-off battle whose outcome no longer concerned them.

"No." Daniel drew nearer. "And sure I'm flesh and blood, sweet lass." Beads of water clung to his shaggy red mane and trickled down his back. He shook his head from side to side, showering his shoulders and the nearby wall with a fine mist.

"And unlike a man of straw, I do not fear fire. I reach out . . . and embrace it." He caught her and pulled the woman into his arms and kissed her. She did not resist.

Her arms encircled his neck, and her lips threatened to draw the life from him. When the kiss had ended, they parted slowly, searching one another's eyes for some sign of how far to let the heat of the moment carry them.

Had there not been a soldier asleep upstairs and Loyal in his bedroom just off the tavern, Daniel might well have spread his cloak upon the nearest tabletop and sweet Kate upon the cloak.

"Oh, dear." She spun around and hurried back down the hall to the safety of her bedroom.

Daniel shrugged and glanced balefully at the tabletop. At least he was dry and had a warm fire. What more could a man ask for? He chuckled softly; the taste of her lingered on his lips.

An ember popped and crackled, drawing Daniel's attention to the hearth, where the flames danced. The blaze was enough to trigger his memory. Flames dissolved, reformed anew, and he stood in his father's bedroom, where Brian Farley McQueen lay still in his bed; Daniel held a letter, one he had been working on for the better part of an hour. Upon this paper he had put his reasons for leaving. Somewhere among those tortured thoughts he hoped he had put the truth. His father deserved that. Daniel placed the note on a table by his father's bed and turned to go. He padded soundlessly across the room and reached the door. And there he paused, unable to cross the threshold. His father deserved more than the truth; he deserved to hear it, to be told by his son.

Daniel returned to his father's side and reached out to wake him. Brian rolled over and stared up at his son. He hadn't been asleep at all.

"So...you've found the courage to face me, eh, and not sneak away like you did when you ran off to war," Brian said.

"You're a clever old fox, Papa," Daniel said.

"Not clever enough to keep you from turning your

back on everything we've built," Brian replied, holding up the letter to the flickering firelight.

"You've built, not me," Daniel said. "I want more than the life I have now."

"More? Because Squire Trevane's prissy daughter cast ye aside for merchant Greene's eldest lad?" Brian shook his head and swung his legs over the side of the bed. "You are not the first younker who's had his heart tramped on by a fair lassie, and you won't be the last, but heartache is no reason to throw your life away."

"You don't understand, Papa."

"There's everything here for you, Danny boy."

"Yessir. Everything but what I want."

"It is that Trevane girl, she's turned your head...."

"No!" Daniel blurted out; then, "Yes...." He walked to the hearth and warmed his hands. "Maybe...at first I, too, thought it was the girl. Then I realized I've felt this way for a long time."

"What are you saying?" Brian growled. "Talk sense to me."

Daniel faced him. The two men stared at one another, father and son, both stubborn and determined to have their way.

"Look," Daniel said. "When you work iron and shape it to your will, it has your mark upon it. Right?"

"Yes," Brian warily consented, suspecting a trap.

"I want a life with my mark upon it. Can you not be understanding this? I want to forge my own life, for better or ill."

Silence reigned, broken only by the crackling flames. Daniel could see the hurt in his father's eyes. He wished there had been another way.

"Well, there it is, then," Brian replied coldly. He turned his back on his son and walked to the window that overlooked the drive and, beyond it, the post road. "I'll speak no more on the matter. Be off with ye."

Years passed in a single breath. Flames shimmered and dissolved like the vestiges of a departing dream. The memory of one hearth became the reality of another.

Daniel surveyed his surroundings; the tavern room, the doorway beyond which a woman he cared for waited and waited, a woman he had already deceived, to his own remorse.

"Well, I've a life with my mark on it now," Daniel said softly. But only time would tell the temper of the "metal" with which he'd worked.

Nathaniel Woodbine had only recently purchased his house on Mulberry and Sixth streets, just a couple of blocks east of the college and academy. It was a handsome, red-bricked, two-story structure that withstood the wrath of the storm. It was the downpour that had roused the colonel from his warm bed and set him on the prowl down the dark halls and stairway and through the spacious rooms below.

The faint odor of tobacco mingled with the aroma of that night's supper. Woodbine paused, his eye scanning the table. He pictured in his mind the men who had only recently partaken of his food. There sat John Adams at one end. And my, how this round-faced, stocky rebel extolled the virtues of George Washington, reciting the Virginian's name ad nauseum as he called for the formation of a Grand American Army to drive the British from the colonies.

Several of the guests, merchants and the like, men of proper breeding and station, championed such a suggestion, and none more loudly than Woodbine himself. It was plain to see that Washington was the best man for the job of commander-in-chief.

The other guests concurred, with the exception of Charles Lee, a British-born mercenary only recently returned from Europe who coveted the command for himself. Much to his displeasure, not a single individual among this gathering of Philadelphia's aristocracy voiced the opinion that Major Lee ought to be considered for the post.

Woodbine paused in the doorway to the kitchen, the memories of the discussion still fresh in his mind, and in the lightning's lurid glare made out the cloth-covered pie tin that Mrs. Patterson, Woodbine's widowed cook, had left on the oak table near the ruby glow of the hearth.

Woodbine made his way across the winter kitchen, retrieved the pie and a silver spoon the widow had left next to the tin, and greedily began to devour the remainder of the mincemeat pie.

Mrs. Patterson knew her master was wont to roam about the house and liked a bit of nourishment for his efforts. Indeed, all the servants were aware of how fitfully the colonel slept and were no longer aroused by the noise of his midnight excursions.

So the colonel, snug in his robes and sleeping gown, listened to the sound of wind and rain and thunder and took comfort in the fact that his support of Adams's proposal might push the Continental Congress toward a decision.

He spooned another helping of pie between his lips and savored the mixture of spices and fruit in his mouth. He judged the conservatory at the back of the house to be the only proper place to view the storm's display. He headed for it, retracing his route through the dining room and then down a narrow hallway that opened into the window-lined conservatory, with its wing-backed, upholstered chairs and comfortable settees arranged around a pianoforte and harp.

Someone plucked a harp string. It was hardly an angel.

Woodbine froze in the entranceway, a spoonful of pie midway to his lips. He dropped the utensil into the tin and slowly ventured toward the center of the room, where a gaunt, rain-drenched figure sat near the harp, his bony digits plucking discordant notes upon the instrument.

"We agreed you would never come here," Woodbine stated nervously. "My God, if someone should see you..." His voice was thick.

"No one did."

"But if someone should...I mean—there are many in Philadelphia, like Colonel Washington, to name just one, who would recognize you." Woodbine glanced nervously about, as if expecting one of his guests to pop up from behind a chair.

The figure by the harp stirred. Tinder sputtered for a moment and then the wick of a candle sputtered into flame. The sallow firelight played upon the sunken cheeks and eyepatched countenance of the uninvited guest. Water dripped from the hem of his cloak and the broad brim of his hat.

"No one saw me. No one will. Now, tell me what you've learned since last we spoke. And be brief; I've had a hard ride." Major Josiah Meeks reached out and snatched the pie tin from Woodbine's grasp. He helped himself to the last of the dessert that the other had coveted for himself.

Woodbine began an account of the current situation, the movement among the continentals to name Washington as commander of the army and the local effort to gather arms and munitions for the troops besieging General Gage in Boston.

The Philadelphian was swift and to the point, as he was most anxious to see Meeks on his way. As yet, no one suspected Colonel Nathaniel Woodbine of being anything less than an ardent patriot. He wanted to keep it that way.

Chapter Eleven

June 1, 1775

The center of Springtown was a collection of businesses and stately two-story brick homes whose lower floors had been converted into shops, all of them surrounding a commons fringed with stately oaks and elms. The commons, or the Green, as folk called it, served as a gathering spot for the whole community. This rectangular plot of ground, lushly carpeted with wild grasses, was already strewn with wagons and tents.

The Springtown Congregational Church, a whitewashed brick structure whose steeple had suffered lightning damage from the recent storms, now ten days past, dominated the north end of the Green, while the remainder of the town square bordered east, west, and south. Over a hundred people had ridden in from outlying farms to participate in the rally in support of the colonial troops besieging the British in Boston.

Among the new arrivals on this first day of June was a wagon from the Hound and Hare Inn.

Daniel McQueen, following Kate Bufkin's instructions, steered the mares off of First Street and onto Main, which bordered the Green on the east. Daniel was astonished at the crowd already decorating the giant old oak tree in the center of the Green. Soon the oak's gnarled branches would be festooned with lanterns, ribbons, and broadsides, and its trunk ringed with patriots full of song and speeches to fuel their courage. Come nightfall and the "liberty tree" would be ablaze with the light of freedom. But this was the Sabbath, approaching noon, and wagons, horses, townspeople, and farm families choked the thoroughfare and reduced Daniel's pace to a crawl. It was better than a country fair, and everyone who believed in the rebel cause was welcome.

The air was thick with excitement that seemed to feed upon itself and expand.

Daniel sighed. "I should never have come."

Kate, at his side, followed his line of sight. His remark had caught her off guard. Had he already tired of her company? Then she noticed big Henk Schraner towering over his brothers where they stood in front of a pub. By the expression on his face, Henk had already recognized the couple on the wagon rolling toward him. Eben and Barnabas doffed their hats in greeting as the wagon crawled by.

Daniel returned the gesture, holding the lines in one hand and waving with the other.

Henk continued to scowl, his gaze smoldering with dislike. Kate noticed how the young man's hands were balled into fists. Daniel had told her of his encounter with Henk in the woods near Sister Hope's farm. Kate had hoped that Papa Schraner might have talked some sense into his adopted son and cooled the green fire of his jealousy. It was obvious nothing had changed.

They left the Schraners behind, and Kate directed Daniel to turn at Second Street at the north end of the commons. A block off the town square, they drew up before a white picket fence surrounding a two-story frame house and a neighboring church. Though not as large as the church in the center of town, Faith Chapel was well attended. About three dozen people were congregated on the front steps and in the yard. Daniel judged they had just concluded a Sunday prayer service. A minister in black frock coat and cleric's collar stood among them, laughing to twice-told tales, empathizing with the newly revealed ache or pain, commiserating with loss, and sharing in the joys of his flock. He was a man of average height, thin, in his late forties. He was wigged, as was the fashion for ministers and barristers and men of high social standing.

"That's Reverend Albright," Kate said. "The barn's out back."

"I'll find it," Daniel told her. "You visit with your preacher friend while I unhook the team."

Kate patted his arm, then climbed down. She hesitated for a moment, and her expression clouded. "You do think Loyal will be—"

"Fine," Daniel completed her sentence in a reassuring tone.

"Sister Agnes and Sister Ruth are there to help him with any guests." Kate had been reluctant to bring her brother into Springtown for the patriotic gathering. She feared all the commotion might serve to unsettle him.

Daniel called out to the mares and shook the lines. The horses obediently fell into step. He rounded the minister's house and located the barn easily enough. It was a small structure, adequate to house the team and keep them out of the elements, but the wagon, like the minister's own carriage, would have to be left outside. A charred patch of earth and soot-blackened debris indicated where a carriage house once stood.

By the time Daniel had found stalls for the mares and left each animal a pitchforkful of hay, he heard Kate's voice and the deep, stentorian tones of the minister in reply ring upon the warm June air. Daniel emerged from the narrow confines of the barn and stood in the sunlight and stretched the kinks out of his muscular frame. He noted once again how pretty Kate looked in her pale green dress and white cotton apron with her bonnet hung loose on her back, away from her heather-gold hair. The ten days following the storm had seemed to Daniel like ten years as the last of May unfolded. One chore had led to the next, and lately the upstairs rooms were taking shape. But underneath every labor, haunting each task, was the memory of her warm kiss on that cold and rainy night when he had held her in his arms in the tavern.

"Reverend Francis Albright," the minister said, extending a pale hand. His grip was surprisingly strong. "Welcome, Mr. McQueen, to our humble lodgings." The minister displayed a good-natured expression, and his eyes were bright and friendly.

Daniel shook hands and glanced from the minister to Kate in surprise. He hadn't intended to spend the night. She only shrugged, avoiding his unspoken question.

"Reverend Albright—uh—Francis has insisted we stay the night," Kate told him. "He has an extra bedroom."

"Oh?" Daniel brightened. One bedroom; now, that did sound interesting.

"And we've plenty of blankets to make you a warm bed by the hearth." Albright beamed, clasping his hands together.

"Oh," came Daniel's dampened reply.

"It's unfortunate you missed our Sabbath sermon," the reverend continued, leading Kate and Daniel around to the front. Albright immediately launched into a discourse on the travails of Job and how the Old Testament story related to the turmoil of the times.

Daniel pretended interest, all the while looking across at Kate, who met his gaze with a whimsical smile. Now, that indeed was a dangerous look, one that meant she was plotting some mischief that would eventually involve him. He felt about as secure as a blind man in a field of bear traps.

And that was a high point, for when Daniel rounded the corner of Albright's house he stopped dead in his tracks. Half a dozen horsemen sat their mounts before the picket fence in front of the parsonage. Three of them were strangers, gruff-looking men in homespun clothes with impassive faces shaded by their battered tricorn hats. The other three Daniel knew only too well.

"I wonder who they are?" Albright wondered aloud as Major Josiah Meeks dismounted and handed the reins of his horse to Black Tolbert. Bill Chaney nudged Tolbert.

A slender, pretty woman in a dark brown dress, white cap, and apron stood at the front gate with an eight-year-old boy who fidgeted in his tight breeches, waistcoat, and buckled shoes. He was the mirror image of his father, Reverend Albright.

Meeks noticed Daniel, Kate, and the reverend. He bowed to the mistress of the house and tousled the hair of the boy, an act which caused the youth immediate displeasure. The gaunt Englishman followed the cobblestone walkway through Mrs. Albright's flower beds and met the threesome halfway.

Daniel glowered at Chaney and Tolbert and rested a hand on the butt of his pistol. The hairs on the back of his neck prickled. He looked around and found Kate studying him. She seemed confused and even a bit alarmed at the way he seemed to recognize the strangers at the gate. She shifted her gaze to take in the horsemen. She had the uneasy feeling she had met some of them before. But where? She glanced directly at Black Tolbert.

The Tory renegade chuckled, as a leer split his features. Kate shuddered. How did she know him?

"Good Sabbath, Reverend Albright," Meeks said.

"And good Sabbath to you, sir," Albright replied, shaking the man's bony hand.

"I and my companions have come to hang a lantern from the liberty tree and offer the strength of our arms to the cause of freedom." Meeks's expression never altered as he offered Daniel his hand and bowed once again to Kate.

"Well spoken, Mr.—"

"Meeks," said the officer. "I am a teacher. And my companions, simple men of the soil. But willing to stand and fight." The major gestured toward the house. "I was told you might have a room to let for some of these good lads."

"I'm sorry. We have nothing save for ourselves and these, our guests," Albright explained. "There ought to be room at one of the taverns. Or perhaps you could camp on the Green. Many families will be there."

Meeks absentmindedly fumbled with the patch over his left eye. His usually sharp features relaxed and he appeared for a moment totally lost in thought. Then he flashed a disarming smile.

"Most unfortunate. Still, what better roof over one's head than the Lord's own starry sky." Meeks patted a coat pocket. "And I've a few coins aching to be spent at the local tavern."

"The Boar's head has a most delectable array of spirits," Albright said, keeping his voice low to avoid his wife's disapproval. He clapped Meeks on the shoulder.

Meeks bristled at such familiarity but held his temper in check.

"The Boar's Head it is. Perhaps I'll see you there later, good Reverend, and you, sir." He focused on Daniel. "I didn't catch the name, but you have the look of a man familiar with war. Will you be casting your lot with the sons of liberty?"

"I work the forge and bend iron," Daniel said. "That is my calling."

"Dangerous work. A man could get burned."

"Only if he's careless."

Meeks laughed softly and then, bowing again to Kate, added, "By your leave," and started back toward the front gate. He mounted his charger and rode off toward the center of town, the folds of his cloak streaming behind.

The horsemen turned from the picket fence and followed Meeks with a precision that decried their supposedly rustic roots. Only Black Tolbert lingered to walk his horse along the front of the house. He drew close enough for Kate to recognize the lust in his red-rimmed eyes. Daniel stepped in front of her, placing himself between Tolbert and the young woman.

The Tory turned and led his mount back toward the center of town.

"I know him." Kate tried to make sense of it and

failed. "I know his eyes," she added, perplexed. She reached out and took Daniel's hand. She felt safe, her hand in his—yes, safe with someone she could trust.

Chapter Twelve

Josiah Meeks found the Boar's Head to his liking. It was a large place, built of stone and dominating a shady plot of ground near the south end of the Green. An imposing structure, it boasted three rooms on the ground floor, with tables set in cool, shadowy corners where men might confer quietly—or in this case shout. Today, the Boar's Head held a noisy crowd of plowmen, tinkers, and woodsmen drawn to Springtown either out of patriotic fervor or simple curiosity and a need for a little excitement. No matter, revolutionary fever was infectious and by midafternoon had spread throughout the gathering. Ale flowed freely and fueled brave songs, brave words, and dreams of glory. A nation waited to be wrested from the British domination, and such men as these were just the ones to do it.

Meeks eased back in his chair, sipped his wine, and listened to the talk around him with a bemused expression on his face. Words were no match for cold British steel, as this rabble would one day discover, to their great dismay. He had chosen a table in the rear of the tavern, the better to watch these rebels. Will Chaney sat to his left and Black Tolbert on the right, his ferret-eyed stare fixed on the buxom tavern wench who carried a pewter pitcher of ale from table to table, filling the tankards as she went and pocketing in her apron the coins left in payment.

Tobacco smoke curled to the ceiling. Men and women sauntered among the tables, exchanging news with strangers, eager for word of the happenings in Philadelphia, New York, and Boston. They cast their shadows upon stone walls adorned with racks of pewter plates and tankards, hunting rifles and powderhorns, and an occasional painting left by a local artist as payment in lieu of money for an outstanding bill.

The three men seated across the table from Meeks were new arrivals he had taken on in Philadelphia. The oldest of the lot was an Irish soldier of fortune, Corporal Padraich O'Flynn, a jovial, ruddy-cheeked Irishman in the direct employ of Nathaniel Woodbine. O'Flynn had a hearty appetite, one he was only too happy to appease at the British agent's expense. A plate of pork ribs held his interest this afternoon.

The other two men, Al Dees and Mose Wiley, were young hotheads eager to prove their worth to Josiah Meeks. They both came from Tory families in Connecticut who had already suffered at the hands of patriots. Barns had been burned and livestock run off. Both Wiley and Dees had resolved to avenge their families' losses, so when Nathaniel Woodbine put them in touch with Meeks the two had jumped at the chance to serve him.

Dees at nineteen was fair-haired, nonchalantly tilting back on the rear legs of his chair. His thumbs were hooked in the wide leather belt around his waist.

His linsey-woolsey blouse was unlaced to midchest. Before joining Meeks's command he and Mose Wiley had been anxious to strike at the rebels but lacked a direction or a plan. The British agent had promised them both that the hour was at hand and he'd lead the young men in a bold strike against these rebels. Dees was more than ready.

Mose Wiley watched O'Flynn work through the stack of ribs and helped himself to one from the platter. O'Flynn glanced up and gave the eighteen-year-old a sharp look as if Wiley had just stolen some of the Irishman's personal property. Wiley grinned and licking his greasy fingers promptly gnawed the meat from the rib and tossed the bone onto O'Flynn's plate.

"You're a brash young pup." O'Flynn glowered. "Best I put you in your place if you aim to run with this pack."

"At your pleasure." Wiley slipped a dagger from his boot sheath. "But mind you, this pup has fangs." Double-edged steel glinted in the confines of the corner.

Tolbert chuckled. He enjoyed a good fight, and he was curious as to the mettle of these recent arrivals. Chaney grinned, and his mean eyes glittered. A brawler by nature, he just liked to see blood flow and didn't care whose.

"Cut him, Mose," Al Dees said, keeping his voice low. "Notch his ear."

"Put the knife away," Meeks interjected. He leaned his elbows on the table, shadow and light painting patterns across his hooked nose and gaunt cheeks. His single eye, like some baleful jewel, gleamed with a chill menace. Wiley tucked the knife back into his boot. O'Flynn shrugged and returned his attention to the food.

Tolbert tore a chunk of bread from the round loaf

before him and began to sate his own hunger. "You think Danny boy caught your meaning?"

"McQueen is no fool. Gullible, yes, but not a fool. He understood," Meeks said. His gaze swept the room, pausing for but a moment on face after face of these rebels young and old, working themselves up for war. They could probably fight well enough, but the colonists had no history behind them, no military tradition, nothing like the army and naval might of Great Britain. This mob would need a leader to mold them together. Perhaps they'd have one soon. But Major Josiah Meeks intended to see such a leader was short-lived. The colonists would need weapons, too: powder and shot, muskets and rifles. There was a supply cached in this area, according to Woodbine. But the merchant didn't know its location. The hidden weapons must be found and destroyed. Meeks considered himself just the man for the job. He dabbed the sweat from his brow with a silk kerchief.

"A warm summer," young Dees observed dryly.

"It will get warmer." Meeks settled in his chair, raised his tankard, and added, "God save the king."

Daniel McQueen had never seen Sicilians before, but their gypsylike lifestyle appealed to him. Families like the Yaquerenos and the Ferillis were free as the wind. They were itinerant craftsmen, knife makers, swordsmiths, and silverworkers who had come to the colonies to ply their trades. Daniel had been skirting the Green when he spied the ornately painted panel wagons and the swarthy Sicilian tinkers who had set up displays of trinkets and finely crafted daggers and knives whose workmanship was unmatched in Daniel's experience.

Dressed in their blousy shirts, vests, and pantaloons tucked in ankle boots, the men paraded their skills and hawked their wares while the dark-eyed women busied themselves with domestic chores. One of the women paused in her work to entertain a small herd of curious farm children. Much to their delight she produced a pair of wooden puppets whose antics left the boys and girls helpless with laughter. Several adults stood in awe of a young man who juggled five brightly colored balls and then switched to daggers whose keen blades and shiny brass hilts shimmered in the sunlight.

"You are fascinated by our knifemakers?" Barnabas Schraner spoke in a gruff-sounding voice at Daniel's side. The Highlander wasn't surprised. He had figured at least one of the Schraners would seek him out. He was relieved it was the eldest son and not Henk.

"Have they come as patriots or performers?" Daniel asked.

"Freedom is the life's blood of their kind. They will fight to preserve it. And aid in other ways, too."

Daniel found the last of Barnabas's statement rather perplexing; the meaning escaped him.

"Giuseppe Ferilli is the patriarch of one family. He's fathered only girls, an even half dozen. As for Pietro Yaquereno, fortunately his Anna has only borne him sons. A good arrangement, yes?" Barnabas chuckled. He averted his eyes from the juggler; he had a weak stomach when it came to a man about to lose an eye or accidently slit his own throat.

"Never have I seen such knives," Daniel said in open admiration for the skill of these artisans. Glancing at their paneled wagons, he wondered what other handiwork they kept hidden from the public. The wagons themselves were impressive; great, heavy conveyances drawn by teams of stout oxen. These Sicilians most assuredly carried their homes with them wherever they went. Despite the outward boisterousness of this lot and their obvious desire to turn a quick profit, the Ferillis and Yaquerenos certainly valued their privacy, for at least three young men in ornately stitched waistcoats stood guard by the wagons and kept the crowd from pressing too close. Even the farm children were shooed away. Two more of the craftsmen stationed at the rear of the last paneled wagon appeared to be engaged in a heated argument. Daniel shifted his stance and recognized the faces of the animated pair, although at first Daniel couldn't believe his eyes. The young one was Tim Pepperidge and the man bearing the brunt of his complaints was none other than Lieutenant Peter Crowe, the militiaman from the inn. Crowe no longer wore the colors of the Virginia militia but had traded his rank for the humble garb of Sicilian tinker. Now, why had he done that, and what had caused the wagon they were standing by to sit so heavy on its axles? More guns and powder for the Daughters of Phoebe's barn? That would explain the presence of the two rebels standing guard.

"Best you cut Henk a wide berth," Barnabas said. "You shamed him, loosing ol' Gideon on him. Seein' you is like pouring black powder on a campfire."

"I am not looking for trouble."

"That's not my point. It's looking for you."

Reverend Albright came in from the backyard, where he'd been singeing the tiny hairs off the chickens he'd just slaughtered. He wore a simple brown waistcoat and breeches and coarse shirt, all the better to keep care of his preacher's attire. He looked more a butcher than a minister, and his hands were stained red with the blood of the hens now ready for the roasting oven.

He handed the birds to Martha Albright, who carried them off to the kitchen table, where she would prepare them for Sunday dinner. Martha kept a steady stream of chatter flowing as she worked. Kate, seated across from her, could only marvel at the wealth of friendly gossip her cousin kept stored for just such a visit. The Martins had a new child, widow Grauwyler was seeing Elmo Dunson, the village cooper, and Abel Merkley's sons had all run off to fight the British in Boston, though some questioned the timing of their patriotic fervor. It was rumored Nels Arnstrom's daughter was with child, much to the scandal of the community.

"If that is the case," Martha remarked, "they had better join the British, for that's the only place they'll be safe from farmer Arnstrom!"

"Now, Martha. The Lord decries an idle tongue," the reverend gently chided.

"Idle, indeed. I haven't stopped talking since Kate and I sat down," Martha said with a wink toward the woman opposite her.

"And where is your Daniel McQueen?" the minister continued, washing his hands in a bucket of well water, which he promptly emptied out the back door.

"Gone to see John Morbitzer about a few rods of blister iron for our forge."

"He'll be back before these hens are cooked," Martha cheerfully added. "Don't worry, Francis, we won't have to delay our dinner."

The reverend patted his stomach, which growled on cue. He crossed to the table and helped himself to one of the biscuits cooling on a platter close at hand.

"Food is for stomachs and stomachs for food, but all will pass away," Albright philosophized as he relaxed in a kitchen chair. His chores were finished, and there was nothing to do but watch Martha spoon bread crumbs and onion stuffing into the hens, preparing them for her roasting pans. Kate was anxious to help. She stuffed the hens and peeled potatoes and kept up a steady stream of innocent conversation, skirting the one topic foremost in the Albrights' thoughts. Just who was this Daniel McQueen? And what exactly was going on between Kate and her hired man?

Chapter Thirteen

Daniel McQueen stood just inside the door of the Boar's Head Tavern and allowed his eyes to adjust to the smoky interior. Sounds and sights assailed him. Tobacco smoke clung heavy as marsh fog to the rafters above the heads of the tavern's patrons. Its pungent aroma mingled with the smells of a stew simmering in a caldron in the fireplace. Abram Rembert, the proprietor of the Boar's Head, was famous for the Friendship Stew he kept heated over the coals; any of the tavern's visitors were welcome to take a bowl and sample the fare. Daniel licked his lips. His mouth had already begun to water, but he refrained from heading right for the caldron. Reverend Albright was expecting him for Sunday dinner, and Daniel promised to return with his appetite intact.

The errand to the local smithy had been a ruse, allowing Daniel to slip away by himself, the better to meet with Major Meeks. The tavern was the perfect place, three rooms full of boisterous strangers and none to notice the likes of Meeks and his conspirators.

Taverns were all the same to Daniel: here a man might find food and drink and perhaps earn the fancy of a comely serving girl. Daniel started across the room and, to his chagrin, garnered the interest of many of the men at the tables around him. They took notice because of his size. He was broader in the shoulders and a head taller than most of the men of his day, and the harsh lessons of the wilderness left an indelible stamp upon his features. He walked like an animal on the prowl, threading his way through the crowd, his eyes alert and searching for the one man he needed to find and wished he would never have to see again.

"Will you be having a jack of ale sir?" said a bright-eyed lass crossing in front of him. She was a pert, diminutive girl whose bodice strained to contain her well-rounded bosom. She carried a tray of leather jacks whose contents sloshed over the sides and left foaming puddles around the tankards. "If you'd prefer something stronger, sir, Master Rembert has tapped a keg of his own brew. The master calls it Pilgrim's Fire."

"Watch thyself, good fellow," a stout, ruddy-cheeked gentleman interjected, overhearing the tavern girl's offer. "Pilgrim's Fire would melt the tines off a pitchfork, mark ye." The gentleman held his belly and laughed heartily, revealing a row of blackened teeth. No doubt, thought Daniel, here was one soul who seemed to have made Pilgrim's Fire his drink of choice. At least if the stubble in his mouth was any indication. The gentleman, though dressed in the sober garb of a Quaker, appeared to have none of the deportment. Perhaps he had fallen away from the ranks of the Society of Friends.

Without waiting for a reply, the man in black staggered off toward a nearby table and slumped unceremoniously into the first vacant chair he came to with nary a "by your leave" to the men already seated to either side.

"Get along, my pretty, for it's business I have with a man," Daniel said. "Mayhaps you've seen him. He's tall, with a lean and hungry look, and wears a patch over his left eye."

"With a face even a mother would long to forget," the girl said.

"The very man. Have you seen him?"

The girl balanced her tray on an upturned hand and pointed to the entrance to the rear room. "He's in there, sir, with his friends—such as they are. Some of them ain't exactly the friendliest sort."

"You're a good lass." Daniel patted her soft arm. He made his way to the rear of the tavern. Behind him, a man moved out of the crowd. Keeping his hat pulled low to hide his features, Henk Schraner fell in step with Daniel and positioned himself to keep the red-headed man under observation.

Meeks was easy enough to locate, and Daniel wasted no time in approaching the Englishman's table. Josiah grinned at his companions and muttered, "O ye of little faith," then ordered them to leave. Al Dees and Mose Wiley shrugged and vacated their seats. Figuring Daniel was one of their own, they regarded him with a certain degree of curiosity, nothing more. O'Flynn, being Woodbine's man, didn't like being ordered about by the major, but now was not the time or place to voice his objections. Besides, the platter of pork ribs held nothing but bones, while the tempting aroma of Friendship Stew beckoned to him from the front room. O'Flynn licked the grease from his fingers and left. Daniel stepped aside, a frown on his face as he tried to remember just when and where he had seen O'Flynn before.

Will Chaney was eager to lure one of the tavern

wenches out behind the tavern or upstairs to a bedroom. Now, there *was* a thought. He nodded to Daniel and hurried off. But Black Tolbert took his time and slowly slid his chair back and stood. A patch of late afternoon sunlight played upon the tabletop between them.

"I ain't afraid of you, McQueen."

"I never said you were."

"When Meeks is finished with us, I'll come for you. And there'll be blood on the earth when I'm done."

"No doubt." Daniel was unmoved by Tolbert's threat. Some words cling to a man and worm their way inside to leave him diminished. But Daniel knew the likes of Tolbert found their brave words sloshed about in the bottom of a tankard, and like the froth from spilled ale, such words dissipated, they didn't last.

Tolbert shifted nervously, expecting more of a reply from Daniel than a somber *No doubt*. He glanced from Daniel to Meeks, who waved him away with a brief flick of his fingers. Tolbert grudgingly swaggered off toward the front of the tavern.

"You prime him like a pistol," Meeks said, amused by the interchange. "Be careful, Danny boy, that you aren't standing in the line of fire when he explodes."

Daniel eased into a chair and sat across from the Englishman. He looked around at the crowd and an idea came to him. "If these lads knew there was a British spy in their midst, they'd tear you to pieces."

Alarm momentarily flickered in the man's gaunt features; then a slow smile crawled across his face and his sole eye looked with cold disregard upon those he considered no more than rabble. He held all American rebels in contempt.

"And General Gage would have your father dangling from a yardarm out in the bay."

The major eased back in his chair and folded his hands across his flat, hard stomach. *Enough idle threats*, he seemed to be saying in that gesture. It was time for business.

Daniel felt the same way. He leaned forward on his elbows, clasped his hands together, and spoke in a soft but urgent tone of voice. "Why did you want to talk to me? I assume that is what the show at Albright's was all about."

Meeks refilled his tankard and then hunched over the table. "You appear to have ingratiated yourself with these rebels."

"I have given no one cause to distrust me."

"Excellent, my good fellow. I have learned of a cache of rifles, muskets, and gunpowder in the area. I must locate it. Have you heard where it is?"

Daniel looked away, focusing on the sunlit patch of ground outside the window. A pair of bluebirds chased one another through the space between the tavern and the cooper's shop next door. The birds dipped and glided; then they flapped their wings and in the blink of an eye whisked out of sight.

"Well?"

"I haven't heard a thing," Daniel said impassively.

"Odd. Maybe you aren't as accepted as you think." Meeks studied the big man's weathered face. His gray eyes were as impenetrable as flint. The major was accustomed to reading the men who served him. He believed he could tell when a man was lying or telling the truth. "Very well." One of the Sicilians' panel wagons is loaded with long rifles. When it leaves, I'll have a couple of my men follow it. We'll let the rebels lead us to the rest of their weapons."

"A gypsy wagon? How did you learn of it?"

"A friend."

Meeks did not elaborate, and Daniel did not press the matter, for fear of arousing the officer's suspicions.

"It's good to have friends," Daniel said.

"He will be well rewarded for the information." The Englishman toyed with the patch covering his eye. "Some men can be bought for money, some for power. And some for a father's love."

Daniel stiffened at the reference. Color crept into his cheeks. "Is that all?" he said. He shoved away from the table and stood.

"Be alert, Danny boy. Events move swiftly now. I believe your hour will soon be at hand."

Chapter Fourteen

"Where the devil is that boy?" Papa Schraner growled. He paced the hard-packed earth in front of the gypsy wagons. The setting sun splashed gold and scarlet on the western horizon and silhouetted the scattered clouds in its dazzling dying light. Dusk meant only one thing to Papa Schraner: The time was drawing nigh for his sons to escort this gun wagon out of town—all his sons.

Schraner clasped his hands behind his back and looked over at the two he could count on. Barnabas and Eben were good lads. Squatting by a cook fire where they nursed stoneware cups of strong black tea, the brothers had remembered to keep their rifles close at hand. Like Henk, they had grumbled over the idea of watching the festivities from afar. Even now a veritable tide of patriots—men, women, and children—inundated the Green. Villagers streamed down streets and alleys and spilled into the emerald park where the great oak waited to be festooned with lanterns.

Barrels of ale had been loaded onto hand carts

and wheeled to strategic spots throughout the Springtown commons, while half a dozen musicians with fife and drum gathered at the base of the oak tree, placing themselves in the center of the gathering crowd.

"Henk knew he was supposed to be here, dammit," Schraner cursed. "I wanted to send all three of you with the wagons."

"He's probably took him a whore and gone off somewhere." Eben scratched at his beard. He cast a knowing glance toward Barnabas, who nodded in unspoken agreement.

"You should not speak so disrespectfully of your own family," Schraner said.

"Henk is not my family, Papa," Eben retorted.

"He is what I say he is!" The older man's cheeks reddened as he struggled to bring his temper under control. He wiped a forearm across his brow. With a look toward the gun wagon, Schraner spotted Tim Pepperidge and Peter Crowe lounging against the wagon wheel. They were pretending to take no interest in the argument. Schraner scowled; he disliked airing family problems in the open where anyone could hear. Crowe had already declared that two Schraner boys was probably enough protection. After all, the whole purpose of disguising the gun wagon was to pass unnoticed from town.

"Surely he wouldn't try to confront McQueen again?" the old farmer speculated aloud.

"It would be a fool's play." Barnabas refilled his cup and took a tentative swallow. The liquid burned the inside of his mouth, and he blew gently across the lip of the cup. "McQueen won't play with him, neither."

"But he's just a brash, headstrong boy."

"In a man's body," Eben piped up. "Leave him be, Papa. We'll see the wagon through."

"Anything happens to that boy, and there'd never be a moment's peace in my house." Schraner slapped his hand into his fist for emphasis. He stared at the oncoming throng as they followed the music of fife and drum to the liberty tree. The world was changing all around him. Life would never be the same again. He clung to the belief that it would be better. But at what price?

As night draped its mantle of darkness across Springtown, torches flared, lanterns glimmered in the branches of the liberty tree. Schraner searched the distant faces in a vain last effort to locate his adopted son. The old farmer suspected he was doomed to failure. He hadn't really expected to find Henk, but being a man of loyalty and purpose, Schraner made the effort, anyway.

"You nurse that bottle as if it were your mother's tit," Will Chaney muttered while watching Padraich O'Flynn sample the contents of a brown glass flask he'd located in his possibles bag.

O'Flynn glanced over at Meeks's henchman. "Why, sure, and whiskey is mother's milk to a thirsty Irishman." He raised the flask as if offering a toast to Chaney, then took another pull, allowing the fiery brew to blaze a path through his innards while he surveyed his surroundings.

The ramshackle barn was all that remained of the Petersen farm. A stone foundation where a house had been stood as a mute reminder to the Indian wars of a decade ago. The barn, too, had lain in ruin until a family of Quakers had begun to renovate the place. That family had abandoned the task and headed west for reasons unknown, though rumor had it that ghosts were responsible for driving them off.

The log walls of the barn had been rechinked and the entire structure partially roofed over. Moonlight flooded the rear half of the barn, warring with the lanterns the men had lit to dispel the gloom at the front.

"They say this homestead is haunted." Al Dees leaned on his rifle. He licked his lips and wished he'd brought along a supply of spirits for himself. He even considered clubbing the Irishman over the head and taking the flask for himself. He indulged his fantasy for a few moments. Then reality intruded. Who was he kidding. There was nothing worse than a hardheaded Irishman. *I'd probably bust my rifle stock on the bastard's thick skull*, Dees cautioned himself.

"Well, if there be a ghost about I hope she stands about so tall," O'Flynn said, holding his hand out from his chest. "And has hair the color o'corn tassels and sweet white breasts for me to lay me head upon when day is done."

"Old fool," Chaney growled. "Your day'll be done if the major catches you tippling that whiskey." Knife and whetstone in hand, he began to trace small circles on the roughened surface of the sharpening stone with the steel blade. A slovenly brawler by nature, Chaney was fastidious when it came to the care of his weapons. No knife blade was sharp enough, no rifle barrel so clean that another swabbing wouldn't increase the gun's accuracy. He was a man of singular purpose gifted with narrowly channeled abilities. He knew how to kill.

"What that Englishman doesn't know will hardly be doing him any harm, eh?" O'Flynn said with a twinkle in his eye. He winked, and a laugh sounded deep in his throat.

"But he does know, which is precisely the point,"

Meeks strode through the doorway. His brown cape flapping, he swooped down on O'Flynn, who froze, flask poised and tilted an inch from his lips.

Meeks's long left arm lashed out and flat-handed the whiskey flask. The earth-tinted glass went spinning off into a nearby stall. O'Flynn staggered backward, lost his footing, and sat down in the dirt, much to the amusement of Dees and Wiley.

O'Flynn scrambled to his feet, his features bunched and ugly with anger. His hand dropped to his knife sheath, but Meeks was quicker. Meeks's hand shot out and clamped in a viselike grip around O'Flynn's throat. The Irishman's eyes bugged out and color drained from his features as Meeks backed him up against a wooden post that supported the roof beams overhead.

"The town is gathering on the Green. It is time to position yourselves along the roads," Meeks said.

Dees, Wiley, and Chaney took up their rifles and headed for their horses as the major continued to issue his orders.

"Chaney, watch the east road leading out of the village. I left Black Tolbert on the north." The Englishman glanced over his shoulder. "You two lads will wait along the south road. Remember, if the wagon comes by, follow it. I must find out where these rebels are hiding their stores."

Padraich O'Flynn made a choking sound; his arms fell limply to his sides in an attitude of submission. The fingers closing off his windpipe eased their hold, allowing a trickle of precious air to flow into his lungs.

"And you'll take the west road," Josiah Meeks finished, his tone silken and deadly calm.

"That...I...will," the Irishman gasped.

Meeks swung around and retreated to the center of the barn. He left his back toward O'Flynn the entire time as if dismissing the man as a threat once and for all. The Irishman, shaken by the sudden, savage strength of the gaunt officer, couldn't leave the barn fast enough. He leaped astride his horse and galloped away.

Meeks heard the man depart. The smell of settling dust mingled with the smoke of the campfire and the aroma of black tea. Things were in place, he thought. And he was optimistic as to the outcome of his plans. There was nothing to do now but wait and enjoy these moments alone.

"Now, you hungry-looking bastard, you can tell me what's going on and how Danny McQueen is involved!"

Meeks, startled, spun on his heels and faced the shadow-darkened ruins at the rear of the barn. Big Henk Schraner emerged into the firelight. His thick lips were curled in a smile. He moved confidently and waved a cocked pistol before him.

"I don't know what the hell is happening here, but I reckon McQueen is involved. I been following you all day to find out." Henk raised the pistol. "And don't get any ideas. I'm no fool like that drunken Irishman. You just keep your distance."

"I can tell you're no fool, whoever you are." Meeks seemed completely unperturbed at this sudden turn of events. A man to whom violence was second nature, Meeks could be surprised but never panicked. This bold intrusion presented a new challenge, one he would have to handle as quickly as possible.

"Who are you? What's McQueen to you?"

Meeks's attitude changed, his shoulders suddenly hunched forward, his expression grew pale. He outstretched his arms as if pleading for his life. "Please. You must let me go."

"Shut up," Henk ordered.

"But you don't understand."

"That's right! But I aim to." Schraner inched closer to the fire and squared his big, beefy shoulders. "I could break you like a twig," he warned the one-eyed man. "And I will if you don't start telling me what I want to hear."

"I'll pay. I've a purse of gold." Meeks patted a leather pouch tied to the broad leather belt circling his waist.

"Gold?" Henk brightened at the sound of clinking coins. "Hand it here."

Meeks dutifully ripped the pouch free and tossed it to Schraner. The throw was short and plopped to the earth at Henk's feet. The brawny youth, on reflex, stooped to retrieve it. He straightened, sensing his mistake.

Meeks shot him. The roar of the pistol filled the barn. Henk tossed his own gun into the air as he was blown off his feet and landed flat on his back in the middle of the barn. Meeks calmly crossed to the fallen man.

Henk felt no pain, just numbness in his chest. He was shocked at the trick fate had played on him.

Meeks began to reload his pistol. Standing over the fallen youth, the British officer added powder and shot to his weapon. He took his time, working nonchalantly, which made his actions all the more horrible. At last he finished, and only then did he take notice of the wounded man outstretched at his feet.

"Who else knows of us?" Meeks asked, pointing the gun at Henk Schraner's heart.

"Go...to...hell." Blood trickled from the corner of Henk's mouth.

"Wait for me there," Josiah Meeks said.

The second gunshot was as deafening as the first.

To Kate it all seemed a kind of dream. Men, women, and children filed through the night-shrouded streets of Springtown as if drawn by an unspoken command. Lanterns, like the stars overhead, flickered and blazed as they dangled from the closed fists of the marchers. This large gathering was unnaturally quiet, as if each participant was made humble in this hour, when life and limb would be pledged to a sacred cause, a pledge sealed by this single, simple act, the hanging of a lantern from the liberty tree.

The pace quickened as the crowd reached the Green. Citizens who had come before stood back, making way for those who would join in the sacrifice. Kate's hand tightened around Daniel's, but the big man kept pace with her of his own volition, his own heart still in turmoil. He felt like a traitor in their midst. He was apart from them, yet among these same brave souls, sharing what they—and she—felt.

Here stood men of the soil, tillers and planters come to sow the seeds of war. Here stood shopkeepers and townsfolk who had longed for a quiet and prosperous life; now they were willing to risk all for that rarest, costliest of commodities, freedom. Here stood the common laborers in their homespun clothes whose callused hands could not even spell the words these men were willing to die for.

The young came, for their spirits hungered for adventure. They were so eager to be a part of something great and glorious—yes, the young, confident of their own immortality.

The old came to the liberty tree, those who had seen the passing of many seasons; they knew what lay ahead, knew what must be risked, and they willingly bore their flames to freedom's fire.

Kate was awed by the immensity of the gathering. Daniel, too, sensed the power surrounding him. The energy of such a throng could become like a rushing river, a wild flood—leading where? He glanced about at the faces drifting from shadow into light, then back to shadow. A year from now how many of these women would be widows, or dead themselves? A year from now how many of these stalwart youths would be carrion comfort on some desolate, battered piece of ground? He raised his eyes to the liberty tree as lanterns were lifted to the budded branches. It was spring, the season of hope and rebirth. Why, then, did he feel dead inside?

"Daniel." Kate spoke his name and turned to him.

It was then that he saw the light of the liberty tree reflected in her eyes.

The crowd surrounded him on every side and pressed forward, carrying him along like an uprooted tree. Images danced like devils in the firelight, and faces from the past mingled in his mind's eye as he struggled to breathe. He saw Josiah Meeks sitting at a table, toying with his eyepatch like he had toyed with Daniel. Meeks dissolved, became Black Tolbert, who drew a pistol from his belt and aimed it at Daniel's heart, and the barrel blossomed black smoke. The image changed. Daniel saw his father dangling from a gallows. Ravens came to feed upon Brian Farley's slowly spinning corpse. As the body turned, Daniel saw the face, the rugged, cinder-burned features that could redden with anger and then crack a smile at the drop of a hat.

His father's eyes were open and Daniel was drawn to the dead man's gaze. Closer, ever closer, as if floating in the air, Daniel was miraculously brought by some irresistible force to stare directly into the wide, lifeless eyes where burned . . .

The liberty tree! Bedecked with tongues of flame, it burned in the eyes of Brian Farley McQueen and would never die.

His father's eyes shimmered, blurred, and then dissolved.... Daniel stood upon the Green, staring into the eyes of Kate Bufkin, and in that moment he knew what must be done and the price that must be paid.

"I'll go with you," Daniel said. Trees die, lanterns fade, but what takes root in the human heart burns with unquenchable fire. "We'll carry the light together."

Chapter Fifteen

Kate Bufkin couldn't sleep. She tiptoed out of bed and padded across the narrow guest room in the Albrights' house. She pressed her face to the night-cooled windowpane and gazed down into the empty backyard. Clouds had covered the moon, and in the distance, thunder rumbled as if the gods were restless beyond the village streets. Well, why shouldn't they be? The people of Springtown had cried out to the heavens this night. Ale had flowed. Music, bright and lively, had underscored the event. Revolution might well be kin to celebration, if the evening's revelry was any indication. She wondered if the liberty tree was still bathed in light. She knew it would always be ablaze in her heart. Kate sighed and once again returned her attention to her surroundings.

Here was a simple room, barely large enough for a narrow alcove bed, a dresser, and a chair. Like the Albrights themselves, the room was simple, honest, and utilitarian. The rug on the floor felt luxurious, and she curled her toes into the thick weave. Kate glanced

at the bedside table, upon which rested a pewter
tankard of milk her cousin had left out for her. Appre-
ciative of Martha's kindness, Kate left the tankard
untouched. Her thirst was of a different nature this
night. A few hours earlier, she had stood hand in hand
with Daniel McQueen before the liberty tree, and as
the fifes played he had whirled her about in his arms
in the center of the Green.

Exhilaration filled Kate's heart. She could still feel
the pressure of his strong arms, still taste his kiss—
and she thirsted for more. A primal passion burned in
the center of her being, and it coursed through her
veins like molten gold. She was helpless to resist
it—and did not want to.

She found her dressing gown draped across the
foot of the bed. The young woman quickly slipped the
garment over her shoulders and tied the ribbons that
adorned the front of the gown. Its hem brushed the
hardwood floor as she stepped into her slippers and
hurried to the door. She cracked open the door and
checked the hallway. It was empty. She eased her own
door wider and stepped into the passage. Kate could
hear the low, ragged sound of the reverend, blissfully
snoring two rooms away. Francis Junior had the room
next to Kate's. The door stood ajar. She peered around
the doorsill, and in the pallid glare of moonlight
seeping through the unshuttered window, spied the
young boy snuggled comfortably in his bed, his small
frame all but hidden beneath a patchwork quilt.

Kate tiptoed past. A loose board creaked underfoot and she froze near the steps, glanced toward the
Albrights' bedroom door, waited to be discovered, and
then sighed with relief. The reverend and Martha had
participated enthusiastically in the demonstration on
the Green.

The young woman continued on to the stairway

and carefully started down. The tolling of the Seth Thomas clock below punctuated each step. Her throat tightened and her heart seemed to skip a beat. Kate managed to stifle a mischievous chuckle. Reaching the lower floor, she paused yet again, hand on the walnut railing. There was still time to hurry back upstairs to the safety of her room. No, she gave up being safe hours ago. Kate took a deep breath and rounded the corner, hurrying across the foyer and into the sitting room where Daniel had arranged his bedding near the hearth.

Embers pulsed and flickered as they slowly devoured the remains of a single log. In early summer, the night air turned cool toward the wee hours before dawn. However, Kate had other ideas about keeping warm. She spied Daniel's huddled form and experienced a tinge of disappointment that he was bundled in his blankets and obviously asleep, when she had lain awake ever since climbing the stairs to bed.

Still, she couldn't remain angry for long. She stole to his side and sank to her knees; she placed her hand on his blanket.

"My dear..." her voice trailed off. More blankets had been rolled and bunched and left beneath the covers to resemble the shape of a sleeping man.

Daniel McQueen was gone!

"Havin' a year up on me doesn't make you any smarter, as I can see," Mose Wiley grumbled as he studied the sky through the branches of an oak tree. "We should keep to the trail."

Al Dees had left the wagon tracks and worked his way up the wooded ridge north of a rainwashed meadow and the Daughters of Phoebe farm.

"What if someone backtracked and spied us?" Dees retorted.

"We kill them," Wiley replied patting the stock of his Pennsylvania long rifle. The flintlock was loaded and primed and as lethal as its young owner.

"Just like that." Dees wagged his head.

A thunderclap caused both men to wince and struggle to bring their skittish horses under control. The geldings trumpeted, rolled their eyes, and fought the riders. But Dees and Wiley had grown up on horseback. They soon succeeded in steadying their nervous mounts.

"Anyways, that wagon's stopped for more than directions. I think here's the place we been looking for." At least Dees hoped so. They'd been trailing the Sicilian's panel wagon for more than two hours. His back ached, and he was saddlesore and rainsoaked from the two cloudbursts they'd ridden through.

Wiley lifted his spyglass to study the farm and the figures, illuminated now by the glare from the open barn doors. "By George, you be speaking the truth, man. They're bringing the wagon inside. What do you think, Al?"

Wiley's companion was silently retracing the route they'd taken from Springtown, knowing Josiah Meeks expected an accurate report. The British officer was certainly not a man to disappoint.

"Al?"

"Shut up!"

"You've no call—"

"Shut up! I see something down there." Dees was bone tired and in an increasingly sour mood.

Wiley glowered and continued to study the barn. He'd take orders from Meeks right enough, but heaven help Dees if he tried to lord it over his younger friend. He felt proud that he had discovered where the rebels cached their weapons and gunpowder. Obtaining such crucial information was a feather in his cap. He peered through the spyglass.

"Looks like a bunch of damn women," he muttered to himself.

Sister Hope nearly slipped in the mud. She managed to brace herself on Gideon's strong back and kept from setting her ample derriere smack in the middle of the mud. She rubbed the back of her neck and glanced over her shoulder.

"You and your suspicious nature," Sister Eve complained. The big-boned farm woman stood aside as Peter Crowe and Tim Pepperidge guided the Sicilian wagon into the barn.

"My neck is never wrong," said Sister Agnes, the beekeeper.

"What about the Huron war party that turned out to be goats in the bramble bush?"

"They were ill-tempered goats, mean as any Huron as I recall," Agnes said defensively.

Sister Eve chuckled and held her broad hands palms up in an attitude of surrender. The levity helped to ease the tension. Every time Eve entered the barn and saw all the munitions stored there, a tightness formed in the pit of her stomach.

Eve had been called by God to form this community of women, called to live in harmony and peace, to promote the teachings of Christ through example. One of those teachings had been a doctrine of peace. Was this any way to live the doctrine? The question bothered her.

Eve followed the wagon into the barn. Eben and Barnabas had already dismounted and brought their horses out of the rain. The brothers quickly doffed their sodden hats as first Eve, then Hope, entered the lantern-lit interior. Sister Eve smiled. She recognized their nervousness. Men were frequently ill at ease in the company of the Daughters of Phoebe. Many considered it unnatural for them to have withdrawn from worldly ways to live in a closed community.

Now it seems the world has come to us, Eve thought as she studied the wagon loaded with rifles.

"We'll not be unloading the wagon," Peter Crowe called out as he freed the team of mares from the singletree and took them to a couple of empty stalls at the rear of the barn. "The hour is close at hand when these rifles will arm the forces of liberty."

"I shall rest easier when we have our barn back." Eve sighed, eyeing the crowded stalls and central aisle.

Crowe and young Pepperidge were forced to ease past the wagon wheels. There was barely room for the two men to sidle past.

"You'll need more than one wagon to load all this." Sister Hope brushed the rain from her gray cloak and shook the droplets from her cowl.

"We'll have them," Barnabas said gruffly.

"And a continental army to receive them, mark my words," Pepperidge enthusiastically spoke up. "With Colonel George Washington to lead us, if those dunderheads in Philadelphia will ever make up their minds."

"Some say it's to be John Hancock," Eben muttered.

"Then we're lost before we set out," Pepperidge countered.

Another figure appeared in the doorway. It was Sister Mercy, who carried a covered basket and a steaming teapot. She lifted her doelike gaze and settled it on Tim Pepperidge, who stared in almost complete disbelief. He had always figured the Daughters of Phoebe to be a bunch of religious old spinsters and widows. Here was as fair a flower as blossomed in any garden, despite her somber gray habit.

"I brought bread and cheese and half a ham," Mercy said. "And something to drink. I thought it would be all right." She glanced meekly toward Sister Hope, who moved to help her, taking the basket from the girl's slender hands.

"Well done, child," Sister Eve commended her. Turning to the men by the Sicilian wagon, she invited them to remain. "You'll be waiting out the rain with us."

"Mighty kind of you," said the militiaman Peter Crowe. He unlatched and lowered the wagon's end gate, which when braced on its two unfolded legs provided a table on which to place the basket of food.

" 'Twas indeed a long and hungry ride out here," Eben Schraner said, trudging across the barn, his older brother at his heels. Eben scratched his bearded jowls, then smoothed back his rain-matted hair and wiped his hands on his linsey-woolsey shirt. He might be the smaller of the two brothers, but he could hold his own at any dinner table and aimed to prove it tonight.

Sister Mercy sliced a wedge of cheese and a slab of ham and added a slice of crusty brown bread to the plate she held. The girl gingerly stepped aside from the end gate and offered the plate to Pepperidge. He blushed, then stiffly bowed, mumbled his thanks, and headed for a stall away from the bemused scrutiny of Crowe and the Schraner brothers. Mercy went with him, drawn by that most powerful attraction of youth.

Sister Eve, being the nominal leader of the religious community, started after her young charge, to remove her from temptation. Hope restrained the larger woman. Eve frowned in anger. It didn't last long, though, for Hope's smile was as infectious as her hold was firm. Eve slowly exhaled, and warmth returned to her features. Though it remained unspoken, both women seemed in agreement that Mercy could not be mothered all her life. Was she not under the Good Lord's protection? And if she chose, even in her innocence, another path from the one she now traveled here among the Daughters, then wasn't that the will of God?

Eben Schraner hunkered down, braced himself against the wagon wheel, and began to devour his food with all the gusto of a man who hadn't eaten in a week. He'd spent enough time on the frontier to learn to fill his belly whenever the opportunity presented itself. He'd spent a winter once in the north woods when meals were few and far between.

He wolfed down a mouthful of bread, ham and reached for his mug of tea, and came face to muzzle with Gideon. In his haste to eat, Eben had forgotten the mastiff's presence. The dog growled and bared its fangs, one by one. Eben's blood ran cold, and he froze, the mug of tea raised chest high.

"I think he likes you," Sister Hope said as she helped herself to a cup of tea.

"Yeah, as what, dinner?" Eben asked hoarsely.

"Maybe he's hungry." Crowe could afford to be amused; the huge hound wasn't threatening him.

"That's what I'm afraid of," Eben said. A swarm of howling mad Hurons couldn't have budged him. Suddenly the mastiff lunged forward. Eben stifled a scream and closed his eyes. Gideon's massive jaws snapped up the wedge of farm cheese from Eben's plate.

Eben opened his eyes and was relieved to see he still had two hands. Gideon, with tail wagging, retreated to a stall, where he happily devoured his find.

"Gideon's partial to cheese," Sister Hope explained. "There's nothing he wouldn't do or fight for a chunk of it."

Crowe and Barnabas, though amused by Eben's plight, suddenly exchanged worried glances and then as one took the cheese from their plates and tossed the morsels to the beast in its stall.

Sister Hope had to turn away to keep from laughing. She walked away from the wagon and returned to the barn doors the men had shut against the rain. She opened one of the big doors a crack and peered out into the night. Her humor faded and the hairs prickled on the back of her neck. Maybe she was just getting old and frail of nerve. After all, who would be out on a night like this?

Chapter Sixteen

Two riders in the gloom guided their mounts by instinct along the mud-slick road toward Springtown. It was hard going, no easy feat to stay in the saddle and keep the horses from losing their footing on the treacherous, wheel-rutted surface. The rain had come and gone. A cool downpour had renewed the creeks and washed the surrounding woods and left them glistening. The moon strove to reveal itself from behind the ominous drifting clouds and cast ghostly shadows upon the road while serpentine silhouettes writhed and played among the brooding oaks. The ghostly aspects of such a summer's night only seemed to spur the men onward.

Al Dees and Mose Wiley rode with reckless abandon. They were young, with delusions of immortality. They were eager to prove themselves to Major Josiah Meeks. They had succeeded in discovering the rebels' hiding place where other Tory agents had failed. The hours in the rain, the rigors of a midnight ride, the discomfort and loss of sleep had all been worth it.

I want nothing more now than to see the look on the faces of O'Flynn and Chaney and Black Tolbert when I tell the major what I've discovered, Dees thought to himself. He was bone tired from the ride and would have searched out a hideaway in which to sleep out the night were it not for his companion. Wiley had the constitution of an ox. He never seemed to need sleep. Dees knew that Wiley would be only too happy to continue on, present their information to the British officer, and garner all the laurels for himself. Dees was not about to let that happen. *If it weren't for me, Wiley would have blundered into the farm and alerted the damn rebels.* So Dees had no recourse but to press on and match his indefatigable companion stride for stride.

Not long now, Wiley encouraged himself, making a mental picture of the road ahead and the village waiting less than an hour's ride along the road. The next landmark along this desolate stretch of road was the wooden bridge across Roemer's Creek. *Just on the other side of this rise, if my memory serves me well. I'll tell Meeks what I've discovered, then find me a jack of rum and a willing wench if there be one in all that cursed village.*

The horsemen cleared the forest, topped the gentle sweep of rolling landscape, rounded a barren knoll, and then followed the Springtown road as it wound down through grassland to a stand of trees half a mile ahead. These woods stretched to either side of the road like silent sentinels guarding the creek in their midst. The tired horses smelled the creek and, anticipating a chance for a drink of the rain-fed waters and perhaps a brief respite, quickened their pace.

"The bridge," Dees shouted. He'd been as eager for the landmark as his companion. Their journey was nearing its end; Springtown seemed within reach. An-

other hour at the most, Dees decided. Nothing would stop them now.

The night's downpour had transformed the normally tranquil creek into a rushing torrent fed by the rains and the runoff from the already saturated ground. But the flat bridge was built of sturdy timbers, and though uncovered, twin rails to either side offered security for the passerby. Wide enough for two horsemen abreast, the bridge could handle only a single wagon at a time. The road widened at either end of the bridge, providing ample room for a freight wagon to pull aside, allowing oncoming traffic to pass unencumbered. Years of travel had widened both clearings, forced back the surrounding woods, and trampled the grasses there.

A cloak-wrapped figure stood among the trees at the north end of the bridge just beyond the clearing. A solitary man, he strove to clear his mind of the turbulent thoughts and images and fears, to free himself from questions and doubts. So much had already happened this night, and more lay ahead. Daniel McQueen had lost Wiley and Dees somewhere along the road to the Daughters' farm and had turned back rather than blunder into a bad situation and make it worse. Daniel was gambling that the two men following the panel wagon would use the same route back to Springtown. He had begun to question his decision to wait at the bridge when the moon cleared a cloudbank and illuminated the road and the approaching riders in its spectral glare. Daniel mounted the horse he'd taken from Albright's barn. He hoped his absence from the minister's house went unnoticed. But that was now beyond his control. He inhaled, slowly exhaled, and cleared his mind.

Daniel rode to the center of the bridge. The animal

was made skittish by the flooded creek rushing below. Daniel gentled the animal with a soothing word and a stroke of his hand. Then he pulled his broad-brimmed hat lower to hide his features and tugged the "scarecrow's" cloak he had brought from the tavern up about his broad shoulders. He drew the pistols from his belt and cocked them, held them at the ready beneath the folds of the cloak.

His "Quakers" were a familiar weight to his hands, the walnut grips smooth to the touch. They had been passed to him by a dying colonial frontiersman during Braddock's murderous retreat during the war with the French and Hurons. The weapons were Daniel's now and to his way of thinking had a kind of life of their own, as if they had chosen him.

No matter now; there was a bloody business at hand, and the guns of Daniel McQueen must prove themselves again.

The splash of iron-shod hooves in the puddles along the Springtown road announced the arrival of Dees and Wiley long before they reached the bridge.

The Tories slowed their mounts and cautiously approached the stranger on the bridge.

"Who the devil is it?" Dees said.

"Maybe that's who. The devil himself," came his companion's hushed reply.

"Then I'll send him packing right back to perdition." Dees cocked his rifle. He cradled the weapon in the crook of his arm. Wiley repeated the action. Then both men walked their horses the few remaining yards to the bridge.

Wiley eyed the surrounding woods with fear and suspicion. He didn't like any of this. His features bunched in a scowl and his hand tightened on the rifle. He was soaked to the skin and angry. He fixed his animosity on the stranger on the bridge who blocked their path and kept him that much longer on the trail.

Daniel sensed their suspicion. He'd have felt the same way, encountering a stranger on such a cheerless night. He tilted his head and allowed the moonlight to wash across his features, the better for Meeks's henchmen to see and recognize him. Daniel felt relief that neither of the riders was Black Tolbert, else this encounter would surely have ended in violence. But if these two had lost the gun wagon's trail there might still be a chance to avoid a fight. It was up to them.

"Who be you?" Wiley called out above the noise of the singing creek.

"Wait. I know you, from the tavern," said Dees, narrowing his eyes. He came forward, still suspicious, but less so now that he recognized the man in the gray cloak. "Did Meeks send you? He needn't have worried. We found out what he wanted to know."

Wiley urged his own horse onto the bridge, determined to ensure he received his full share of credit. But Dees blocked his progress, claiming the right of first passage for himself.

"You found the farm?" Daniel asked. His muscles tensed, the guns beneath his cloak familiar as old friends.

"I . . ." Dees began; then, remembering just how nasty and dangerous a disgruntled Mose Wiley could be, he corrected himself. "We tracked through mud and rain. Watched 'em bring the wagon into a barn. There were several women about."

"We didn't see any men on the place," Wiley interjected, striving to be heard. "That's my kind of farm," he added with a wink no one could see.

"We're on our way to tell the major," Dees continued. "Meeks will want to burn them out. You going with him?"

"No," Daniel said softly. "And neither are you."

He waited, allowing his words to sink in and watching both men for their reaction.

Dees, the first to realize what was happening, tensed. His mouth went dry as he chanced a quick glance toward the surrounding woods. "There's two of us," he warned. "Stand aside, or we'll cut you down."

"What the . . . ?" Wiley muttered from behind, the last to understand the situation.

"Go to the devil!" Dees said, and brought his rifle to bear as Daniel snapped up his pistols and fired. A thunder shattered the night. Deadly orange flame blossomed beneath the pale moon.

Dees was struck in the skull. The impact knocked him from horseback; his rifle discharged harmlessly into the air. His lifeless body landed in the creek and was borne off by the swirling currents.

Daniel's second shot shattered the stock of Wiley's rifle and sent it flying from his hands. Wiley panicked and whirled his horse around, but the startled animal reared and pawed the air with its forelegs. Wiley lost his grip and tumbled from the saddle. He landed in the mud, staggered to his feet, and reached for the pistol in his belt as Daniel bore down on him.

Wiley dragged the flintlock free, cocked it just as Daniel cleared the bridge, and dove from horseback. He landed on Wiley, and both men fell heavily in the mud. The gun's muffled roar sounded. Flaming gunpowder singed the front of Daniel's shirt as he rolled clear of the Tory.

Daniel grabbed at his belly; for a brief moment he thought he'd been shot. But he felt only mud and the sting of burned flesh.

Wiley lay on his back. His mouth gaped open as

he sucked in air. He raised his head, looked down at the front of his shirt. He couldn't see anything, but his chest felt as if his ribs had been kicked in. His whole upper torso was moist, and numbness was spreading through his limbs.

"You've done...me," he gasped. "By my...own ...hand...." His head tilted back, and his eyes grew round and cold as the moon above.

Daniel checked the road north and south. There was no one about. He dragged Wiley's body into the woods and left him beneath a bramble bush out of sight of the road. It was the best he could do under the circumstances. Daniel's own mare was waiting down by the creek bank. Daniel joined the animal by the water's edge. There he reloaded the "Quakers." And there he clung to the knowledge he'd done what needed to be done. He could not have allowed Dees and Wiley to return and place Sister Hope and the other Daughters of Phoebe in peril.

At last he remounted and guided the mare back onto the road. The other horses had already wandered off into the woods. More than likely they'd return to the village on their own. Two saddled, riderless horses were bound to attract attention, but there was nothing to do for it. Daniel swung his own mount north and rode toward Springtown. There was no turning back, from this night on. For Daniel McQueen, the war had begun.

Chapter Seventeen

It was a tired horse and rider that rode through the deserted streets of Springtown in the gray dawn of a new day. Daniel sure didn't feel new. He felt about as used as year-old moccasins.

He kept to the back alleys away from the Green and the village center, taking an indirect route that was a few minutes longer but bound to attract less attention. The village had spent itself in celebration and everyone was still asleep in this last moment before dawn. As Daniel made his way to Albright's place he struggled with the next decision: whether or not to return to his bedroll and pretend to wake with the others in the house. There was always the chance of alerting them prematurely. The reverend might not be a sound sleeper. Better not risk attention. He could clean up in the barn and pretend he had just awakened when the others came down for breakfast. He yawned and worked the kink out of his shoulders. Somehow, today, he was going to have to steal a little time to rest.

Daniel had another problem even more important than sleep. He had taken the first step against Josiah Meeks. But that was only the beginning and the trail ahead was a dangerous one. He was loath to defy Meeks openly. The life of his own father would surely be forfeit by such a course. He was playing for time, hoping to find a way to stop Meeks, confide in Kate Bufkin, rescue Brian Farley McQueen, prevent the murder of George Washington, and keep the cache of weapons hidden by the Daughters of Phoebe from falling into the hands of the Tories.

No problem. A weary grin lit his mud-spattered features. He guided the mare behind a stone house and across the back lot, where a dozen cocks, alerted by his intrusion, strutted around the perimeters of their individual pens and crowed a challenge to this new-comer. Daniel winced at the noise and urged the mare to quicken the pace. He hurried through the yard, rounded another outbuilding, and approached Albright's house from the rear. The ground underfoot was soft and doughy and the hooves of his mount threw up great clods in its wake.

Daniel rounded the barn and reined to a halt, surprised to find not only Reverend Albright awake but Kate and Martha on the top steps at the back of the house. They weren't alone.

Two men with rifles stood at the far corner of the parsonage. Another pair stood in the doorway of the Albrights' barn, the reins of their horses in their hands. Papa Schraner was one of the men by the barn. He appeared momentarily caught off guard by Daniel's arrival. Daniel heard Kate stifle a gasp and saw her dash back into the parsonage.

Schraner stepped forward, his rifle cradled in the crook of his arm. He was the first to speak.

"Surprised to see you come riding back into town. You're a bold one, McQueen."

Daniel glanced toward the men by the parsonage as they cocked their rifles. Something was wrong. He didn't like it. But the mare he rode was exhausted, so escape was out of the question unless he took a fresh horse. Schraner's black mare was a fine-looking animal. All Daniel had to do was get past the rifle of its owner....

"Is there some trouble?" Daniel asked.

"Where have you been?" Schraner asked.

"I took a ride," Daniel offered lamely. "My horse threw me," he added, aware of his own muddy appearance.

"Rode where?"

"Noplace special. Why?"

"Henk is dead," Schraner said. He gestured toward the man next to him. "Samuel here found him, shot twice and left dead in an alley." He waved a hand toward the weapons tucked in Daniel's belt. "I would like to see if your guns have been fired recently."

"No need to check," Daniel cast a wary glance toward the two men on horseback by the house. They seemed reticent to approach. Maybe they were waiting for a command from Schraner, or perhaps even more help was on the way. "I fired my guns a few hours ago."

Schraner's face hardened; muscles tremored along his jaw. Sorrow gave way to fury.

"At what?" he asked.

"Wolves."

"Haven't been wolves in these parts for years."

"These were strays," Daniel replied. Henk could have been killed by anyone, though Daniel had to admit he was the likely suspect. But whatever his sympathy for Papa Schraner, he didn't intend to allow the village constable to clap him in irons. Not with so much at stake. And what must Kate think? He looked over at Reverend Albright and Martha, both of whom were more than a little confused by this turn of events. Kate had yet to reappear, Daniel noted with sinking heart.

"You'll be coming with us," Schraner said.

Any moment the old man might lose control. Henk had been a Schraner, no matter that the bond was not by blood but in name only. Papa Schraner was determined to see justice done. As far as he was concerned, his son's murderer sat astride the lathered mare only a few feet away.

"I had nothing to do with Henk's death, Mr. Schraner," Daniel replied. "But I'll not be coming with you." He waited, unable to make his move, unwilling to endanger a grief-stricken father who was behaving no different than Daniel would were the roles reversed. Yet there was too much at stake to risk waiting for the magistrate while incarcerated in the Springtown jail. Daniel had to be free to handle Meeks in his own way.

But how in the name of heaven was he going to escape this confrontation without... He never completed the thought. Suddenly a large oil lamp came sailing through an open upstairs window and crashed a few yards in front of the riflemen by the corner of the house. The lamp exploded into flames on impact, slivers of glass spattering the area.

The riflemen scurried out of harm's way while Schraner and Samuel turned on reflex at the exploding lamp.

It was all the distraction Daniel needed. He drove his heels into his spent mare and the animal lunged forward, slammed into Schraner, and knocked him flat on his back. Daniel caught up the reins of the black, vaulted from his saddle, and leaped onto the other animal.

Samuel spun around and charged forward, hoping to drag Daniel from the saddle. A well-placed boot sent the smaller man sprawling. Daniel slapped the black across the rump, and the animal galloped away from the barn.

Daniel touched the brim of his rain-battered hat in a gesture of courtesy to Martha Albright as he galloped past the reverend and his wife.

"I'll be back!" he shouted.

Rifle fire erupted behind him. He winced and ducked low in the saddle. The deep-chested mare hit its stride. The black was born to run, and once they had cleared the alleys and fenced gardens, Daniel gave the animal freedom to do what it did best.

Houses and barns fell behind, meadowland sped by. The woods ahead offered concealment, but first he'd keep to the road and put as much distance as possible between himself and any pursuers. He was bone weary. His legs were numb. He'd have to find a place to hole up and rest, but not now. He thought of the well-timed lamp falling from the window. It had been Kate. She had to have known why Schraner was there and that Daniel had stolen away during the night. Yet why had she helped him?

"Hell and damnation!" Schraner bellowed as he paced the ground at the foot of the steps. He glared through the back door at the two women seated in the kitchen.

"There's no cause for such language." Reverend Albright tried to exert a calming influence over the situation.

"No cause?" Schraner bellowed. "Don't try me,

Preacher!" He glared at the empty yard as if it were to blame for his helplessness. Samuel had been dispatched to round up another horse. The other two men had been sent to hurry along Constable Mueller. Schraner paced the ground in an ever-tightening circle. Suddenly he lunged past Albright and up the steps, where he opened the back door with a bang and stood in the doorway, glaring at Kate.

"If that murderer escapes it will be on your head," he said. "You are not above the law, Kate Bufkin."

"I know that as well as I know Daniel McQueen had nothing to do with Henk's death." Kate was not about to be cowed by this man, no matter how righteous his anger. She had puzzled well and good over Daniel's strange absence. She had not been able to explain it to herself. The man had secrets he was not yet able to share, of that she was certain. And when Schraner and the others arrived with news of Henk's murder and demanding to talk to Daniel, her heart sank and she feared for his life. Yes, his conduct was suspect and disconcerting at best, but not for one minute did she believe him responsible for the killing of Schraner's foster son.

"How can you sit there and say such nonsense after what has happened?" Schraner blurted out. His whole face turned red as a berry. He looked as if he were about to explode.

"He ran from men already convinced of his guilt." Kate remained steadfast, her gaze unwavering before the equally resolute farmer.

Yet it was Schraner who at last backed down, unable to break down the young woman's defiance. The farmer muttered something. Kate thought she heard him say "witch," but it might have been something even more insulting.

Schraner retreated down the steps, shoving Albright aside. He nearly sent the good reverend sprawling.

Kate heard the sound of approaching horses, then half a dozen riders appeared outside the back door. One of the men led a horse for Schraner, who lost no time in mounting up. Constable Mueller, a thickset, balding man in his mid-thirties, tried to issue a few orders, but Schraner cut him off and rode away, exhorting the men in his wake to come along.

A rumble of departing horses shook the dishes on the kitchen shelf and set them clattering. Then the men were gone, leaving Martha and Kate to sit across from one another in awkward silence.

Martha finally spoke up. "Oh, Kate... why, why?" She reached out and took her cousin's hand. "My dear, what do you know of your Mr. McQueen?"

"I know I love him," Kate said.

"Ah...." Martha nodded, and she clasped her hands together as if in prayer.

"Mama... I heard horses," a little boy's voice sounded from the front room.

"It's nothing, dear, go back to bed," Martha called out. Then she returned her attention to Kate. Her smile was warm, her eyes sympathetic and conciliatory. "My dear, is this 'love' worth going against your family, your friends—is it worth endangering everything you've worked so hard to build?"

"Yes," Kate said. She stood and started from the room.

"And you have no regrets?" Martha asked, a note of motherly disapproval in her voice. She had hoped to talk some sense into the younger woman.

"Maybe one," Kate replied, pausing in the doorway.

"Yes." Martha brightened. Perhaps there was hope after all.

"Sorry about the lamp." Kate headed up the stairs

to gather her belongings. It was time to start for home.

Reverend Albright entered the kitchen. He crossed to his wife's side to place a hand on her shoulder.

"Well, dear, did you bring your headstrong cousin around and show her the error of her ways?"

"Oh, shut up!" Martha snapped. The discussion was ended.

Chapter Eighteen

June 8, 1775

Barnabas Schraner squirmed beneath his blanket as if trying to throw off the nightmare that plagued him. He was reliving a moment from childhood. He was twelve years old again, transformed and carried on the winds of his dream to the past. He had been feeding the chickens and was starting back toward the farmhouse, where his own dear mother was baking pies for a neighbor's barn raising. Barnabas spied a snake, a black racer, gliding across the yard. He had seen his father once take a snake and crack it like a whip, popping the head off. Without weighing the consequences, Barnabas had hurried over to the snake and grabbed it by the tail end of the constrictor's five-foot length. It seemed simple enough. He whirled the reptile over his head and cracked it like a whip. The snake shot forward, then recoiled right toward the twelve-year-old's throat. The snake was not only intact but furious. It lunged for Barnabas, who was forced to whirl the snake overhead to keep the racer from catching hold of his youthful attacker. Each time the boy "cracked the whip" the black racer would come flying backward straight for the lad's exposed throat, forcing the boy to repeat his actions while the snake, still quite whole, grew angrier and angrier.

In life, Barnabas, the boy, had finally just released his hold and sent the black racer sailing across the yard. In the dream, Barnabas tried to release the snake but the cursed reptile remained in hand. The boy couldn't get rid of the damn thing and so had to continue to whip the indestructible snake out away from his body while growing wearier and wearier, dodging the snake and whirling it away. As he repeated the effort and slowly weakened, the nightmare unraveled to its dire and predictable end, an end which Barnabas managed to escape by bolting awake.

His eyes opened and he saw the branches above him. Reality seeped into his consciousness, and a twitch of arthritis in his left hip reassured him he was most definitely a grown man—not a boy of twelve—with a grown man's aches and pains.

After such a nightmare, even life's discomforts were welcome. He knew where he was now, about twelve miles north of Springtown, camped in a grove among the colony's green hills. With his brother Eben and Tim Pepperidge he had searched the northern woods for sign of Daniel McQueen. After learning of Henk's death on their return to Springtown, the Schraner brothers and their patriotic young friend had grabbed a half a day's rest, then started out in pursuit of McQueen. Parties of other townsmen ranged the surrounding countryside but to no avail.

Barnabas hadn't been surprised at their failure so far. Daniel had struck him as one to whom the wild country was a familiar haven. They weren't going to find Daniel unless he wanted them to, Barnabas had explained to his father. But Papa Schraner insisted they try.

Now here we are, Barnabas told himself, *the eighth of June. And nothing to show for six days of riding except sore backsides.*

There was a farm that needed tending to. He and Eben ought to be home. *We've ridden a wide circle east, south, and west and come up empty-handed. North is bound to be no better.*

Barnabas closed his eyes a moment and inhaled the aroma of frying bacon and brewed tea. They had a crusty round loaf of bread left over from supper with which to sop the grease and make a meal along with the fried meat and tea. Pepperidge, being the best cook of the three, always stood the last watch so it fell to him to prepare the morning meal.

"Ah, this is the way to start a day, now, there's a good lad." Barnabas rolled over on his side to face the campfire. Through the flames he spied Pepperidge sitting across from him. The seventeen-year-old was securely bound, ankle and wrist. He wore a sheepish expression on his face. But that wasn't the worst of it. Eben Schraner was also bound and gagged and propped shoulder to shoulder against young Pepperidge. Eben's face was mottled with fury and shame at being taken without a fight. Barnabas suddenly thought to inspect his own limbs and discovering he was yet unbound, reached for his rifle—only to find it was gone.

"I figured you'd need your hands free to eat," said Daniel McQueen, freezing Barnabas in midreach.

Barnabas slowly turned to face Daniel, who was seated on the trunk of a fallen white pine. He offered a plate of bread and bacon in one hand, his short-barreled pistol in the other. Barnabas had his choice, death or breakfast. The eldest Schraner brother didn't have to belabor the matter. Hell and blazes, the bacon smelled mighty good. He grabbed for the plate.

"Good choice." Daniel took up another plate and, balancing it on his knees, ate with one hand while keeping one of his Quakers cocked and primed.

Barnabas gnawed a chunk of greasy bread as he surveyed the campsite. Their weapons were piled on the ground about seventy feet away. Daniel must have stolen into camp in the wee hours, dispatched Pepperidge, and then taken their rifles and pistols while the brothers slept. He could imagine Eben being rudely awakened with a gun to his head.

"I never heard a thing, Barnabas," young Pepperidge said meekly. "I'm . . . uh . . . real sorry."

"*Mmmmmhhagh!*" Eben added disgustedly, making his opinion known despite the gag.

Next, Barnabas focused on his captor. Daniel's unruly red hair was gathered and tied at the back of his neck. The lower half of his bronze features were hidden behind a nine-day growth of beard. He looked tired, his shirt was torn and dirty, and yet there was a flash of merriment in his eyes, perhaps at Schraner's expense.

"What do you want?" Barnabas said.

"I have it." Daniel finished off the last few morsels, set the plate aside, and crawled over to the fire, where he helped himself to a cup of tea. For a moment, his back was turned.

Barnabas tensed and carefully began to ease his plate aside. This might be his only chance.

"I wouldn't try it," the man at the campfire said without even looking back. "Besides, I took your flints. They won't fire till you add new ones."

No chance at all. Barnabas glumly resumed eating.

"Why'd you stay around these parts?" Barnabas asked. A guilty man ought to have skedaddled. All one need do was flee to a colony farther south or north to be beyond the reach of any pursuit from Springtown. Staying just didn't make sense. It was a fool thing to do.

"I have business here."

"Like with Henk."

Daniel handed Barnabas a cup of "Liberty" tea, a drink brewed from various roots and plants and ground cherry bark, it was a strong, bitter drink that could burn the sleep out of a man and stand him on his toes.

"Henk's death was none of my doing. Now, leave me alone. Call it off and go home." Daniel gulped his tea, then stood and started to walk away from camp. "I scattered your horses during the night. That ought to slow you awhile."

Barnabas winced, then glared at Pepperidge, who shrugged and smiled sheepishly.

"How do I know you aren't no killer?" Barnabas shouted.

Though Daniel had vanished into the woods, his words drifted back through the forest:

"You're alive, aren't you?"

Chapter Nineteen

June 11, 1775

> Any blacksmith, iron worker, or gunsmith of
> the City of Philadelphia who is willing to
> supply the Colony with any number of fire
> arms, completed by the 1st day of November,
> may apply to the Subscriber in Philadelphia
> who has been appointed by Assembly to offer
> Bounty and Encouragement for such labour
> he has engaged.

June 1, 1775
Carpenter Hall   Wm. Rutledge, Esq.

Daniel McQueen read the broadside beneath his
breath. The missive had been posted beneath a wooden
signpost that sported two placards. The topmost sign
read ROAD TO YORK, with an arrow pointing north. The
sign beneath read PHILADELPHIA, with an arrow pointing
toward an impressive array of shops, houses, and ware-

houses, many two and three stories tall, arranged in an orderly sprawl along the banks of the Delaware. The carefully ordered streets were alive with carriages, horsemen, and people afoot—everyone on their way somewhere, each to his own destination. A forest of masts rose in the harbor, where barks and frigates were anchored.

From the hill, Daniel could take in most of the city at a glance. It never failed to fill him with wonder. The colonies were no longer primitive settlements clinging to the eastern shores of North America. They had come of age and now must be tempered in the crucible of war.

Daniel knew of such things: furnaces, anvils, molten metals, and the sacrifice a man must make to produce anything worthwhile and lasting. That was why he had come to Philadelphia on this morning. He had followed a circuitous trail from the countryside around Springtown, allowing the black mare to rest as much as possible and taking two days to reach Philadelphia.

Daniel studied the city that lay before him and wondered how he was going to find George Washington. After all, Virginia colonels traveled in different company from Scottish blacksmiths. Yet Daniel was certain that once he found Washington, he'd be able to arrange some kind of meeting with the Virginian.

But where to begin? The man by the broadside had pondered the problem throughout his journey and come to only one conclusion. He would try Nathaniel Woodbine. Daniel had no great liking for the man, especially for the merchant's financial hold over Kate Bufkin; still, Woodbine was a patriot and colonel and no doubt moved in the same circle as Washington. It was worth a try. As for finding Woodbine's house, well, someone must know. He'd begin with the local artisans, who were constantly being employed by such men of means. It seemed a good enough plan.

Perhaps, Daniel told himself, *my luck is about to change.*

Colonel George Washington stretched his long legs before him, loosened the buttons on his uniform, and settled back to enjoy the dessert young Sexton Rutledge brought from the kitchen. The nine-year-old boy, first-born son of Dr. William Rutledge, had taken it upon himself to bring a second portion of sweet pumpkin pudding to the man he idolized.

Washington tousled the boy's sandy hair and then made a great show of inhaling the pudding's aroma and smacking his lips in anticipation.

"Your son makes a grand forager," the colonel said with a chuckle. Young Sexton's chest swelled with pride. He returned to his father's chair.

"Bill Rutledge, you tell your wife that I used to think my own Martha's pumpkin pudding was the best in the colonies, but I've been forced to reevaluate my thinking. I have found this custard to be more than a match, and I'm having a second helping to prove it." Washington spooned a delectable spoonful into his mouth.

Today he felt at peace with the world around him, though the world around him was hardly at peace with itself. That was why he had come to Philadelphia. He wondered how he'd leave—as a colonel in Virginia's home guard or as the commander of this fledgling nation's army.

Dr. William Rutledge, a Philadelphian of influence and wealth, sat across from Washington in the parlor. The good doctor had parlayed several tracts of land into a considerable fortune by selling off the least valuable and selectively exploiting the resources of the rest. He was a man of modest appearance, average in height, unassuming in demeanor, at least when relaxing among his peers. But place him in any arena of competition, be it financial, political, or a game of whist, and the mild-mannered, unassuming physician became as combative as a gamecock—another sport he fancied, as did Washington.

But breeding cocks and fighting them had not initiated their friendship. The two men had marched side by side during the French and Indian War. The field of battle had forged a bond more lasting and truer than bloodlines and heritage between these two friends.

Rutledge yawned and rubbed his eyes, then leaned forward, elbows on his knees. He lowered his voice as Sexton went across the conservatory to plunk random notes upon the harp.

"Seriously, George, what think you of our host and ally?"

Washington frowned a moment. He had hoped this visit would remain cordial and pleasant. Nathaniel Woodbine had opened his house to many of their mutual friends, patriots all. These two men seated in the conservatory had been the first to arrive, and the colonel from Virginia, victim of a sweet tooth, had walked right over to a table laden with custards, pies, and honey cakes, many of which had been left earlier by Edythe Rutledge and her household staff after Woodbine's own cook had taken ill.

"You have embraced him." Washington hesitated to commit himself, like any good man of the soil, without assessing the situation one last time.

"He furnished the last shipment of powder and rifles out of his own pocket. I have met few so willing to be of service," Rutledge conceded. Trustworthiness was a rare quality to find in a man.

"I know you trust him," the Virginian said, taking another mouthful of pudding. "That is good enough for me."

"He has won me over. I wish some of those obstinate men at Carpenter's Hall were as dedicated," Rutledge complained. "Vermont wants Artemas Ward, Massachusetts insists Hancock is the man to lead us. Such obstinacy."

"Come, now, Bill," Washington chided. "Nathaniel invited us here to relax. The only decisions I wish to make are which sherry to drink and how many games of whist I shall allow you to win before I take every coin you have on your person." Washington scratched beneath his wig and set the bowl of pudding aside.

"Then you feel luck is with you?" Rutledge challenged good-naturedly.

"It is never farther than my pocket." The Virginian fished a round, shiny coin about the size of a silver dollar from his waistcoat. It was an English crown.

"Tell me of it, sir," young Sexton said, returning to the side of the man he worshiped. He sat on a stool at the Virginian's feet. Washington seemed pleased to have an audience for his tale.

"This, my lad, is a sterling silver crown, a proper English coin, mind you, worth over two pounds. It came to me as did my luck on the long and bloody retreat down Braddock's Road, after the death of the general himself."

"You kept the retreat from becoming a rout, George," Rutledge added.

Washington ignored the compliment and continued his story. "It was the morning after the day the French and their Huron allies had sprung their trap. It had rained all night and the road to safety was a quagmire. We were under constant attack and I had begun to lose hope of ever seeing the Blue Ridge

Mountains again, when suddenly I spied this gleaming bit of silver shining in the churned mud. I picked it up and wiped it clean."

He held the coin so that it reflected the sunlight streaming through the open windows. His memories harkened back to a long-ago war. Now another war was at hand, one whose outcome he must place in the hands of God and hope for the best.

"What happened then?" Sexton asked, his eyes wide with interest.

"Well, the Indians didn't get me." Washington grinned and clapped the boy on the shoulder. "And this has been my lucky coin ever since." He returned the crown to his waistcoat and patted the pocket. "Now I carry my luck with me wherever I go."

"Hrrumph! Maybe I should just write you a note of debt first thing and save myself the trouble of losing at cards," Rutledge said.

"Just as long as you include another of Edythe's custards," Washington replied with a laugh.

The good doctor would have joined in had not Nathaniel Woodbine chosen that precise moment to reenter the conservatory. The normally easygoing merchant appeared flustered and anxious to impart some news of grave importance.

In contrast to his two uniformed guests—Washington in the outfit of the Virginia Militia and Rutledge in the colors of the Philadelphia Drum and Fife Corps—Woodbine was comfortably attired in a ruffled white shirt, sleeveless brown waistcoat with gold brocade, and dark brown velvet breeches. The polished buckles on his shoes shone.

"Gentlemen, I have just received news that Hancock is relinquishing his claim to the post of commander-in-chief. Adams has just sent word. Even now the deliberations in Congress continue. But the feeling is that Pendleton of Virginia and Sherman of Connecticut will be swayed to follow Hancock's lead!" Woodbine held up a decanter of Irish whiskey. "This calls for a toast."

"A premature one," Washington cautioned, though it was obvious in his voice that word of Hancock's decision had caught him off guard. "There's still old Artemas Ward...."

"He swears too much," Rutledge countered.

"And Charles Lee," Washington said.

"An able leader," Rutledge conceded.

"But an Englishman despite his newly purchased plantation," Woodbine reminded them. "No. The Congress is a suspicious lot. They'll bandy his name about, but in the end, they simply do not trust him." He raised his glass of whiskey in salute.

"To our commander-in-chief!"

Sexton nudged his father, who poured a measure for the youth. Washington sighed, feigning disbelief but secretly excited and alarmed at the prospect of leading the army.

"I accept your praises in the spirit they are given." He downed his own glass of whiskey and sucked in his breath at the liquor's potency. Young Sexton's eyes streamed tears, but he managed to swallow and keep the burning liquid in his stomach when he wanted to double over and retch.

Washington rose from his chair, towering over his companions, and bid them peace and farewell.

"You're leaving?" Woodbine was surprised by the Virginian's behavior. "But the party. It is in your honor. What will I tell the others? Your friends?"

"Tell them the truth," Washington said. "That I have gone to sit in the garden behind the German Lutheran church, where I hope, alone, to collect my thoughts."

The sudden change in mood left Rutledge and Woodbine all but speechless. Washington donned his hat and started out of the room. Woodbine hurried to escort the Virginian to the front door. Before long the merchant returned to the conservatory. He held out his empty hands.

"Well, what do you make of that?"

"I gave up trying to second guess that man long ago," the physician said. "Which is why George continues to beat me in cards and chess."

"When word spreads concerning Hancock the others will mob the hall," Woodbine said.

"And we'll be left here to entertain ourselves." Rutledge helped himself to another glass of whiskey. He waved Sexton away when the boy stepped forward, as his mother had instructed him, to caution his father against overindulgence. But for William Rutledge the first whiskey had but awakened a thirst for more, much more.

Woodbine was only too happy to comply, out of his professed friendship for the physician and because William Rutledge was the one man in Philadelphia who knew where these rebels had hidden their guns.

In the garden behind the German Lutheran church, a solid structure of timber and gray stone that thrust its whitewashed steeple toward the sky, Colonel George Washington found a stone bench near a bed of pale pink and scarlet roses. He liked roses. And he liked the solitude of this garden, with its vine-covered walls and shaded walks. He studied the stone tablet set in the ground like some ornate headstone. There were ten such tablets, one for each commandment. Each tablet bore a similar guildmark etched into the slate surface. However, Washington didn't need the artisan's signature to know the tablets were the workmanship of one man. The stone carver was a notoriously bad speller, and though the commandments were handsomely wrought, each table contained a misspelled word or two.

Washington sat across from THOUS SHALT NOT COVET THY NAYBORS WIFE. *Words of wisdom*, the Virginian thought with a smile. He leaned back against the rock wall; the vines cushioned him as he allowed the day's news to sink in. So Hancock was no longer the formidable obstacle he had been since Washington arrived in Philadelphia back in early May. John Hancock was the golden lad of the assembly, a favorite of the New Englanders. The notion of being commander-in-chief had most assuredly appealed to the man. But at long last, common sense had prevailed over vaulting ambition. Hancock, it seemed, had at last admitted he wasn't the man for the job and given Washington his all-important vote of confidence. Sooner or later the delegates from New Hampshire and New York would follow suit. Washington felt it in his bones.

He had sought the post of command for so long, how odd that the enormity of the challenge had only now begun to sink in. There was some small measure of consolation. *If I fail*, he thought, *it will be one of the grandest failures in the history of man.*

Washington laughed softly to himself and, fishing a small, bone-handled folding knife from his coat pocket, glanced around for something to whittle. He heard the creak of the iron gate leading into the garden and noticed a travel-worn man enter from the street. Washington paid him little mind; his thoughts were of home and hearth and the woman who waited for him there. Martha Washington possessed a degree of courage few people even suspected she had, much less understood. Whatever the outcome of this war, his sacrifices and his fate would be hers. She would have it no other way.

Daniel McQueen waited in the shadows and checked the garden walkways. Reassured he and the Virginian were alone, Daniel started down the path. He'd found Woodbine's house easy enough after a few well-directed questions at a local tavern, the Shepherd's Crook. Daniel had tethered his horse in a wooded lot across from the merchant's circular drive and would have made his way into Woodbine's study if another carriage had not pulled up bringing a most illustrious guest, none other than George Washington himself. Daniel had resolved to wait the colonel out in hopes of catching him alone. Now his patience had paid off.

Daniel moved tentatively at first, awed by the powerful presence before him. He stopped a few yards from the Virginian and drew back against the trumpet vines. He shrugged his cloak back off his shoulders, freeing the guns in his belt. Not that he intended to use them, but the Quakers were a reassuring presence, and there was no telling who might be the next to enter the garden in pursuit of this lonely man.

Washington looked up from his reverie of leaves and roses and troubled future and saw his visitor.

"Yes?" he said in a deeply melodic tone. "Have you come to see me or to converse with the bees?" A smile played across his lips.

"I've come to warn you," Daniel said. Once choosing this course, there was no turning back. Better to have done with it. "Your life is in danger. You are marked for death. British spies have brought men into the colony to kill you."

"How do you know this?"

"I am one of them."

A twitch of the muscles around Washington's eyes was the only indication he had heard Daniel. He noticed the brace of pistols Daniel carried in his belt. Daniel kept his hands away from the walnut grips of his guns.

"Since you're talking instead of shooting, why not walk with me and tell me more?" The Virginian stood.

And they walked together, this tall colonel and this broad-shouldered blacksmith. They left the church grounds and continued on toward the waterfront. Daniel explained how he had been brought into the affair and the hold Meeks had over him. It took a lot of talking, but the Virginian was a good listener.

"Josiah Meeks—I know the man and had hoped never to encounter him again." Washington dabbed at his forehead after they'd covered a half dozen blocks. He found himself liking this blacksmith. By warning Washington, Daniel could well be signing his father's death warrant.

The sun, having reached its zenith, began its downward slide into the middle hours of the afternoon. On such a lazy day men were wont to close their eyes and abandon the duties of the day for a brief rest or perhaps a sojourn at a favorite pub. Rest was the farthest thing from Washington's mind, unless it was the threat of eternal rest.

"Where am I to meet my fate?"

"I was to wait for you at the Hound and Hare Inn along the Trenton Road. But if Meeks suspects you've been warned, I don't know."

"Well, we shall just have to keep Meeks guessing as to my motives," Washington replied. The humor left his features. He stopped in his tracks and placed a hand on Daniel's brawny shoulder.

"You have taken a great risk for me, Daniel McQueen. I wish I could return the favor. But alas, I am powerless to act in your father's behalf. His life is in God's hands."

"And Josiah Meeks's," Daniel added bitterly.

"Many good men will die in the days to come," Washington said, his voice tinged with sorrow. "Maybe you and I..."

The two men continued in silence until they reached the waterfront warehouses, piers, and the wide, watery expanse of the Delaware. The people around them mirrored the sentiments of the time. Among the traffic of carriages, freight wagons, and those afoot, most paid no heed to the Virginian, much less the red-bearded man in the ragged gray cloak standing at Washington's side. Like the colonists who wished to remain aloof from the coming struggle, these city folk were concerned with the day's business, nothing more. However, other townsmen stopped to notice Daniel and the colonel, and once Washington was recognized, word quickly spread throughout the waterfront.

Everyone knew the delegates at Carpenter's Hall had been deliberating on the qualifications of this man and a handful of others as to who was best suited to command the army. It was obvious, as Daniel accompanied Washington along the waterfront, that the men and women there were divided in their admiration for the Virginian. A trio of merchants haggling over the price of whale oil paused in their argument to openly glare at Washington as if he were some pariah. They were in the minority, however.

Far more of the locals, from common laborers to tradesmen and a few well-to-do gentlemen, found time to approach the tall, introspective Southerner and wish him well and offer their support. Washington's reputation as a man of courage and integrity set well with them. They knew why he had come to the city and prayed he would leave as commander-in-chief of the nation's untried army.

Again Washington moved on, seeking a back street

and greater privacy. When nothing presented itself, he chose a pier instead and walked out upon the long planks. Daniel, drawn along by the Virginian's personal magnetism, followed him onto the pier. They stood together at the end of the dock, a perfect place for fishing. Washington stood with his hands folded behind his back, apparently deep in thought. Then he spoke.

"I feel as if we have met before, my bold friend."

"Braddock's Road," Daniel replied. "I was thirteen. But big for my size. I marched with the Green Mountain volunteers."

"A mere boy!" the Virginian exclaimed. A memory returned from the bloody time of a handful of frontiersmen standing their ground while the British regulars around them broke and fled before the onslaught of the Hurons. Had Daniel been among them, a boy posing as a man and doing a man's work?

"I carried my own rifle," Daniel boasted.

"Yes." Washington smiled. "I am certain you did." He stared out across the river. What did he see in that distance?

"There is a new wind blowing," Washington said, looking out at the ships crowding the harbor. So far the British had not been successful in their blockade. But Washington knew things could get worse; they always did. "It is like a storm cleansing the land. It will bring a new order to the world, a country the likes of which has never existed." Washington looked at Daniel standing at his side. He saw a son of the Highlands, a man of gristle and bone, of shrewdness, courage, and bold action. "Our new nation will have need of such men as you if it is to prevail."

Daniel's cheeks reddened at the compliment. How quickly he had confided in the colonel before he had a chance to think or caution himself. *As for my part,*

Daniel thought, *I'm just glad to be aboard, whatever happens.*

"What are your plans, my young friend?"

"I'll return to the Hound and Hare. There is a woman there to whom I owe the truth."

"I see," Washington replied, bemused. Even revolutions had to stand aside for love.

"Don't take the Trenton Road, sir," Daniel said. "Whatever else happens."

"I'm not the commander-in-chief yet."

"You *will* be. We both know it."

"Perhaps," the Virginian conceded. "But if it is so, then I must choose the quickest route to my troops."

"No matter the risk?"

"We are both at risk, my young friend. Each of us travels a perilous road."

"Then—until our paths cross again," Daniel said, starting back down the pier.

Washington was caught off guard by Daniel's abrupt departure. He remained at the end of the dock as Daniel hurried past broken barrels and fishnets and an overturned johnny boat whose hull needed repair.

"What will you do?" Washington called to the departing figure. He felt a kinship for the younger man. Daniel's responsibilities, though far more personal than Washington's, were no less weighty.

Daniel whirled around, and his somber gray cape fluttered about him. "What needs to be done. The same as you, sir," he called out, then resumed his course, retracing his steps back to Woodbine's house and the grove of trees where he'd tethered the black mare.

Chapter Twenty

An hour after sundown, Padraich O'Flynn settled his chunky frame into the sumptuously cushioned chair Nathaniel Woodbine provided for the guests who came to his study. O'Flynn, dressed in the uniform of the New York Militia for his visit, had entered the house by the front door and had even been introduced to William Rutledge—although the good doctor, being "in his cups," would no doubt forget the corporal's name upon sobering up. At Woodbine's insistence, Rutledge had been led upstairs to a guest room to sleep it off.

The merchant entered the study and placed himself behind his desk. He was dwarfed by the walnut-topped desk and the shelves of leather-bound books behind him. Upon those hallowed shelves the merchant kept such treasures as Percy's *Reliques of Ancient English Poetry*, Blackstone's *Commentaries on the Laws of England*, Walpole's *The Castle of Otranto*, and the works of Thomas Gray and Jonathan Swift. He folded his hands and listened as O'Flynn recounted the events of the past ten days and what Meeks intended for the future.

Woodbine was unable to conceal his distress as O'Flynn recounted how, with Josiah Meeks, he had found the corpse of Al Dees caught in the roots of a willow along the banks of Roemer's Creek. Mose Wiley was nowhere to be seen and more than likely had been washed away in the flooding waters.

Meeks had buried Dees and returned to Springtown. It was there he learned of Daniel McQueen's near capture upon returning from a mysterious night ride. It was no great leap of the imagination to see that Daniel was responsible for the deaths of Wiley and Dees. How had this happened? What had caused him to betray Meeks?

The only good thing to come out of all this was that Daniel stood accused of Henk's murder. As long as the good citizens of Springtown were looking for Daniel, they wouldn't be searching out Henk's real killer.

But where was Daniel? No one seemed to know. As long as he was free he was as dangerous as a loose cannon on the deck of a ship.

After listening to the Irishman's story Woodbine allowed O'Flynn a brandy. The Irishman swirled the amber-brown contents beneath his nose, then gulped the drink while Woodbine looked on in distaste. Brandy was to be savored, like the pleasures of a woman. But Woodbine returned his attention to the business of war.

"More men have arrived from New York," Woodbine told him. "You will take them with you to rejoin Major Meeks."

O'Flynn grimaced. "Beggin' your leave, Mr. Woodbine. But ain't there another who could go between

Meeks and yourself? That Englishman is a haughty bastard and I've no liking for him."

"Our English major will have little time for games. Indeed, the news you bring to him will please him greatly and place him in our debt."

"Then you've learned where the rebels have stored their guns?" the Irishman leaned forward in anticipation.

"From Rutledge himself, the drunken, trusting fool." Woodbine rubbed his hands together. "We'll have the guns and Washington, too. It will be a blow these treasonous rebels will never recover from."

Glass shattered in the foyer outside the study. The noise brought both men to their feet. Padraich O'Flynn filled his hand with a pistol from his coat pocket.

Woodbine paled as he rounded his desk and led the way to the door. O'Flynn's ruddy cheeks seemed to quiver as the muscles along his jaw tensed, relaxed, then tensed again.

"Rutledge?" he whispered to Woodbine.

The merchant merely wagged his head no and pointed toward the ceiling. He had personally escorted the physician and his son to one of the guest rooms upstairs. Then who was this intruder, and how much had he overheard?

Woodbine reached the door, quickly pulled it open, and darted into the foyer. The diminutive merchant did not lack for courage, O'Flynn thought to himself as he maneuvered past his employer.

A three-legged mahogany table lay on its side. Just beyond it were scattered the pieces of what had once been a bowl of Stiegel crystal that the "Baron" himself, Heinrich Stiegel, had engraved with miniature parrots.

Woodbine saw that the front door was shut and bolted from within. That meant the culprit was still in the house. He stared at the wreckage of his beautiful bowl with fists clenched, and in a soft, murderous voice said, "All right. Come out, damn you."

A blur of motion caught his attention near the stairs. O'Flynn snapped up his pistol but held his fire as a charcoal gray cat leaped down from beneath the banister and landed near the shattered glassware.

Woodbine and O'Flynn sighed in relief.

"Damn cat belongs to my cook," Woodbine said. "It's a good ratter but not worth the price of that bowl." He glared at the feline, who, impervious to the merchant's dislike, padded off to explore the sitting room across the foyer.

"At least it can't tell anyone what it overhears in its prowling," O'Flynn said. "Though I knew a man in Dublin who I'm told could converse with cows and hogs and even a goose or two—depending upon how much whiskey he had imbibed."

Woodbine returned to the study and O'Flynn came right along behind the merchant. His prattle never slackened as the door to the study swung shut.

Only then did another shadow detach itself from the stairway and take itself, one labored step at a time, up to the second floor. For there had been two prowlers afoot in Woodbine's townhouse: a gray tomcat and a frightened young boy who had crept from bed and made his way to the kitchen in search of an extra shortbread cookie.

Sexton Rutledge reached the upstairs hallway and, fearful of knocking anything else over, forced himself to walk to the guest room where his father lay asleep. He reached the door. It opened at a touch. He slipped inside and hurried to the sleigh bed where his father, William Rutledge, lay snoring. Sexton grabbed the sleeping man by the shoulders and shook him. The doctor mumbled something unintelligible.

"Father, wake up. Please, Father," the boy said fearfully. "Woodbine's a loyalist. A loyalist! Father!"

He gave the unconscious man a sound shake but could not rouse the physician from his stupor. Woodbine had capitalized on the man's weakness, plied him with liquor, and then cajoled the secrets from him. Sexton hadn't seen his father like this in a long time, but he remembered all too well he was powerless to wake the man. There was nothing he could do save wait. Wait. The boy crawled into bed alongside his father.

Nathaniel Woodbine thought he was so very clever.

"Well," Sexton whispered to himself, "we shall see about that. Wait until morning, after Father and Colonel Washington hear my story."

That same evening, many miles from Philadelphia, the Hound and Hare Inn was the scene of a much more private and personal debate. Kate Bufkin sat across from her brother, a chess board between them. But Kate's mind was hardly on the game. Her thoughts kept drifting from chess strategy to a handsome Highland rogue with flashing eyes and flaming red hair, whose strategy she couldn't even begin to guess at. Whatever the reasons for his actions, she loved this bold adventurer—and so be it.

"Your move." Loyal Bufkin wiped his mouth on the sleeve of his shirt. He took another bite of his pork sandwich and watched his sister for some indication that she had returned her attention to the game.

Kate's hand drifted above the board, then committed her queen. The young woman's golden hair looked darker by lantern light than it really was, and when she leaned forward, her unbound tresses spilled forward to conceal her features.

"I'll take your queen," Loyal cautioned, his mouth full. He folded his forearms on the table to prop himself over the chess board, where he loomed like some Greek god above the earthbound struggles of his pawns. Kate retracted her move and made another.

"You'll take my queen," Loyal commented in the same tone of voice. *My God, she has blundered into victory,* he thought, and then sighed with relief as she absentmindedly took back her threatening knight. She had barely heard him. She chose another piece at random and completed her move.

"You can't do that!" Loyal protested.

"Why not, for heaven's sake?"

"Because that is my bishop."

"Oh." She returned the black bishop to its former position. She pushed away from the table and went to the hearth. Grabbing an iron poker, she reached into the flames and adjusted one of the logs.

It was a small but cheerful blaze, just enough to take the edge off the night, which in mid June didn't take much. Despite the warmth which grew uncomfortable the longer she remained by the fire, Kate stood, transfixed by the dancing flames.

"Kate..." Loyal called softly. He glanced down at the chess board and saw he was winning; it was one of the few times. He hated to leave the game now. Maybe she'd come back. He repositioned the slab of pork between the two crusty halves of bread. "Kate..." He looked around the empty inn. The Schraners had spread the word of how Kate had helped Daniel escape from Springtown. Loyalties ran deep. The Schraner family had settled this part of Pennsylvania, and they had helped other families who had moved into the area, built their farms, and at last come together to form a town with real churches and a school.

Kate Bufkin, on the other hand, was a relative

newcomer, and though well liked, she could not command the same sympathies as Papa Schraner.

There was little traffic on the Trenton Road, none of which turned into the Hound and Hare for lodging. She suspected the eldest Schraner's influence behind this as well. Eben and Barnabas had come by yesterday and all but admitted this was the case and openly apologized. They told her their father wouldn't bring charges against her but was determined to punish her for helping "Henk's murderer" to escape. Barnabas had doubts about Daniel's guilt, and Eben reflected his older brother's influence. But the brothers' sympathy was all she could expect.

"Kate . . . come and finish the game," Loyal said. "What else is there to do?" His voice sounded hollow and rather lost in the empty room. How many times had he wiped the tables or checked the wicks in the whale-oil lamps or dusted the bottles and jugs and tankards behind the walnut bar? He'd lost count. And what was the point—to provide service for their phantom guests?

"What else?" Kate repeated, facing her brother. She crossed the room and stood at his side. "I don't know. Except I shall go mad waiting."

"He's fine, Kate. Daniel's safe wherever he is. I'm sure of it. You just have to believe, is all."

Kate's smile was forced, but at least she tried, and she patted her brother's arm, then hugged him. And to his dismay walked away again after threatening his king with her queen. "I left the butter churn out back near the root cellar; I better carry it down where it is cool."

"Want me to go?"

"No. You stay here and try to beat me," she teased.

"I should never have taught you this game," Loyal muttered. Leaning forward on his elbows, he pondered his next move. No game was ever like another. That was the excitement. There was always a surprise, an unseen development or a dilemma to be confronted.

Poring over the checkered field of play with its arrangement of pieces all carved by his hand, Loyal did not hear the rear door close. Nor did he notice the front door open.

Kate was halfway to the root cellar when out of the darkness of night she heard the barn door bang against the outside of the building. The noise alerted her. She had barred the door shut that morning after carrying a cartload of corn out of the bins to the hogs. At the gentle pressure of a summer's breeze the door swung to and fro on its hinges, and the empty doorway was a yawning patch of darkness that suddenly blossomed with pale amber light as someone within struck tinder and lit a lantern.

Kate gasped, and broke into a run. It was him! It had to be! She forgot everything else. Emotion ruled her now. She lifted the hem of her dress to quicken her pace and hurried toward the barn. The lamplit doorway was a beacon to her. She was furious at him for his absence and overjoyed he had returned. Daniel had left her with a heart full of questions. It was time to find out the truth of this man whom she had come to love. Yes, it was time for the truth.

She crossed the yard, darted through the doorway, and spied a shadowy figure standing just inside the near stall.

"Daniel McQueen! It's high time you show yourself. I was worried to death not knowing whether or not I'd see you alive...." Kate stopped. The blood in her veins turned to ice.

Josiah Meeks bowed to her, doffing his hat. His single eye glittered, and his lips curled back in a feral smile as he left his horse and advanced on her, all gangly and dangerous.

"Daniel, is it?" he mocked. "Did you hear, Tolbert? The devotion in her voice."

"I heard." A voice came from behind her which brought her to a halt after a single step backward.

"What do you want?" she asked, recognizing Meeks from his visit to the parsonage in Springtown.

"I want McQueen. And you'll help me get him, my little darling."

Kate spun on her heels. Too late. Black Tolbert blocked her escape, his keen eyes hungrily ranging her figure, lingering on her bosom and the graceful lines of her neck.

"Take her into the inn. If she tries to escape," Meeks said, in his most gentlemanly tone, "kill her."

Chapter Twenty-One

Black Tolbert was thirsty, and he didn't like the way Josiah Meeks was rationing the Hound and Hare's supply of liquor. He had been pacing the tavern for the better part of the morning. By noon, Meeks had tired of Tolbert's edginess and ordered him back outside to check the area around the tavern again and work off a little steam. Tolbert grudgingly obeyed and headed for the front door. He noticed Loyal Bufkin watching him from a table near the bar.

"What are you looking at?" he snapped.

"The stars in the heavens, the birds in the trees, the fishes in the seas, He made them all," Loyal said, a beatific gleam in his eyes. His fingers toyed with the bandage circling his skull.

"You're crazy as a loon," Tolbert muttered, and stepped outside.

Kate Bufkin, seated at the same table as her brother, rose and stepped behind him to examine his bandaged head. The coarse cloth was stained dark red where the blood had seeped from Loyal's head wound.

Will Chaney, on first entering the tavern the night before, had viciously clubbed poor Loyal senseless after he had refused to answer any of Chaney's questions. Loyal looked up at his sister and patted her hand. "There is a special providence in the fall of a sparrow, Kate. The major doesn't believe it yet, but he will. They all will."

Josiah Meeks was standing at the bar, a glass of Madeira in his hand. A permanent scowl had settled on his features ever since the discovery of Dees and Wiley. How could he have played this so wrong? What sort of man was Daniel, and what had he found so damn important that he'd forfeit his own father?

Meeks left the bar and stalked across the large, empty room. His boots rapped solemnly upon the hardwood floor. His long, bony arms flopped at his side as he approached Kate, who remained at her brother's side.

This rebel wench is a beauty, but no woman is worth sacrificing a life for, Meeks thought in his characteristically unromantic way. Women were a diversion, pleasant enough for nights of peace, but wholly in the way in time of war.

"I have given you ample time to reflect on the nature of truth," Meeks told her. His voice, though threatening, remained gentle, coaxing, filled with false affection, which made his actions all the more offensive. "Think, now. Where is Daniel McQueen?"

He made a show of inspecting Loyal's bandaged brow. "Fortunately your brother has a hard head. Then again, Will Chaney wasn't really trying." Meeks indicated the other would-be assassin asleep on another table. Chaney's rifle lay alongside him within easy reach in case of trouble. Chaney stirred for a brief moment, smacked his lips, raised his head to look around, and then settled back onto the feather pillow he had taken from Loyal's bed.

"When Chaney wakens he's apt to be in a nasty mood," Meeks warned. "He has ways of making a man talk. But you don't have to suffer. Tell me what I wish to know of Daniel McQueen and I'll send Chaney back out to the hogs."

"You see Daniel McQueen as if through a glass darkly," Loyal said, gravely serious.

"I bloody well see him not at all." Meeks slapped Loyal across the face. "And neither will you. Ever again."

"No. Leave him alone. He's telling you the truth," Kate blurted. She placed herself in harm's way, between her brother and the Englishman.

Meeks relented and backed away. He smiled, and his single eye held all the warmth of early frost.

"I believe you," Meeks finally said. "There, you see, my dear. I am not the black-hearted villain you surmised. I can be charitable even to my enemies." He rubbed his hands together, and the leathery sound reminded Kate of bat wings brushing one another. He scratched the tip of his hooked nose, then fished a long-stemmed clay pipe from inside his waistcoat. "Especially charitable when they serve such an elegant Madeira." He started back to where he'd left his wineglass, sliding his right hand along the top of the bar as he went.

"Danny won't come here!" Kate said, defiant to the end. "Why should he? And what has he to do with the likes of you?"

"More than you can imagine, my dear." Meeks lifted the Madeira to his lips and took a sip before continuing. "Danny and I soldiered together. Aye, that's it. Brothers at arms." Meeks finished the Madeira and wiped his mouth on a silk kerchief he kept tucked in his sleeve. How reed thin and hungry the brooding major looked at first glance. Yet the longer Kate was around Josiah Meeks the more she sensed the strength in him. Like a rod of cold iron there seemed no give in the man. She feared for Daniel's safety. The major obviously intended nothing but harm for him.

"How long do you intend to stay here?" Kate left her brother's side and, crossing behind the bar, brought out the stoneware bottle of wine. She refilled Meeks's glass. She could see no point in confrontation when an extra glass of wine might bring her everything she wanted to know.

Meeks knew when he was being plied with drink, and her tactic amused him. He accepted the refill and lit his clay pipe, blowing gray-blue clouds of aromatic tobacco smoke toward the rafters.

"I shall stay as long as it suits me," he answered.

"And if other guests arrive?"

"They won't. We have blocked your drive. Anyone who stops will be promptly sent on their way. Unless, of course, it's Daniel McQueen." Meeks's eyes grew hard. "I shall welcome him."

Across the Trenton Road opposite the Hound and Hare Inn, Daniel aimed one of his Quakers at Black Tolbert and enjoyed the fantasy of blowing the brigand's head off. It wasn't a bad way for Daniel to pass the time of day as he lay in the shadow of a baneberry patch and peered between a break in the overgrown stone wall at Tolbert.

Tolbert stood before the barrel of hard cider set atop the courtyard wall. A tankard in his hand, Tolbert helped himself to the inn's supply of hard cider. All the while he filled the pewter tankard, the Tory renegade kept a fearful eye on the front door lest Josiah Meeks appear and catch him in the act.

Daniel lowered his pistol and placed it on the ground alongside him. He cursed Major Josiah Meeks beneath his breath. Tolbert wouldn't be here alone. No doubt the major was inside, and Daniel knew no good would come of the Englishman's presence.

Tolbert strolled across the courtyard and stood beneath the wrought-iron arch he had forged. A stone's throw from the road and Daniel's place of concealment, Black Tolbert leaned against the gate and tilted the tankard to his mouth. As he poured the bitter cider down his gullet, his nut brown waistcoat parted to reveal a pistol and a tomahawk thrust through his wide leather belt.

"Enjoy your drink, you bastard," Daniel muttered.

He licked his lips and had to rub his belly when his stomach began to growl. He winced and shifted position. The ground had made for a hard bed the night before when an hour outside of Philadelphia Daniel had pitched camp in an apple orchard. Exhausted, he'd slept through the morning, allowing the black mare to rest before riding the last few miles to the inn. Caution had caused him to hold back and approach the Hound and Hare by the most discreet course. The woods across the Trenton Road offered the most concealment. After picketing the mare in a draw well back in the trees, Daniel had walked and crawled to the fence. Now, with Black Tolbert so close at hand and the idea of Kate in danger, it took all of the Highlander's self-control to keep from charging the inn, guns blazing.

What had Meeks in mind now? Daniel had more questions than answers. First things first: He had to find out how many men were with Tolbert. That meant an inspection of the barn to count the horses. As for the inn itself—well, he'd be of no use to Kate dead, so a daylight assault was out of the question.

The man behind the fence would have to be patient and bide his time until nightfall. There'd be a stalking moon tonight, and Daniel McQueen intended to put it to use.

Chapter Twenty-Two

Black Tolbert returned by the side door from a brief sojourn to the barn to check on the horses. He had relinquished the watch to Chaney and now moved quickly past the bar with its array of libations. He wasn't interested in liquor anymore. Two tankards of hard cider sloshed in his belly. He had another appetite now; he headed straight for the winter kitchen, where Kate Bufkin was preparing food for her unwanted guests. Meeks would not allow her to use the summer kitchen just outside the back door of the inn, for he feared she might try to run away—a foolish fear, as far as Kate was concerned. She would never leave her brother behind. Her back was to Tolbert when he entered the kitchen. She was leaning over a table and offered a tempting sight as she prepared the meal. Smooth and arrogant and brittlely handsome, Black Tolbert was just drunk enough not to care if he got into trouble with Meeks. Such a comely wench was worth any risk. He remembered how he felt the first time he'd set eyes on her, during the pretended robbery by the covered bridge. He'd wanted her then. And by God, he'd have her now.

Tolbert shut the door as he advanced on the woman, quietly and confidently past barrels of corn meal, salt, and molasses, past salt pork and dried peas and dried gourds neatly arranged upon a shelf close by. Close enough to smell her, Tolbert grinned and in a silken voice broke the silence. "Well, now, my sweet. Trundle your skirt up and stay as you are. And we'll both have sport aplenty before I'm through." He reached for her hips.

Kate straightened up at the sound of his voice. She slowly turned from the salt pork she had been slicing. The young woman brandished a butcher knife whose curved steel blade was over a foot long and gleamed wickedly.

"Come ahead, prince of pigs," she replied. "I've carved this bacon, why not yours?"

"So the cat bares her claws," Tolbert said. He dropped his hand to the gun in his belt. "I can play your game. You'll spread yourself on that table or take a pistol ball in your pretty head."

"Enough," Meeks said from behind him. The kitchen door banged open and the officer stepped to one side, keeping the doorway clear. "Keep watch upstairs. Call out if you see the Irishman."

"Dammit, Meeks," Tolbert snarled.

"Go on. And keep your eyes open. I sent Chaney out to the courtyard. You stay in the window. If anyone comes along the road—"

"Meeks! Soldiers coming. It's O'Flynn and his men," Chaney called from the front door. His stubbled cheeks were flush from excitement; the front of his shirt was splattered with freshly spilled cider and clung to his round belly. "They're riding like the devil's on their tails. And they ain't alone. Woodbine's with them."

"Woodbine! Damn. There must be trouble." Meeks glanced at Tolbert. "Get your rifle and head to the barn. Saddle the horses."

"You're trapped," Kate taunted. "Nathaniel Woodbine and his militia will ride you down no matter where you go." She placed her fists on her hips and glowered at the Englishman. "Better you lay your guns here on the table and surrender while you have the chance."

Meeks reached out, caught her by the arm, and dragged her from the kitchen, forcing her to walk alongside him as he crossed the inn to the front door. "Come along and watch me surrender." He pulled her outside and propelled her halfway across the courtyard.

Daniel McQueen had begun to work his way along the fence in an effort to place himself out of view of the inn before he crossed the Trenton Road and headed for the barn. The sudden appearances of Josiah Meeks and Kate in the courtyard halted him in his tracks. He darted down and remained in view of the Hound and Hare. He recognized the rumble of approaching horses. Moments later he caught sight of Woodbine and his militia. Daniel's heart soared and he forgave Nathaniel Woodbine all the terrible sins he had attributed to the merchant.

Quakers in hand, he readied himself to charge the inn at the first sound of gunfire. His heart throbbed in his chest. With the prospect of rescue, the danger for Kate only heightened. Daniel could only hope Woodbine's men held their fire. But then, how would Woodbine even know these were British agents? Daniel had to warn them, but in some way that wouldn't risk Kate's life.

Daniel was struggling to formulate a plan when Woodbine and his men dismounted at the arch. Woodbine left his men, hurried through the gate, and clasped Josiah Meeks's outstretched hand as if he knew the Englishman—as if they were accomplices! Meeks and Woodbine spoke for a moment, then Woodbine turned to Kate and said something. She raised a hand to slap him, but Chaney stepped up from behind and caught her arm. He pulled her back into the inn. Woodbine and Meeks trailed along behind.

Daniel crouched back under cover. He stared at the brace of pistols in his hands, his mind reeling with the shock of what he had seen. *Not that I ever trusted Woodbine. . . . Damn! I never felt so helpless in my life. What the devil is going on? Meeks is a sly fox. I'll have to stay a step ahead. But how?*

Maybe there was a way. Maybe one desperate chance. If one of the men in the inn made a mistake.

Nathaniel Woodbine gulped his ale and continued his story while Meeks stood with one arm resting on the mantelpiece and listened. He wasn't the only one, however, for Kate Bufkin sat nearby in a state of utter shock. The truth of Woodbine's treachery had left her speechless, and she had begun to despair, whereas before she had been able to resist the major's mental tortures. He had told her of Daniel McQueen, and how he had involved the blacksmith in a scheme to kill the new commander-in-chief of the Continental Army as soon as the Congress announced the appointment. He had also described his hold over Daniel, dangling the prospect of his father's execution like a man dancing from a gallows rope. Oh, but Meeks had been so very pleased with himself. He had even bragged of his part in the murder of Henk Schraner. It amused the major to no end that Daniel had been blamed for the crime.

Yet, even after learning all the British agent had to say, Kate still managed to cling to the hope that Meeks could be stopped. Her faith in Daniel had never wavered—until Woodbine's arrival. Here was no deliverer but simply another piece in Josiah Meeks's puzzle of deceit. Now Kate stared into her folded hands upon the tabletop as Woodbine revealed the depths of his betrayal of the cause he had professed to serve.

"Don't ask me how, I just knew," Woodbine said. "That very morning, something in Bill Rutledge's eyes told me he had somehow learned of my true loyalties."

"A man drinks to excess, he is bound to act a bit queer the following morning," Meeks replied.

"And well I thought as much. But to be sure I left shortly after the good doctor rode away. I joined O'Flynn and my lads in another part of the city and dispatched the Irishman to watch my house, but from a discreet distance. I had already left the city, trusting in my own intuition. Sure enough, about an hour from the inn, O'Flynn caught up to us. He had ridden two horses into the ground just to catch us." Woodbine paused to drain the contents of his tankard.

"And?" Meeks pressed. It appeared he had little regard for the merchant; he mistrusted any man who frightened so easily.

"I was right. By midmorning, a dozen armed men surrounded my house. They took my servants prisoner and were waiting for me, when O'Flynn decided he'd seen enough."

"And I have heard enough," Meeks said. "We shall have to abandon one of our plans. We obviously cannot remain here and wait for Washington. But we can destroy the arms and supplies. Now, I have narrowed the possible farms the rebels could be using down to two. The Schraner farm and the Grauwyler farm both offer concealment and ample protection. Schraner has two sons, and he is an old Indian fighter himself. The Grauwyler widow has five sons, all of them patriots."

"You are wrong," Woodbine said. It pleased him to correct the Englishman. O'Flynn was right. Meeks was too damn haughty. "The guns have been right under your nose. The Daughters of Phoebe have hidden the rifles and gunpowder on their farm. Their barn is the rebel's armory."

"Impossible," Meeks retorted, facing the merchant. "There are no men around. Who's to guard the weapons? Surely not a bunch of old hens. Why that's the last possible place I'd ever..." Meeks had started to say "use," but "look" would fit as well.

Woodbine could see he had convinced Meeks, or the Englishman had suddenly convinced himself. Either way, it didn't matter. The merchant had done everything required of him. Now it was time to salvage what he could of his own property and wealth until the rebels were crushed.

"I am leaving you my men. They are in my employ, but I have told them to follow you." Woodbine slapped his tankard down on the table. He caught Loyal staring at him. Kate's brother contemptuously shifted his gaze. Woodbine walked over to the young woman. "I pity you, Kate, for you have hinged your fortunes to that which can only bring you ruin."

She made no reply. Brave words failed her. ·

"Where are you going?" Meeks said.

"I shall take whatever gold and silver I can from my estate," Woodbine said, "and continue on to Boston, where I shall seek safety with General Gage and his troops until the hostilities have ended."

Meeks handed the merchant an oilskin packet. "These papers will see you are brought directly to General Gage. Give him my compliments, and tell him what I am about. These papers will also guarantee you are placed under his personal protection. You have done well, Nathaniel. Once these rebels are dancing a gallows jig, you shall be amply rewarded. Perhaps the governorship of one of His Majesty's colonies. . . ."

Woodbine beamed with pleasure and started for the door. "I'll take a fresh horse from the barn, if I may." He paused and looked around at Kate. He touched his hand to his tricorn hat and with a flourish of his pea-green cape, left the room.

Meeks turned to Will Chaney. "See that O'Flynn and his men stand by their mounts, and be ready yourself. We will yet deal these traitors a crippling blow."

"What about her ladyship there and her crazy brother?"

Josiah Meeks turned to Kate. He strolled over to the woman, touched her hair, and stroked her cheek. "Horses for them as well. M'lady wouldn't miss this for the world." He laughed. The rebels had finally outsmarted themselves. It had been a clever, even courageous ruse, to hide the rifles where they were least protected. But the ruse had backfired. There was nothing to stop him now but a bunch of women. Yes, it was indeed worth a laugh.

Twenty minutes later and two miles down the Trenton Road, Woodbine slowed his mount to an easy walk. The last thing he wanted to do was ruin the animal on the wheel-rutted trail and risk being set afoot with so many miles before him. Pursuit might well be forthcoming out of Philadelphia and could overtake him if he lost his horse. For now that he had a good start, he was safe. But he had to be careful and keep from panicking. *Take it easy, now,* he cautioned himself. *No one is going to catch you.* He'd be safe in Boston long before word of his loyalist activities reached the ears of his fellow colonists. Even then, he wouldn't be alone. There were plenty of others who felt like him. It was just that right now, as he studied the way ahead, he wished he'd brought a few of his men with him. He pulled back on the reins and the mare slowed its pace even more.

Here the road cut through a thicket of black walnut and stately elms. It was a particularly well shaded, heavily wooded stretch and always a pleasant find on a warm summer's day, for the cool, shadowy canopy the trees offered could be most refreshing to a hot and weary traveler. But to a fearful man pursued by phantoms of his own imagination, the way through the thicket seemed ominous indeed. *I will not turn back.* Woodbine drew a pistol and nudged the mare with his bootheels, and the animal obediently continued along the road. Warblers sang in the branches overhead. Squirrels chattered at his intrusion. Somehow, the music of nature began to soothe him and ease his tension.

Woodbine relaxed, grateful he had managed to overcome his momentary cowardice. The mare quickened her pace. The edge of the grove lay just ahead, where sunlight washed the wheel-rutted path and amber fields stretched off to either side. He returned the pistol to its saddle holster and resolved to enjoy the rest of the journey.

Suddenly, a shadow detached itself from the grove and Colonel Nathaniel Woodbine was no longer alone on the Trenton Road. It all happened so quickly he had no time to react. One moment he was enjoying a solitary reverie and the next, cold fear numbed his limbs and safety seemed far away.

"You forgot to say good-bye." Daniel McQueen held a pistol to Woodbine's head.

Chapter Twenty-Three

The Daughters of Phoebe had set a fine table that afternoon, in front of the common house, laden with round loaves of bread, a platter of roasted chickens, a tureen of creamed onions, and boiled potatoes.

Daniel McQueen arrived right between grace and gravy, leading his prisoner. Woodbine made a pathetic sight. The diminutive merchant was securely bound and forced to cling to horseback by his thigh muscles alone, an effort that left beads of moisture on his bald pate. Daniel had gagged the man with the merchant's own periwig.

All the Daughters of Phoebe were seated at the table. Even Sister Constance, a rail-thin wisp of a woman whose parchment skin stretched over a skeletal frame and whose gray dress hung loose upon her. Sister Hope-Deferred-Maketh-the-Heart-Sick stared in dumb amazement at the red-bearded Scotsman as he reined the weary black mare up to the table. She placed her hands on her broad hips and blurted, "Glory be!" She voiced a surprise they all felt. Sister

Mercy looked over her shoulder and loosed a startled cry as the dust settled over them. She cowered against Tim Pepperidge, who recognized Daniel, leaped to his feet, and snapped up his rifle. Daniel rode in close to the young man and kicked him square in the chest. Pepperidge went sprawling over the table, scattering loaves of bread and overturning a bowl of potatoes before tumbling to the ground.

Gideon came charging up, his ferocious growl filling the air. But the mastiff skidded to a halt inches from Daniel's bootheels. The dog sat back on its haunches, studied the red beard, then altered its course. Woodbine drew up his legs and issued a muffled cry of horror as the huge dog regarded him with all the affection of a favorite meal.

Pepperidge crawled to his feet and tried to bring his rifle to bear on the intruder, only to have the weapon ignominiously snatched from his grasp by Daniel.

"Damn it, lad, I'm not your enemy. Save your powder for the Tory war party that's coming to raid the farm."

"Sweet mother of God," Sister Agnes exclaimed.

"Raiding . . . here?" Sister Ruth protested. "But why? I mean, our secret—"

"Isn't secret any longer," Daniel said. "Thanks to Mr. Nathaniel Woodbine here." He jabbed a thumb in the direction of his prisoner. "Now, I don't know how long we have. I cut across country to get here, while the Tories will probably keep to the road. They could come riding down Cobb's Hill at any moment!"

Daniel glanced over his shoulder, fearful that even mentioning the possibility might have summoned Meeks and his loyalist raiders.

"I don't believe you." Pepperidge was angry and

humiliated at the ease with which Daniel had disarmed him.

"Me neither," Sister Ruth said.

"I think perhaps you're after the guns," Pepperidge added.

"Then you'd be dead now," Daniel retorted belligerently, and returned the rifle to the astonished young man.

"I believe him," Sister Hope said, bounding down the steps with an agility that belied her amply padded frame.

"As do I." Sister Eve emerged from the front door of the farmhouse. She held a blunderbuss in the crook of her arm. At close range it could rip a man to shreds with its load of pellets and bent nails. Daniel eyed the weapon and the big-boned woman in gray who headed the religious sect.

"I thought you were women of peace," he commented wryly.

"We are," Sister Eve replied. "I was aiming at your legs."

Daniel grimaced. "With that cannon it would be kinder to shoot me in the head and save me the trouble of bleeding to death.

"Well, I think he brings us nothing but trouble," Sister Ruth protested sourly.

"Oh, Ruth, that's because he's a man. You blame every man for the grief your no-account husband caused," added Sister Constance, ending with a dry, rasping laugh at Ruth's expense.

The widow scowled and would have left but for Sister Eve, who ordered her to remain at the table until a plan of action could be agreed upon. If the farm was to become a battleground they had to have some idea of what to do. Sister Ruth grudgingly returned to her place, her orderly, placid existence forever in a shambles.

"Take to the woods," Daniel told them. "Staying in the farmhouse will place you at the Tories' mercy."

"And where will you be?" Sister Hope said, adjusting her habit and straightening her apron.

"In the barn. Maybe Woodbine here will buy me a little time. Meeks can't afford to risk the life of such a prominent loyalist."

"And if he doesn't buy you time?" Sister Agnes, the beekeeper, called out.

Daniel shrugged. The answer was obvious. He'd put up a fight. Meeks would probably torch the barn. When the flames touched the powder, the munitions, the barn, and Daniel McQueen would disappear in a blinding flash. It would be one hell of an exit.

"I'll stand with you," Pepperidge said in a chastened tone of voice. He didn't understand any of this. But it seemed Daniel wasn't the renegade Papa Schraner claimed. "If you'll have me." He wore a sheepish expression on his face as if he half expected a rebuke. Sister Mercy placed a hand on his arm, then realized how such a gesture must seem and drew her hand back as if burned. She glanced about to see if anyone had noticed. No one had.

"I'd be glad for the company," Daniel said. "But I had hoped you would ride to the Schraner farm. You might even make it back here in time."

"The Schraners are selling off a pair of mules and a milk cow. Eben said they're expecting a dozen or so men to show up to bid on them," Pepperidge said excitedly. "Maybe more!"

"I can ride good as any man," Sister Mercy spoke up. All the older women turned toward her. She drew herself sharply erect, throwing back her shoulders. "I shall ride the back trail over Cobb's Hill. And if Cherry Creek is dry, I can even save another half hour."

Daniel glanced at Sister Eve, who nodded her

consent. "Very well, lass. Our fortune, for good or ill, is in your hands." He reached down and clapped Pepperidge on the shoulder. "We have work to do, my fine fellow. Maybe we'll teach these Tories the price of guns."

It was warm, even in the shade of the barn. Carrier pigeons cooed and fluttered restlessly among the rafters. A bee whirled and darted through the dancing dust to torment the bound man near the entrance.

Nathaniel Woodbine never spent a more miserable hour. His arms ached from lack of circulation. His mouth was dry as grit, and a bee was threatening to sting the tip of his nose. Where the blazes was Josiah Meeks? The major was obviously taking his own sweet time, for he had yet to arrive. Of course, as far as Meeks knew, he was on his way to raid a cache of weapons guarded by a bunch of helpless women. The rebel guns were his for the taking. Why hurry? He was no doubt resting his horses in case his small force should need to make a speedy getaway from the farm. Back at the inn Meeks said he intended to burn the women out. There was no telling who such a fire might attract. Yes, Woodbine could read the major's mind. Such a precaution made perfect sense, for any situation but this one. Meeks had unwittingly allowed Daniel to instigate a plan of defense. Woodbine swallowed. Gad, his throat felt raw. At least Daniel had possessed the common decency to remove Woodbine's periwig gag.

The merchant was securely tied to the back of the Sicilian panel wagon, and through the open doors of the barn he watched Daniel prepare a special surprise for any would-be attacker.

Daniel had tapped a pair of powder kegs and

poured two separate powder trails fanning out from the front of the barn to a distance of about fifteen feet. Each powder trail ended in a keg of gunpowder. Daniel buried the kegs beneath mounds of rocks and splintery logs and pouches of lead shot, anything to make a nasty spray of shrapnel.

While Daniel completed his explosive line of defense, Pepperidge unpacked a crate of Pennsylvania rifles whose octagonal barrels were long as a man was tall and sheathed in stocks of burled walnut. He loaded and primed each weapon. The young patriot worked quickly and efficiently, despite his trembling hands. He carried several of the rifles to the loft, where he and Daniel would be able to fire down on their attackers. He arranged another dozen rifles to either side of the main doors. The ability to shoot without having to stop and reload might well save their lives. If the Tories came at them from every side, the defenders of the barn would have a problem. Two men couldn't face thirteen at the same time. Pepperidge paused in his work to consider the possibility of such an attack. His hand holding the brass powder flask paused before pouring a charge down the muzzle of the flintlock rifle gripped in his left hand.

Woodbine sensed the misgivings in the lad and hoped to turn them to his advantage.

"Water . . . please," Woodbine rasped.

Pepperidge eyed the merchant with a skepticism he always reserved for the wealthy. He walked across to a nearby water barrel and returned with a dipper of cool spring water. He held the dipper to Woodbine's lips and allowed the loyalist to drink. Water trickled down the man's chin and spattered his dusty vest and round belly. Woodbine no longer cared about etiquette. He was a desperate man. Any moment, Josiah Meeks would come hurtling down on the farm and burn the buildings to the ground regardless of the fact that Nathaniel Woodbine was being held prisoner.

"There's still time, my young friend," the loyalist continued in the gentle, soothing tone one might use to charm an unhappy child. "I have no animosity toward you. No indeed, for I, too, was young once and made mistakes aplenty."

Pepperidge met the prisoner's gaze. The words seemed to be sinking in, at least as far as the merchant could tell. He pressed on, hoping to win the youth to his side.

"There is much of the world you haven't seen, so much you haven't done. Death is such a pitiful waste . . . for both of us." Woodbine wondered if he was reaching the young man. Was that fear in his eyes? "I am a man of means. I will be even more so because of my loyalty to His Majesty. You could share my good fortune. Yes . . . you. Set me loose and we shall warn the others, and your brave act will be generously rewarded by General Gage himself. I promise it." Woodbine flashed his most winning smile. "Now, what say you? Are we partners?"

Pepperidge shrugged and finished loading the rifle. He primed the piece; then, with the rifle butt on the ground, he folded his arms and leaned against the barrel.

"I'd rather die poor and free than live rich with the taste of British bootheels on my lips," he replied. "But you sure talk pretty." Reaching down, he took the dirty, straw-covered periwig off the ground and shoved it in the bound man's mouth. Woodbine spat out the wig, his eyes wide and round. His cheeks turned blood red, and for all his lack of size he seemed capable of bursting his bonds.

"You're going to die. You're all going to die! Do you hear? Die!"

His voice carried outside, where Daniel was finishing with the powder kegs. He didn't know if his makeshift mines would kill anyone, but they were bound to be noisy as the devil. He straightened, sensing the approach of the woman across the yard. Daniel frowned in anger and concern. Hope and Eve should have already secured a hiding place in the woods. He had seen Ruth and Agnes with Sister Constance abandon the farm and take the carriage into the forest. They were safe. But these last two Daughters were finding one excuse after another to linger at the farm. They came toward him, carrying blankets draped across their shoulders. Gideon trotted at Hope's side, his tail wagging in the breezeless heat. It was a good day to take a fishing pole and lie by a creek bank and try not to catch fish. What better way to pass the time than to doze beneath a cloudless sky and let the warm sun seep into tired muscles and leach one's cares away?

Daniel wiped the sweat from his brow on the sleeve of the shirt he wore open to the waist. Moisture glistened on the red curls covering his chest. He'd tied back his long hair with a strip of leather, but a wayward strand escaped. His hands were bruised and dirty from his labors.

Gideon trotted up to Daniel to receive an affectionate pat on the head and a scratch behind the ears. The mastiff slobbered over Daniel's outstretched arm and muzzled a pouch dangling from the Scotsman's belt. Daniel untied the pouch and removed the last strip of jerked venison he'd been living on for the past few days. Gideon hungrily devoured the snack and eyed the pouch for another.

"Gideon," Sister Hope warned, and the mastiff turned and looked at her, barked, and then trotted off into the barn to see if Pepperidge had any handouts.

"I'll saddle a couple of horses for you," Daniel said to the two women.

"No need," Sister Eve replied. She was big and homely, a woman born for hard work; she had little of the femininity of the others. But she was not without dignity, and she was not without courage. "Hope and I are staying."

"I don't understand." Daniel began to argue, sensing he'd already lost.

"As you said, we have Mr. Woodbine. His presence among us should give your British major pause."

"I did not explain the entire situation, dear lady," Daniel said. "I remained by the inn until Meeks and the Tories departed. They took Kate and Loyal Bufkin with them as their prisoners. I hope to buy their freedom with Woodbine. Once I do that, Josiah Meeks will be free to attack."

"Oh," said Sister Eve.

"I see," said Sister Hope.

The two women exchanged glances and then looked back at Daniel.

"We're staying," they said.

"But you will not fight," Daniel protested.

"There are water barrels in the barn," Sister Hope explained. "We can soak these blankets and fight the flames, leaving you and young Master Pepperidge to man the guns."

"It is our farm," Sister Eve pointed out, thick arms folded across her chest. That point was irrefutable.

Daniel sighed in resignation. Like Kate, these Daughters of Phoebe were as stubborn as they were brave. Hope and Eve marched past him and into the barn. Pepperidge was leaning against the outside wall of the barn, a rifle cradled in his arm, a bemused expression on his clean-cut face. It was obvious he had overheard

Daniel's failed attempt to change the women's minds and steer them to safety.

Daniel acknowledged the younger man. On his way into the barn, he paused beside Pepperidge and spoke in a lowered voice. "Phoebe must have been one hell of a woman."

Pepperidge grinned, and the two men shared a moment of humor. Then Pepperidge's eyes hardened as he looked beyond Daniel to the road circling Cobb's Hill. A plume of dust drifted above the treetops. Daniel swung around, saw the dust cloud, and allowed a deadly calm to settle over him. So they had come at last.

"Is it . . . ?" Pepperidge's voice faded as he barely managed to swallow.

"Josiah Meeks," Daniel said.

Chapter Twenty-Four

Now that Meeks had at last found Daniel McQueen, he wasn't sure what to do with him. Padraich O'Flynn and the rest of Woodbine's men had fanned out across the road and into the pasture on either side. Cobb's Hill lay behind them, and about seventy yards ahead by the barn waited two men, Daniel astride the black mare and Woodbine on the brown mare he had ridden from the inn.

Meeks centered his spyglass on the two and muttered aloud, "Woodbine, you fool." So much for an undefended barn. There was a wise old adage about such a turn of events, but damn if he could recall it.

"The merchant don't mean piss to me," Black Tolbert said. He held one of the many torches the Tory raiders had made along the way. It was a branch two inches thick and a yard long. At one end, dry grass had been tied in a bulb and soaked with whale oil. He glanced at Will Chaney, who nodded in accord.

"Ride them down and burn the place, says I," Chaney added.

"And cause the death of one of the most influential men in the colonies?" Meeks glanced back at O'Flynn and the other of Woodbine's men now under Meeks's command. "The Irishman would be sure to tell the tale. No doubt those other hirelings as well. Such stories might well drive other loyal colonists into the ranks of these rebels."

"You saying we ought to just ride away?" Tolbert grumbled. "Tails tucked betwixt our legs?"

"I am suggesting, my thickheaded friend, that we return Mr. Woodbine safely to our ranks. McQueen hasn't the only prisoners." Meeks turned his horse and walked back along the road until he drew abreast of Kate Bufkin and her brother where they waited under guard. Meeks touched the brim of his tricorn.

"Will you be having a jack of ale, sir?" Loyal asked as if standing in the Hound and Hare rather than sitting a horse on a farm road. Meeks studied Kate's brother for a moment but made no reply. Obviously Will Chaney's blow had addled the poor man's senses. Meeks would have released Loyal except for the fact that his presence seemed to keep Kate in line. The major turned his attention to the woman. Kate Bufkin tried to look more confident than she felt. She had enjoyed seeing Meeks caught off guard at not finding the farm totally undefended. What worried her was that Daniel might be all alone. If that was the case, he was hopelessly outnumbered. She glared at the one-eyed major with all the hatred she could muster.

"Ah yes, but of course. I am the villain of the piece." Meeks glanced toward the barn. "And that man below some knight in shining armor, the hero of the ballad, battling for love and honor." The major laughed softly—then his gaze turned cold and hard as steel. "But to me, my girl, you are the villains, you are the traitors to His Majesty, King George. You and your rebellious friends threaten everything I hold most dear, and I will do everything in my power to bring your plans to ruin." Meeks stiffened in the saddle. "We shall see if Danny boy is willing to bargain for your life." He shifted his gaze to the two men stationed to either side of the prisoners. "When I signal you, start these two forward."

The two men held their rifles ready as if daring Kate or her crazed brother to try something. Loyal examined the man to his left, shook his head in dismay. "Blessed be the peacemakers, for they shall see God," he said. "My son, salvation is at hand. For you. And I bet you've a thirst. Folks say mine is the best hard cider. Will you be joining me in a cup?" He held up an empty hand.

"You crazed idiot, shut up now or I'll lay into you with my rifle," the man growled.

Loyal shrugged, glanced aside at Kate, and winked. Kate looked at her brother in wonderment. Was all this an act? He'd certainly fooled her. But why? What was Loyal planning now that everyone thought him a helpless, addled fool? Now she was really worried, and she had every right to be.

"What's happening?" Tim Pepperidge said from the hayloft.

Daniel watched with interest as Josiah Meeks rode away from his command and came alone down the road to the farm. The major covered about half the distance to the barn and then reined in his horse and waited, a solitary figure in the warm afternoon.

A few high, feathery clouds dotted the otherwise barren azure sky. The warmth of the sun poured down, thick as the honey from Sister Agnes's bees. It stifled sound as it cast a hypnotic spell across the landscape of the afternoon. Daniel stretched, worked the tightness out of his shoulders. It was a pity to waste such a lazy afternoon; there ought to be time for a quick swim in the spring, time to lie upon the bosom of earth and be refreshed. He turned his face to the sunlight, closed his eyes, felt the heat upon his cheeks and forehead. It was a feeling similar to standing at a forge and working the bellows, turning bar iron into a white-hot, malleable substance to be worked with hammer and anvil. His skills, those his father had taught him, had been of little use lately. More so, his self-honed talents for war had been called upon. He missed the honest grime and sweat, the toil of the furnace, the shaping of black iron into useful tools or works of simple beauty. Perhaps one day he would again stand before a forge. . . .

"You aren't so smart now," Woodbine said smugly.

Daniel, his thoughts shattered, beheld the hapless loyalist with eyes that smoldered like the embers of his imagined forge. Before such a stare, the haughty grin crawled off Woodbine's face; the man gulped and shuddered.

"If Woodbine tries anything, shoot him down," Daniel called out to the young rebel in the loft.

"I have my rifle aimed at his head," Pepperidge's voice drifted down.

"Be careful. I don't trust that Englishman, from what I can see of him," Sister Hope said from the doorway of the barn.

Daniel urged the black mare forward. He rode across the yard, where a red-winged chicken, an escapee from the coop, scratched in the dirt looking for food. At Daniel's approach, the hen scampered off toward the safety of the barnyard pens. Sheep blissfully grazed in the meadow, oblivious as the dairy cow and rooting hogs to the mounting tension.

Daniel turned onto the farm road and covered the

distance to where the British major waited. Meeks's long arms hung at his side. His brown cloak, worn even on such a hot afternoon, draped loosely over his tall, spare frame. Neither man dismounted; they faced one another on horseback.

"You have been a disappointment to me, Danny boy," Meeks said.

"Ride away, Major. Leave the girl and her brother and ride back to General Gage. Then both of you go home. This isn't your country anymore."

"I counted on your being a practical man," Meeks continued. "And a loving son...not to risk your father's life."

"Maybe I found something more important than his life," Daniel said. "Or mine." He wasn't good at these word games. Already he felt as if he were being led. The Englishman was toying with him, trying to trick him into a rash act that could only end in ruin.

"So I no longer even have that hold over you." The major sighed. "Well, 'tis for the best. I would have felt like a knave betraying your trust and not keeping my part of our bargain."

"What do you say now?"

"Only that the day Brian Farley McQueen was arrested, his treason was obvious, you know, still warm from the forge. Well, your father put up quite a struggle. He was killed trying to escape."

Daniel doubled over, as if struck; for a brief moment his eyes squeezed shut as the enormity of this revelation sunk in. Meeks reached for one of the saddle pistols holstered in front of him by his right leg. Daniel glanced up and dropped a hand to one of his Quakers. Meeks shrugged but didn't try for the horse pistol. He did not need to; it was plain he had already wounded Daniel, shaken him to the core.

"You're lying," Daniel managed to say through clenched teeth.

"Not hardly. On my honor—"

"You have no honor!"

Meeks did not intend to debate the issue. Better, he thought, to strike at the wound again. "Your father is dead. But learning of his death and the circumstances of your estrangement from acquaintances who did not share your father's seditious tendencies, I thought to capitalize on them. You have never failed, Danny boy, to impress me with your daring and skill and quick mind. I thought you were an excellent choice to help me carry out my orders." Meeks pulled the silk kerchief from the sleeve of his coat and dabbed at his nose. "I see I was wrong."

It took every last ounce of strength to hold himself in check. Daniel wanted to drag the Englishman from his horse and strangle him, break his neck, cut the black heart from his body. Meeks had shown himself to be a liar, yet there was something in the man's voice that caused Daniel to believe him. Perhaps it was not so much the major as knowing his father. Brian Farley McQueen had been a volatile, proud, unyielding man. He had loved his son and yet so rarely had expressed it. Only looking back had Daniel at last been able to see and understand the little ways his father had demonstrated his true feelings for his son. Brian McQueen would never have gone with the British soldiers without a fight. And he would have fought to the death.

"Now, then, it seems we are at an impasse. You have something I want. I have something you want," Meeks said. "I'll make it simple. I shall start Kate and her simpleton brother toward the barn. You will allow Woodbine to ride out to meet them. Of course, if you do not send Woodbine out, I shall have my men open fire on the girl. Her life is in your hands. Simple?"

"Yes," Daniel said hoarsely. He looked toward the hills, hoping in vain to find the Schraners and other patriots riding to the rescue. But all he saw was a hawk circling above the trees. There was no one coming. He would have to defend the farm with his army of an untried youth and two middle-aged women. Despite the pain of his loss he suddenly laughed aloud. It was the one reaction that caught Meeks completely off guard, and he looked at Daniel with renewed wariness as one watches the mad. He slowly had his horse retreat a few paces.

"But know this," Daniel said. "If not today, Josiah Meeks, then the next, I *will* kill you." Daniel turned the black mare and rode back the way he had come.

The time for talk had ended.

Chapter Twenty-Five

Kate and Loyal started down the farm road at the same time Nathaniel Woodbine rode away from Daniel's side. The merchant was no longer tied, but Daniel had ordered him to hold his mount to a steady walk until he had reached the halfway point and crossed paths with Josiah Meeks's prisoners.

"Keep your rifle on him," Daniel called to the loft, and Tim Pepperidge answered with a wave of his hand. While there were a few moments left Daniel hurried back into the barn and found Sister Hope standing by the wagon and Sister Eve at the rear of the barn, her blunderbuss at the ready. Sister Hope was seated on the back steps of the Sicilian wagon with her faithful Gideon at her side.

"There's still time to get out of here. You could miss a lot of trouble."

"Trouble and I are old friends." Sister Hope scratched Gideon behind the ears. Her face took on a worldlywise expression. "Pity the only man I've ever known who has never told me a lie turns out to be a dog. But I have my life here among the Daughters, and it is a good life. If it must end, then let it end here." She rolled up her gray sleeves and unfolded a blanket to immerse in the water barrel. If the barn caught fire, Sister Hope-Deferred-Maketh-the-Heart-Sick was ready. Daniel had to smile; he knew he'd get the same response from Sister Eve. He looked down the length of the barn. The big-boned woman in gray by the rear door waved to him, and Daniel returned the gesture. He rechecked the guns in his belt and crossed back to the front of the barn.

The Tories had positioned themselves as if awaiting the order to charge the barn. No doubt they would as soon as Woodbine was clear. Daniel watched Kate and Loyal draw close to Woodbine. They had maintained as even pace, matching the merchant's horse stride for stride.

Kate could feel the eyes of the raiders boring into her back. Meeks had not seemed to mind losing her. Perhaps he intended to capture her again before the day was out. Well, he wouldn't take her without a fight.

"Kate?" Loyal drew abreast of his sister.

"Don't worry, Loyal."

"My little sister, always watching out for big brother."

"I haven't minded." Kate studied the round-shouldered, balding man who as a boy seemed so bold and capable. Suddenly she realized he was behaving quite lucidly and was aware of his surroundings.

"I shall always love you," Loyal said. "I think Daniel McQueen is a good man. Stand by him."

"That blow on your skull did no more than raise a lump. You've been pretending all this time. Why?"

"A fool is never taken seriously. A fool isn't even searched." With that, Loyal doffed his tricorn hat and slapped it across the rump of Kate's horse while loosing a bloodcurdling scream.

"Loyal!" Too late. Kate held on tight as her gelding galloped full out. Loyal did the same to his own mount and soon was racing pell-mell over the wheel-rutted path leading to the barn. A few yards ahead, Woodbine, sensing some kind of betrayal, urged his own horse to a gallop. The prisoners rapidly closed on one another.

Kate, leaning low on the neck of her racing steed, only caught a blurred glimpse of her mother's former lover as the merchant sped past. Loyal quickly closed the gap, but at the last possible moment he veered his own mount, tugged viciously on the reins, and brought his horse in front of Woodbine's. The animals collided and went down in a flurry of flashing hooves.

"Treachery!" Josiah Meeks roared. "Black treachery! Ride them down! Burn the place, I say. Burn it to the ground!" He drove his bootheels into the flanks of his charger and the animal bolted forward. Black Tolbert and Will Chaney took off after the major. Padraich O'Flynn looked about at the men drawn up to either side of him.

"Well, men, it's a fight we came for, and a fight we have. And merry, but I'll not have the major say we held back! Come on, brave lads, and earn the silver you have been paid!"

As one, Woodbine's militia charged across the meadow, torches aflame, rifles primed, sabers gleaming in the sun. There was not a faint heart among them. To a man they were eager to fight.

"Oh, God," Daniel muttered, as Loyal sent Kate charging toward him. "Oh, God," he repeated as Kate's brother slammed into Woodbine and the two riders went down. Daniel grabbed the rifle closest to him and ran out of the barn as Josiah Meeks and his raiders broke ranks and began their attack in a ragged line.

Kate had lost her reins and had caught a handful of mane; she held on for dear life. The animal headed straight for the barnyard and was not about to stop or turn back, however desperate Kate's efforts to return to her brother's side. Daniel had to place himself in the path of the frightened beast about fifty feet from the barn. The gelding tried to cut by him, but Daniel caught up the reins and forced the animal to slow its pace enough for Kate to slide out of the saddle. She started back the way she had come. Daniel caught her by the arm.

"Let me go!"

"No. You can't help him," Daniel said. Loyal and Woodbine were locked in a desperate struggle. "If Meeks catches us out in the open we won't stand a chance!" Some of the oncoming riflemen loosed a volley. Lead smacked into the walls of the barn, dug gouts of earth around the struggling men, and fanned the air inches from Daniel and Kate. Daniel snapped off a shot with his own rifle, tossed it aside, and half led, half dragged Kate the remaining ten yards to the momentary safety of the barn.

Woodbine struggled up out of the road and spat a mouthful of blood and dirt.

"What are you doing? Fool, you could have killed us both!" Loyal dove into the smaller man and knocked him over on his back.

"A fool, yes, but clever enough to hide a knife." Loyal snatched a knife from his boot top as he forced Woodbine down. The merchant saw the glint of sunlight on the steel blade and panicked. He twisted and turned and flailed.

"Tell me about the cider. I make the best hard cider in the colonies. Our friend, our betrayer!"

"I've always been your friend," Woodbine shrieked as he managed to block the knife in its descent.

Loyal heard the drumming hoofbeats of the approaching horses. Men with guns and torches were riding him down. Rifles and pistols blossomed black smoke. In that instant of distraction, Nathaniel Woodbine gave one last herculean effort to save his life. He grabbed Loyal by the scruff of his waistcoat and pulled. The merchant rolled loose, knocked Loyal aside, and rose up on his knees as gunfire thundered over the meadow and rifle balls filled the air. But he was free, damn it. Free!

There came a sickening whack and a crunch of bone. The merchant's head jerked to the left as blood spilled from a ghastly wound just above his ear. Woodbine dropped forward onto Loyal's chest, killed by his own would-be rescuers.

Daniel stood in the shadow of the barn. The summer air was thick with the smell of straw and manure and horseflesh. It wasn't the most romantic of places, yet there was so much he wanted to say and so little time to say it. Balls splintered the wood as the Tory raiders charged the barn.

"Daniel, I have to help my brother," Kate pleaded.

Daniel took a rifle and shoved it into her arms. "It's too late."

Kate staggered into the doorway. Sister Hope hurried to her side.

"Poor dear. There's a love," the older woman said, putting an arm around Kate.

Back in the road, one horse was down. Loyal and

Woodbine were an unmoving pair sprawled upon the ground.

"No. Oh, please, no," Kate cried weakly, her eyes filled with tears. But she did not break. A dark and angry expression transformed her beauty into a mask of rage. She raised the rifle and fired in the direction of the oncoming Tories. She lay the rifle aside, started to reach for another, and changed her mind as Daniel loosed a shot that dropped one Tory from horseback. The raider's left foot caught in the stirrup and the man was dragged, screaming, across the meadow and toward the woods.

"I'll keep them loaded," Kate shouted, and poured a charge down her rifle barrel, following with patch and ball that she rammed home.

Daniel lifted another rifle to his shoulder, fired, methodically replaced it with another. From the loft, Pepperidge worked through the rifles he'd carried up from the wagon. But he was hurrying his shots and sacrificing accuracy. Still, he accounted for one more kill, a sun-darkened Welshman who dropped his torch and clutched at his chest as he rolled from horseback.

Daniel sensed the trouble before he heard Pepperidge's groan. The Highland rebel ran to the center of the barn as young Pepperidge dropped to the floor of the loft and rolled over the edge. He managed to catch hold of the top rung of the ladder and break his fall, though his agonized cry rose to the rafters. Daniel rushed to his side and lowered him to the ground. The front of his shirt was sticky as blood seeped from his punctured right shoulder.

"I'll tend him." Sister Hope knelt close by, tore a swath from the hem of her skirt, and applied pressure to the wound.

"Am I going to die?" Pepperidge said through clenched teeth.

"Heaven's no," Sister Hope chided. "Imagine you'll live long enough to snatch our Sister Mercy from the nest." Her eyes were wise and knowing as she beamed down at the wounded lad. He looked surprised. "Silly one, did you think you invented those feelings? I may be old and thick as yesterday's pudding, but I'm just as much a woman as I ever was." She winked and lowered her voice. "Maybe even more so."

Daniel trotted back to the doorway, where he paused to fish a tinder box from his belt pouch. He caught his breath, then darted through the doorway and scrambled to the twin trails of gunpowder he'd drawn upon the ground. The Tories were forty yards away and coming at a dead run. He could make out Chaney and Black Tolbert, but Meeks appeared to be lagging behind now, allowing the raiding party to carry the attack. Daniel worked the strike box and ignited the powder trails, then darted through a hail of lead to the safety of the barn. He stumbled, and Kate, fearing him wounded, ran to the doorway to help drag him to safety. An enemy ball missed her by inches. Daniel waved her aside and scrambled to his feet. He caught the startled woman and forced her into the nearest stall. They tripped and fell, landed on the piled straw in a tangle of arms and legs. Outside, two dancing columns of smoke sputtered toward the kegs while the Tory raiders closed the gap. Thirty yards—twenty—fifteen...

"What are you doing? Have you lost your senses?" Kate blurted out, spewing straw and trying to extricate herself. "Daniel McQueen, are you mad? This is hardly the time for a roll in the hay!"

One explosion followed by a second thunderous clap shook the walls and blew a thick cloud of dust through the open doorway. Beyond the walls, horses neighed in terror and human voices rose in cries of agony.

Josiah Meeks had seen the powder trails and shouted to his men to alter their attack. Had he been in the lead he might have turned them out of harm's way. Then again, he might have been killed in the explosions. Even a hundred feet from the powder kegs he was knocked off his horse. But being an expert horseman as well as a seasoned soldier, the Englishman managed to keep a tight grip on the reins of his horse. The animal tried to bolt and pawed the air. Meeks tightened his hold and let his weight bring the animal's head down. He'd underestimated Daniel.

And now the damn Highlander had turned the tables on him.

"My God, a blacksmith. Am I to be beaten by a blacksmith?" Meeks growled.

"And by a fool," a voice said from behind him.

Meeks looked around and spied Loyal Bufkin lurching toward him. Kate's brother was wounded: He'd been trampled by Meeks's horsemen, his ribs were broken, and blood flecked his lips. But he was still alive and he still held his knife.

The major reached for a saddle pistol. He drew the weapon as Loyal, seeing he couldn't reach the Englishman in time, hurled his knife. Meeks fired as the knife blade sank into his thigh. Loyal doubled over and dropped to his knees.

"Bastard!" the major howled as he drew the knife from his flesh and tossed the weapon aside. "You wretched idiot!" The world spun, and he clutched the saddle to keep from falling. Pain took his breath away, but the major endured it. He holstered one pistol and drew another.

Loyal slowly rolled over on his side, the world turning dark. He saw his mother and father walking toward him. He ran to their arms. By the time Meeks's second shot struck him, Loyal Bufkin was beyond feeling—or caring.

Daniel wiped the grit from his eyes and staggered from the stall to the Sicilian panel wagon, where he found another brace of pistols he'd placed on a barrel of knives. With his Quakers in his belt and these heavy-bore pistols in hand, he bolted toward the front of the barn and the dust-choked doorway.

"Daniel..." Kate called to him.

He turned. He was soot-streaked and his shirt was torn, he had two weeks of beard and his thick red hair was matted with straw, but to Kate's eyes, he was grand. There would be no other man for her.

"Don't you be getting killed, Daniel McQueen," she said. He hesitated as if searching for a reply. "Go on!" Kate told him. She began to reload the nearest rifle. Daniel disappeared into the billowing dust.

Daniel narrowed his eyes and stalked across the barnyard toward the still-smoking craters where the powder kegs had been buried. A horse galloped past him in blind terror. A dead raider lay sprawled in front of him.

"You've done me," said Will Chaney in a pain-filled voice. "Ohhh..."

A few paces from the dead man, Chaney sat in the dirt with his wide eyes staring. His face was contorted in agony, his lips curled back from his yellow teeth as he sucked in air through his locked jaws. It was the only way he kept from screaming. Chaney's leg was bent at an awkward angle and a white shard of bone jutted obscenely through his pants leg above the knee. Blood seeped from a nasty gash on his forehead and spattered his dust-caked coat. Beyond him a horse pawed fitfully at the dirt, belly ripped open. The animal's rider lay sprawled in death beneath his flailing mount.

Daniel sensed movement on his right and instinctively ducked. A saber sliced the air and missed him by a hair's breadth. He turned and fired. The swordsman staggered and fell to his knees with a belly wound. Another shot rang out. For a moment, Daniel and this next assailant stalked one another through the slowly dissipating cloud of powder smoke. Pistol fire stabbed through the cloud. Daniel emptied his second pistol at the muzzle blast and heard a groan. A Tory staggered toward him, visible now. The man dropped his pistols and flopped face forward in the dirt. Daniel tossed the heavy-bore pistols aside and drew his Quakers. The fight wasn't over yet.

"Follow me, lads," Padraich O'Flynn called to the two men behind him as he led them at a gallop around the corner of the barn. Since the front of the barn had proved too formidable, with exploding powder kegs and the like, the Irishman figured to try his luck on the rear of the barn. And pure luck it had been that caused him to swerve away from the open doorway that had seemed so inviting. The two men who followed him believed fervently in Padraich's luck, for they had emerged unscathed by the explosions.

"There be a door back here?" one of the men called out.

"More than likely," O'Flynn said, and as the rear of the barn came into view he knew for certain. "Yes, by heaven." He glanced over his shoulder and saw with dismay that neither of his companions carried a torch. The Tories had dropped their brands and armed themselves with long-barreled pistols. A torch did little good against a man with a gun, and these two weren't about to attack unarmed.

"Damn your eyes, we've nothing to burn the place with."

O'Flynn and his men dismounted. The rear door of the barn opened onto a hog pen. O'Flynn was forced to crawl over the low fence and trek through hog wallow to reach the door. A sow and her piglets scurried to the opposite end of the pen, complaining at the invasion with a series of grunts and squeals. The smell didn't bother the Irishman, but the two behind him wrinkled their noses in grimaces of distaste.

They hesitated at the fence line and stared down at the mud and manure.

"C'mon, lads. Don't hang back. Hell, I've woke up in worse places than this." O'Flynn reached the back door, which to no one's surprise was bolted from the inside. The Irishman unslung a hatchet from his belt and began to hack away at the hinges.

"Go away," Sister Eve said, her voice drifting through the oaken door.

O'Flynn stiffened at first at the sound of the voice. It took him a few seconds to realize it belonged to a woman. He grinned. It was just like Meeks had promised, a farm full of nothing more than frightened old spinsters. The Irishman peered through a crack in the slats and could make out a woman's silhouette in the dim light. He wondered if she was pretty. No, she couldn't possibly be. Why would a comely gal hide herself on such a farm?

"Unbolt this door, me darlin'," the burly Irishman said. "Nary a lady has anything to fear from the likes of Paddy O'Flynn."

"Go away and leave us in peace."

"Open the door," O'Flynn repeated, his tone of voice darkening. His boots sank in the mud underfoot.

He was tired and ready to be done with this day's work.

"Open the door!" he shouted, and began to hack furiously at the hinges. He slipped and dropped one knee into the muck. His hand sank into excrement as he tried to brace himself. "Damn," he muttered, and pulled himself erect.

O'Flynn drove the hatchet into the door with such force the blade caught and held in the wood. He kicked the door and beat his fists against the wood with enough force to crack the wood. But his hands were bleeding and the door still standing when he had finished. His two companions watched from the fence, uncertain whether or not to join the Irishman.

O'Flynn slogged back a few paces, drew his pistol, and fired, blowing loose one of the hinges.

He loaded the pistol and fired again, this time missing the top hinge but shooting a hole through the door. He listened, hoping to hear a woman's moan of pain. He added powder and ball to the flintlock and had it primed and ready to shoot in less than a minute.

"This is your last chance!" he shouted.

The blunderbuss thundered like a cannon from the confines of the barn. The blast blew a gaping hole through the door and flung Padraich O'Flynn backward, where he skidded to a lifeless stop in the mud at the far end of the hog pen. The two men by the fence glanced at one another and then, reaching a mutual, unspoken decision, returned to their horses and rode off toward the trees.

Back at the barn, Sister Eve peered through the hole in the door. "God forgive me," she said. After adding an "Amen," she started to reload.

*   *   *

Kate shot the first man who charged through the dust into the barn. He was a gruff-looking brigand of average height and solid build. He managed to hurl his torch into the piled straw in a stall to his left before he was slammed against the doorsill, rebounded, and collapsed in the yard outside. Hope was closest to the stall. She abandoned Tim Pepperidge and attacked the rapidly spreading flames with her water-soaked blanket. The blaze proved too much for her. The straw was dry and brittle, perfect fuel for the flames.

A second torch, hurled by an unseen hand, came flying through the door and landed on the steps of the Sicilian wagon. Kate dropped her rifle and ran to the water barrel. She armed herself with a soaked blanket to combat this new enemy before they were all blown to bits. Sister Hope renewed her efforts and despite her size moved with ungainly speed and finally vanquished the fire in the stall. Breathless, lungs heaving from exertion, her round cheeks beet red, she crossed the barn to the Sicilian wagon as Kate slapped out the last burning step.

"I'll fight the fires," Hope gasped. "Best you see to your—" A man stood in the doorway, a bemused expression on his face.

Kate saw the mixture of anger and fear in Sister Hope's face and turned to face this new threat.

Black Tolbert first surveyed the interior to assure himself this was no trap. Then he entered and waved the women aside with the flintlock pistol he held in his left hand. In his right, a torch sent oily black smoke curling to the rafters. His once fine coat was torn, and the waistcoat, too, was in tatters. His finely chiseled features were bruised and burned. His red-rimmed eyes streamed water. The back of his coat was singed and continued to smoke, which gave him the appearance of a creature recently loosed from some hell of fire and brimstone.

"Stand clear of the wagon," he said. His lower lip was puffed and swollen. "Move away from the wagon." Neither woman moved. "Stand clear!"

As if impervious to his threats, the two women stood their ground, their blankets in hand. Black Tolbert raised the pistol and pointed it directly at Sister Hope. "Move!" They remained motionless. Over by the stall to the left of Tolbert and near the wagon, Pepperidge tried to reach for one of his pistols, but the movement sent waves of searing pain shooting through him and he groaned.

Tolbert heard him and shifted his aim. "Very well, then. If you are not afraid to die, are you willing to be the death of your young friend?" Tolbert trained his pistol on the wounded man.

"No!" Sister Hope said, and charged forward, catching everyone off guard. She lashed out with her sodden blanket and knocked the pistol aside. Kate made a hopeless dash for the rifles. Tolbert was momentarily knocked off balance, for Sister Hope outweighed him by eighty pounds. He stumbled back against the barn wall. He recovered enough to club Sister Hope with the shaft of his torch, singeing the woman's gray habit as he struck her again and knocked her to the ground. It was the worst thing he could have done.

"You cursed old bitch!" He spat and contemptuously shoved Hope aside with a brutal kick.

Kate was halfway to the rifles when she heard a deep-chested growl and caught a blur of brown fur and bared fangs as Gideon came from the rear of the barn and launched himself upon the foolish man who had harmed Sister Hope.

Tolbert tried to protect himself. Panicked, he fired at the enraged animal and missed. He tried to club

Gideon with the torch, but the mastiff dodged the flames and dove into the man. His massive jaws clamped around Tolbert's arm. Bone crunched as the mastiff hauled him to the ground. Tolbert shrieked for his life. But the only one who could have helped him was still dazed from the blow she had suffered.

Gideon dragged the man around the floor of the barn and shook him. Then, like any good hunting beast after crippling its prey, the mastiff switched its hold and went for the throat.

Tolbert's scream came to an abrupt end.

Using a strip of cloth torn from his shirt, Josiah Meeks finished tying a tourniquet around his leg above the knife wound. At last, with the bleeding stanched, the Englishman was able to redirect his attention to the barn. Like diaphanous brown veils lifted by a summer's breeze, the dust and smoke cloud dissipated slowly. The barn with its hidden cache of weapons was intact. Worse, the remnants of his command, those who weren't wounded or dead, rode off at a gallop toward the safety of the woods.

To make matters worse still, Daniel McQueen was standing in the center of Josiah Meeks's ruined plans. He looked as if he were waiting—Yes, the damned blacksmith was waiting for him.

"Now it's my turn, is it?" Meeks said, steeling himself against the pain. He laughed and swung his mount around, held his steed to a contemptuous trot. He calmly rode away from the farm as if unwilling to demean himself by dueling with a man of such humble station as Daniel.

"Josiah Meeks!"

The major never looked back.

Daniel started to run after him. He was several

yards along the wagon trail before common sense took hold. It had to end today, it had to be done with; the major was too dangerous a threat to be allowed to live. There would fresh horses in the barn. *My God, the barn!* He quickly shoved Meeks to the back of his mind and retraced his path across the barnyard.

Kate met him at the doorway with a roan gelding that she had just saddled. Daniel was taken aback at the sight: Kate's dress was torn, and there was blood on the hem and her cheek was smudged with charcoal, but she was alive.

"Some of us are hurt, but none of us too seriously," Kate said.

"Thank God," Daniel replied.

"And Gideon," Hope added, emerging from the shadows. Pepperidge was there, walking along between Sister Eve and Sister Hope. The mastiff, its muzzle caked with crimson, loped along behind the Daughter of Phoebe.

"This is Sister Eve's horse. She claims he can run," Kate said. "I have never known her to lie."

"Perhaps I should stay here until the Schraners arrive," Daniel said.

"And allow the man who caused all this to escape?" Kate said, astonished. She looked around at the carnage. Her own brother lay dead out in the meadow. She held the reins out to the man she loved.

He took them.

Chapter Twenty-Six

This sixteenth of June was an uncomfortably cool, rainy night in Philadelphia. The townspeople had every reason to avoid the glistening streets and keep vigils by the light of warm kitchen fires surrounded by friends and family to debate the merits of this day's auspicious events. And indeed, those townspeople with loyalist leanings remained behind their closed doors. They weren't missed. Despite the inclement weather, the city streets were alive this night with patriots who were abuzz over the announcement that the Continental Congress had finally proclaimed General Washington commander-in-chief of the army.

Church bells had pealed throughout the city, filling the night air with a melodic message of hope. So while two thirds of the city avoided the streets, the sons and daughters of liberty celebrated and showed General Washington their support. It was all spontaneous as patriots flocked to the center of the city and crowded into favorite taverns, and at every street corner perfect strangers greeted one another and their common spirit of optimism dispelled the gloom of such a rainy night.

So it happened that the one-eyed "parson" standing across from the City Tavern on Walnut Street was greeted time and time again by townspeople and militiamen who passed him on the cobblestone walk. He spoke to them in turn and gave his blessings and wishes for their good health. Then Josiah Meeks tugged his broad-brimmed hat low to hide his features and moved along the block, never really leaving the area of the City Tavern. He was waiting for the man he had followed there. Meeks dug his hands in his pockets, touching the pistol hidden in the folds of his coat.

"I seen him go in," said a shipping clerk, who paused to peer above the wire frame of his spectacles at the churchman. He noticed Meeks's broad white collar. "Lutheran, are you?"

"Calvinist, my good fellow," Meeks replied with forced levity.

"Ah well, as I said, I followed General Washington right into the tavern, him with his gold braid and blue uniform. I toasted his health, right there in front of God and everybody. To a man they raised their tankards right along with me." The clerk puffed out his chest, enjoying his moment in the presence of greatness.

"May the good Lord bless him," Meeks said.

"Well, you know, you could go give him your blessing to his face," the clerk suggested. "But you best hurry. I heard talk that he was going to leave, maybe to home. Although I heard tell he often goes off by himself. But I don't know where."

Meeks did. It had been one of the last things Woodbine had told him, how the courtyard of the German Lutheran church was Washington's favorite place for private reflection. The question was, would the general be foolish enough to seek the solace of his garden tonight? With such momentous events taking place he just might. But if not, then Meeks would have to hope for another opportunity to catch the new commander alone. He might have to strike at Washington's house, no doubt a suicidal act.

"That's his phaeton, drawn up in front of the tavern." The clerk pointed to a carriage across the street. This also was information Meeks knew. Again he held his tongue and wondered if this pale little man would ever cease his prattling.

It had not been the best of times for the major. But he had managed to elude capture and with his disguise had no trouble in losing himself among the people of this city of over thirty-five thousand. He had taken a room at a boarding house in the heart of town and waited and watched for his moment to cut down the new continental commander. It had come as no surprise to him when he heard the news, an hour after the Congress had announced its selection.

Meeks adjusted his stance and pain stabbed from his infected leg to his scalp. The wound needed tending—and soon. But Meeks had more important matters to attend. He might only get one chance at the newly appointed commander. He had to make it count. What happened afterward was of no consequence. After the debacle at the farm, the Englishman was more determined than ever to accomplish his primary mission. He braced himself on his black walnut cane and pulled his black coat about his shoulders to ward off dampness. He waited.

A trio of soldiers sauntered along the street. They wore the blue uniforms of the Virginia Militia and were on hand to protect their illustrious commander. Meeks noticed how they scrutinized everyone standing along the street. Perhaps they were looking for a man with a patch. They wouldn't find him, for Meeks had replaced the patch with a glass eye. If he kept a narrow gaze and avoided the glare of the soldiers' lanterns, Meeks could fool them.

As the men approached, Meeks lowered his head and gave the illusion of praying. The soldiers passed him by and Meeks released the breath he had been holding.

The clerk straightened and stepped forward almost into the street as a tall, blue-uniformed figure stepped out through the front door of the tavern and was outlined in the lantern light flooding through the front door of the tavern and was outlined in the lantern light flooding through the doorway.

"It's him. By heaven, there he is again—General Washington. You mark my words, Parson. This has been a great day. If you hurry I can introduce you. After all, I practically know him now. Come along—" The clerk turned to guide the minister by the arm but found himself reaching for an empty wall. "Well, I never. Such odd fellows, these Calvinists—"

The parson had ridden away on a horse from a nearby hitching post.

Washington's team waited patiently at the hitching post on Cherry Street in front of the German Lutheran church. Scudding gray clouds clung to the starlight. A gusting breeze wandered among the stone tablets and the trumpet vines and stirred the drooping branches of the willow in the corner of the courtyard.

Josiah Meeks, looking for all the world like he belonged in the shadow of the church, limped away from the front window of the sanctuary and made his way past the pews to the side windows. His bootheels and cane went a-rapping and tapping on the hardwood floor.

Meeks had followed Washington's carriage past the Carpenter's Hall. Acting on information gleaned from Woodbine, Meeks had ridden on ahead to the church and hid his horse in a thicket of willows. After breaking a window at the rear of the chapel Meeks had let himself inside. To his great relief, the phaeton arrived bearing its illustrious passenger. Even in the feeble light, Meeks managed to catch a glimpse of white periwig and gold braid on the blue uniform.

Meeks heard the creak of the iron gate and watched the tall, powerfully built Virginian walk to a stone bench and take a seat in the middle of the garden near the roses that provided a flash of color to offset the green vines and gray stone walls.

Meeks wiped the sweat from his eyes and for a moment considered chancing a shot from the window. No, it was better to be sure. He tugged the pistol from his coat pocket and made his way to the door that opened onto the garden. The hinges were well oiled and opened silently. Major Josiah Meeks chose his steps wisely, avoiding the broken twigs and branches that littered the garden path as he approached the Virginian from behind. Leaning on his cane, it did not take long for Meeks to cover the distance, keeping to the shadows, passing the misspelled commandments.

Eight feet from the man on the bench, Meeks steadied himself and aimed his pistol at the general.

"Pray to your God, General Washington. Better yet, go to meet him in person," Josiah Meeks said, savoring his moment of triumph. The man in the blue coat stiffened, slowly stood, and turned to face the Englishman. With his left hand he removed his tricorn and periwig to reveal a mane of unruly red hair and a face that the major knew only too well. In his right hand he held a pistol, sleek and deadly and aimed at the Englishman's heart.

"No," said Daniel McQueen. "You go—and dance with the devil." The gun in his fist blasted fire.

Josiah Meeks turned pale. A cry sounded from deep in his chest as he stumbled and twisted and fired his gun. The ball went wild and hit the wall across the courtyard. Meeks staggered from the path and trampled a bed of roses as he stumbled toward the vine-covered wall.

I can pull myself over and lose myself in the mist, if I can just reach the wall. . . . But he had to endure the crushing weight in his chest. *Just endure it.*

He sank to his knees and braced himself on a tablet. His vision blurred, then momentarily cleared—and he read the words, all properly spelled, THOU SHALT NOT KILL.

He tried to laugh, but his throat was full of blood. He spat and turned to Daniel.

"You—?"

"Yes, me—just a blacksmith." Daniel tucked his pistol back in his belt.

"Nobody . . ." Josiah Meeks gasped. He bent forward and his forehead touched the cool ground, and there he died.

Daniel heard a twig crack and the gate creak open, and Washington was there, wrapped in a dark gray cloak. He glanced from Daniel to the Englishman crumpled among the leaves and the flowers.

"It worked, I see. Though I was loath to let you risk your life in my stead," the general said.

"It was my duty," Daniel said. "The possible loss of a commander-in-chief far outweighed the loss of a blacksmith." He removed the blue coat and handed it back to its rightful owner as half a dozen soldiers led by Bill Rutledge filed into the courtyard.

"Not to me, good sir," Washington said evenly. He fished something shiny from his coat pocket and, taking a knife from the soldier nearest him, carved on it, then flipped it to the man who had saved his life.

Daniel caught the coin and held it up; he recognized it as an English crown. GW had been scrawled upon its silver surface.

"For luck," the general said, putting on the uniform he had passed to Daniel back at the City Tavern.

"Won't you need it?"

"Not anymore," George Washington said. The realization had come to him on the ride to the church. "You will be my luck, McQueen. And other men and women like yourself. My luck and the life of our new nation."

Daniel flipped the silver crown in the air, caught it, and dropped the coin in a buckskin pouch dangling from his belt.

"That's fine with me. I'll be there for you." But right now, he had a past to bury, old wounds to heal, and the woman he loved waiting for him at an inn on the Trenton Road.

"Uh...General, do you reckon as you and this new country of ours could get along without me, just for a few days?" he asked.

"We'll try." George Washington clapped Daniel McQueen on the shoulder and walked with him, out of the churchyard and into history.

A Note From the Author

The Medal is a series of novels that chronicle the exploits of the McQueens, a family whose devotion to the dream of what America can be involves them in our nation's most turbulent decades. Passing along their own unique "medal of honor" from one generation to the next, the McQueens embody the proud spirit of the country they serve.

GUNS OF LIBERTY is the beginning of their story.

I write about frontier America and who we are as Americans. I write about the opening of the West and the tragedies and triumphs of those who have gone before. With every landmark paved over to make a new industrial park or shopping mall, we lose a little more of our precious identity. What's the point of rushing to the future if we lose the richness of where we've been? So I'll continue to tell my tales and spin my yarns and do my part to keep the legends alive and if you find pleasure in them, well my friend, I am satisfied.

(Kerry Newcomb lives in Ft. Worth, Texas, with his wife and two children.)

The McQueen clan, established in the Revolutionary War era by the intrepid Daniel McQueen, will fight for liberty and for American values in war after war. Their lives, and our nation's history, are chronicled in the Bantam series.

THE MEDAL

Written by bestselling frontier author Kerry Newcomb, The Medal is full of action and military lore. The next title is

SWORD
OF
VENGEANCE

available July, 1991 wherever Bantam Books are sold.

(Turn the page for an exciting preview of the second book in the series.)

July 4, 1811

Kit McQueen laughed as thirty-six inches of watered steel blade missed decapitating him by inches. He ducked and, lowering his shoulder, rolled against his attacker's legs. The momentum of the attacking Turk carried him up and over the balcony railing. The Turk cried out in astonishment and tossed his broadbladed tulwar aside as he fought to catch a handhold on the railing. But luck had abandoned him, and the captain of Bashara al-Jezzar's janissaries dropped out of sight and crashed into the spring-fed pool below. Kit heard the splash of water followed by a sickening crunch as the captain's head slapped against the marble fountain built along one side of the spring.

Kit heard footsteps behind him. He swung around and leveled his pistol at Bill Tibbs, his fellow privateer.

"Please don't kill me, Christopher," Tibbs pleaded, and held out his hands in mock supplication.

Kit grinned and shook his head. "It's tempting.

But I still might need your help before this night is through."

There came a hammering on the harem's bolted doors, and from the hall passageway sounded the savage outcries of the pasha's guards, who at any moment might break into the room and tear the two infidels limb from limb. Elsewhere in the city port of Derna, the rumble of distant cannons and rifle fire signaled the revolution against the pasha's rule was still in progress. Fortunately, the insurrection had drawn most of al-Jezzar's janissaries into the streets.

"Where are the jewels?" Tibbs asked, realizing for the first time that his companion was empty-handed.

Kit gasped, a look of alarm washing across his sun-darkened features. "I thought you had them."

Tibbs looked horrified. "I took the lead to ensure our escape route while you pilfered the treasure house. Good God, have you lost what we climbed the cliff for?" Then he knew he'd been set up as Kit roared with laughter and pointed toward the wall behind his fellow thief. A large leather pouch dangled from a wall bracket that supported a heavy silk tapestry depicting the pasha in all his finery sitting astride a white charger and trampling his foes beneath the animal's flashing hooves. Kit did not feel the least bit guilty stealing from Bashara al-Jezzar, for the old brigand was one of the Corsican brotherhood who had been preying on American ships for several years. It was high time the thief got a taste of his own medicine.

Tibbs hurried over to retrieve the bag of stolen booty. With a sharp tug he worked the pouch loose and saw it drop to the floor. The pouch fell open, and the ruby-encrusted hilt of a scimitar along with a necklace of gold clattered out onto the sandstone floor.

"The Eye of Alexander!" a man gasped from a nearby doorway. Kit looked around and noticed a bald, robe-clad eunuch staring at the scimitar from the entrance to the private quarters of the pasha's many wives. Several young women, dark-haired and doe-eyed, their perfumed flesh in various stages of undress, tittered among themselves and gestured toward the intruders. Such women were kept in seclusion and allowed only the company of eunuchs until they were summoned to al-Jezzar's bedchambers to await his pleasure, though there was seldom pleasure to be found in the nobleman's jaded and often cruel embrace. The women crowded the entrance despite the eunuch's efforts to force them back. The aroma of incense, burning spices for which Kit had no name, wafted into the corridor and clouded the senses of the intruders, luring them to enter and lose themselves to desire. For here were two young men fit to fan the fires in any woman's heart, be she Turkish princess or slave. Bill Tibbs, at twenty-eight, was a tall, strapping fellow, whose stark white skin was in sharp contrast to his pitch-black, shoulder-length hair. His eyes were deep-hued, his gaze often guarded and yet ever scrutinizing, always trying to gain the upper hand. Kit McQueen stood several inches shorter than his towering friend. And yet it was to him that many of the women offered their inviting glances, for they had seen him move with catlike grace and quickness and they sensed an aura of untapped power about him. His mane of scarlet curls was partly hidden by a bandanna of yellow silk, and his eyes were as bronze as his well-muscled torso. A gold ring glimmered in his right ear. He was younger than Tibbs by a couple of years, but that didn't keep the larger man from deferring to his partner's judgment. It was an influence Kit tended to exude in moments of crisis. He caught Tibbs by the arm as the man started toward the women, drawn by lust and a hunger for the forbidden and exotic fruits of the pasha's nubile garden.

"Bill . . . we don't have much time."

"I don't intend to be very long," Tibbs replied, a lascivious smile upon his face.

"You must not take the Eye of Alexander," the eunuch interjected in his high-pitched voice. He placed his round, flabby frame between the privateer and the harem women. "I don't know who you are or how you gained access to my honorable lord's domain, may he live a thousand thousand years and be blessed with the strength of a thousand thousand stallions—"

"Oh, shut up," Tibbs said, and shoved the pasha's servant aside.

"But you must hear me. The sword is the Eye of Alexander the Great, given to that most illustrious one by the priests of Persia after he conquered all the world. Cursed be the infidel who disturbs its rest among my lord and master's treasures. So it is written."

"Cursed be the fool who doesn't take it when he has the chance, old one," Kit said. "I do not blame you, old one, for trying to protect the pasha's belongings. But we are only stealing it from one who stole it himself. So the curse, if any, rests with Bashara al-Jezzar." Kit managed to catch the leather pouch of necklaces and gold anklets and the jeweled sword as Tibbs casually tossed it back over his shoulder. Tibbs caught up the nearest woman, a mere girl of sixteen, and lifted her into his arms. The silks and bangles she wore rubbed against him, and she pressed her small, pointed breasts against his lips as he held her in the air and then lowered her, running his tongue along her neck and up to her ear.

Kit shouldered the leather pouch. He could hear the wooden bolt begin to splinter in the court below.

"You don't understand," the eunuch continued to entreat, but no one was paying him any mind.

Kit hurried over to the balcony just as the courtyard door caved in and the pasha's guards, who had been alerted to the intruders' presence, crowded through the doorway. A wheel-lock pistol roared and blasted a fist-sized hole in the balcony.

Kit returned the favor and fired his heavy-caliber flintlock into the center of the janissaries, who were packed together by the door, struggling to untangle themselves and head for the stairway. Kit aimed low; he didn't want to kill anyone unless he had to. The heavy lead ball from his pistol took down three men with a variety of crippling wounds before its energy was spent. The fallen men only served to further block the entrance. A pistol shot rang out from behind Kit, and the privateer spun around in time to see Tibbs standing over the eunuch. Blood streamed from Tibbs's ear. The eunuch was propped against the barren sandstone wall; he had dragged the pasha's tapestry down around him like a burial shroud as he slid to the ground, blood oozing from a nasty wound in his round belly.

"The bastard bit me," Tibbs said.

"You didn't have to kill him," Kit snapped angrily. He had shipped with Bill Tibbs for the better part of two years. They had been friends and trusted shipmates aboard the sleek little Baltimore clipper the two men had pooled their resources to purchase. In all that time Kit had found only one thing to complain about with his friend, and that was Bill Tibbs's temper. The man had a short fuse, and he seemed forever primed and waiting for the right spark to set him off.

"C'mon," Tibbs said sheepishly, and clapped Kit on the shoulder. He blew a kiss to the harem women, who had recoiled in horror at the sight of the dying eunuch. Tibbs broke into a run. Kit took a step toward the pasha's eunuch. The man's eyes were already glazed over. But he was still breathing.

"I'm sorry," Kit whispered. Then the clatter of swords and rifles below spurred him into motion. He charged the top of the stairway curving up from below. The stairs were crowded with a dozen of the pasha's heavily armed harem guards. Their naked swords were thirsty for the blood of infidels. To the lead janissary, Kit seemed to come out of nowhere, a blur of motion like a pouncing tiger. The soldiers in the courtyard struggled to bring their rifles to bear on the daring young thief. Kit never gave them the chance. He stiff-armed the balcony rail, and pivoting on his strong right shoulder, he leaped up and drove both booted heels into the lead janissary, a Turk in a black burnoose and flowing robes. The guard was hurled backward and began a chain reaction that toppled the entire column of men on the stairway. Weapons were discharged into the air as the soldiers tumbled over one another all the way to the courtyard below.

Kit hit the floor running. Something slapped the pouch on his back and clanked against the metal inside. He nearly lost his balance but managed to reach the door hidden behind another tapestry at the end of the corridor. Tibbs was waiting for him at the top of the winding stairway on the other side. The quick-tempered thief held a crudely drawn map that he had purchased from an old beggar in Constantinople, a withered relic of a man who claimed to have been in the pasha's service. The beggar had been a harem guard who had been discovered with one of al-Jezzar's wives, summarily castrated, and driven out into the desert to die. However, he had survived and, remembering the location of al-Jezzar's own private escape passage, had furnished a map for the two American privateers.

It was in Constantinople, too, that the privateers had heard the rumors of an impending assault on Derna by al-Jezzar's enemies. They had timed their own intrusion to coincide with the attack on the city.

"We promised we would leave the map with Salim's name upon it for Bashara al-Jezzar to find," Kit reminded his friend. Tibbs nodded and placed the parchment outside the corridor, where the guards and the pasha would be certain to discover it. The beggar of Constantinople would have the last laugh, after all. Kit removed the pouch and fingered the bullet hole in the center of the bulging surface. A gold anklet had turned the rifle ball and saved Kit's life. He nodded to his companion and led the way down the stairs. He risked life and limb on the narrow tread as he descended at a run. Rough stone walls sped past as Kit circled around and around, as if burrowing like a corkscrew into the very earth. Only there was light, not darkness, at the end of his journey—light and the smell of the salt sea air. A few minutes later Kit emerged from the base of the villa onto a wide ledge carved into the face of a cliff overlooking the sparkling blue expanse of the Mediterranean, some three hundred feet below. What had looked like an impossible sheer cliff face was, on closer examination, a narrow footpath chiseled into the stark surface. The narrow switchback was just wide enough for one man to edge along the wall, angling back and across all the way to the water's edge. Though a precipitous journey, it promised to be a far easier task in daylight than it had been in the predawn hours.

Anchored thirty yards offshore, the *Trenton* rode easy on the wind-rippled surface of the bay. The *Trenton* was a Baltimore Clipper, only seventy feet from bow to stern and armed with a swivel cannon amidships. Half of the clipper's crew, six heavily armed men, waited by a johnboat at the orders of the clipper's captain. The landing party was ready to fight or run at a moment's notice, whatever the *Trenton's* joint owners required.

"The janissaries probably will start shooting at us from the walls once they discover what we've done," Kit said, dabbing the perspiration from his face on the sleeve of his loose-fitting linen shirt.

"But they are poor marksmen, these Turks," Tibbs said. His features were sweat-streaked and smudged with black powder.

"And they might even pry loose a few rocks to drop on our heads," Kit said in a sage voice.

"No problem, my good friend; the pasha's curse will be our good fortune." Tibbs lovingly stroked the bejeweled hilt of the scimitar jutting from the leather pouch. Then he reached inside his leather belt and removed a silver flask embossed with his family crest, a mailed fist holding a cross. He passed the brandy to Kit, who grinned and lifted the flask in a toast.

"To Alexander's luck," he said.

"To Alexander's luck," Tibbs echoed.

Nothing could stop them now.

Thirty-five days later "Alexander's luck" played out. After a particularly violent and stormy night, the morning tides washed the wreckage of the *Trenton* onto the seaweed-littered sandy shores of northeast Spanish Florida, two miles north of the thriving mission of St. Augustine. Fragments of a shattered jib, several barrels, a freshly carved coffin, and patches of a sail littered the shore, along with planks of wood ripped from a reef-shattered hull and a section of mizzenmast as long as a man was tall. A johnboat had also been left by the storm-swept waves that had lashed the coast in the hours just after midnight. The rowboat now rested on its side and was rocked to and fro by the surf. Two men lay as if dead in the bottom of the boat, and a third was sprawled in the froth where the waves played out upon the beach. A leather pouch lay at his side, tethered to his right arm by a single strap. His matted red hair was patched with mud and dried blood. Little Maria, an eight-year-old, brown-skinned, hazel-eyed bundle of curiosity and courage, gingerly approached the wreckage the winds of fate had wrested from the sea.

"Go on, Maria," the boy behind her said. Esteban, her brother, was older by five years. He was already grown, as tall as many of the men in his village, but what he had gained in size he had lost in courage, and he held back. These Yankees had been touched by the sea, or worse, by the Angel of Death that the padre told of in his stories. Either way it was best, Esteban decided, that he not touch such men. Far better to send his nosy sister to tempt fate, and if she withered and died on the spot...well...where was the loss? No doubt his mother would make more sisters. Maybe she even carried another sister for Esteban right now in her swollen belly as she baked the bread for the padre's noonday meal.

"Go on, Maria. What is there?" Esteban called out. "Are you afraid?" he chided.

"I am not!" the little girl retorted, taking offense at even the mere suggestion of fear, though, to be sure, her insides were about to turn to jelly and her bare legs trembled as she crept up to the johnboat and peered over the battered bow. She saw the two men up close, and yes, they were indeed Yankees, but as to whether they were alive or dead she could not tell. One of the men was very big, with large hands matted on the backs with black hair, and his black-bearded features were red and peeling from sunburn.

The other man was average in height, as best as she could tell; he lay curled up like a baby in his mother's arms, only his mother this time was the bottom of the boat. He was bearded, too, a thick, brown beard and his mouth was open and she could glimpse a line of broken yellow teeth. His thinning brown hair was plastered to his skull. There was a knot on his forehead, a swollen, purplish mound that was flecked with blood. Both men wore torn shirts and breeches tucked into high-topped boots. The larger of the two men had a brace of pistols jutting from the broad leather belt circling his waist.

"Senor?" the girl found her voice and spoke to the men in a soft whisper. After all, she did not wish to wake the dead. Neither of the men stirred, for which she was profoundly grateful. Esteban might like the Yankee's pistols, but then let him come and take them.

The girl backed away from the boat and crossed over to the red-haired man lying facedown in the sand. He was smaller than the others, only a little taller than Esteban, but she could see he was powerfully built, for his shirt was in shreds and his shoulders and back, even in repose, were corded with muscles. She knelt by his side, her eyes on the pouch whose strap was looped around his sun-bronzed right arm.

Esteban took a few tentative steps closer and repositioned himself, the better to see what Maria had found. He craned his neck forward, and his bare feet trampled a pattern of nervous circles in the moist sand.

"The pouch, Maria, the pouch. Open it."

"I will," Maria hissed back, angry at her brother's incessant instructions. She had her own way of doing things and was not about to be rushed. The pouch appeared to be waterlogged. She reached for the corner flap, attempted to untie the fastenings, and eventually succeeded. Overhead, a flock of gulls began to gather in lofty spirals. These scavengers of the coastline were willing to wait their turn because their turn always came. Their high-pitched cries filled the air like the banter of shrewish spirits caught between heaven and earth and complaining about the quality of both.

Maria reached down and picked up a six-inch-long, fanlike shell from the sand underfoot. Using the shell, she lifted the pouch flap and gasped as the golden sword hilt fell into view. Sunlight played upon the finely worked grip, and the rubies seemed to pulse as if with a life of their own, like embers waiting to burst into flame. They drew her like a moth. Esteban, too, once he caught sight of the sword, moved closer, youthful greed overcoming his cowardice. Here was something special, and he couldn't allow his younger sister to claim what ought to be rightfully his.

"Take it out, Maria. Let me see." The boy inched toward his sister and the red-haired Yankee who must surely be dead. "Bring the whole pouch to me."

"Perhaps we ought to bring the padre."

"Foolish girl," Esteban snapped, and he trotted the rest of the distance and drew up alongside his sister. "The padre will take what we have found and give it to God ... or worse, hand it over to Sergeant Morales and his men. Is that what you want?"

Maria was somewhat impressed by her older brother's argument. She had to admit he made a lot of sense. She did not like Sergeant Morales. Every time he paid a visit to the mission he caused trouble. Once he had taken her mother inside the jacal and would not allow the children to enter, and when her mother appeared later she was crying and Maria knew the sergeant had hurt her. Father Ramone had been furious, too. No, she was not about to hand over anything that was hers to the sergeant. And as for God, well, she had seen the golden cup that the padre drank from during Mass, so it seemed to her God had enough pretty things.

"I want the pretty red stone," she said.

Esteban grinned. He envisioned buying his sister's silence with a single stone and keeping the rest of this treasure from the sea for himself.

"Yes—yes, a pretty red stone," he agreed, and shoving the eight-year-old aside, he caught up the pouch and attempted to drag it free of the dead man's arm.

The arm suddenly tensed, and the "dead" man partly rose from the sand and turned a bruised and swollen visage toward the startled children. He pulled the pouch from their grasp violently and snarled, "No!"

Esteban screamed and released the pouch, his blood turning to ice water. Maria screamed alongside her brother. She didn't remain there long. A second later, and she was scampering down the beach and calling out, "Father Ramone! Father Ramone!"

Esteban whirled around and lost his footing in the sand.

"Wait," the voice behind him ordered. But the boy was not about to obey the entreaties of a corpse sprung to life. The red-haired man reached for him, and the boy screamed again, leaped away, and ran for his life. He could sense the other dead men leaping out of the boat and pursuing him down the beach, their dead arms flapping, and leering at him with their hideous, pointed teeth. The image gave wings to his feet, and the boy soon caught up to and passed his sister. Maria cried out to him to wait for her, but alas, she had become expendable once again. So she plowed the moist sand with her chubby little brown legs and ran for her life. Ghost crabs scurried out of harm's way.

The two children headed inland and spooked a flock of sanderlings, sending them winging into sky.

Kit McQueen watched the brother and sister disappear beyond a rise topped with beach grass and seaside goldenrod.

"Oh, hell," he muttered, and sank to his knees. He had to brace himself on all fours as he tried to make sense of his surroundings. His head ached terribly. He remembered the storm. Like a fool, Captain Clay had tried to outrun the elements to shore and, misjudging the speed of the storm, had been caught in treacherous waters. He had fought to turn into the wind and lost when the Trenton had ripped its hull open on a submerged reef. Caught and buffeted by the gale, the clipper had capsized. Kit had managed to survive the catastrophe and through sheer luck and determination had found one of the johnboats, climbed aboard, and managed to retrieve two of his shipmates from the black waters.

Kit doubled over and retched, leaving a puddle of muddy water on the sand along with the contents of his stomach. His head throbbed. He staggered back from the water's edge, noticed the johnboat, and managed to stumble over to the battered craft. He rounded the bow and saw that Bill Tibbs and Augustus LaFarge, the Trenton's first mate, were sprawled in the boat. He reached down, probed LaFarge's neck, and felt no pulse. The sailor was stone-cold dead. But Bill Tibbs moaned, and his eyelids flickered as Kit shook him. Kit tossed the treasure pouch onto shore, then caught Tibbs underneath the arms, dragged him out of the boat, and stretched the big man out upon the sand well away from the lapping waves. Kit stumbled, then braced himself on his friend's shoulder and gasped for breath.

"Christ almighty," he muttered, and gingerly felt

his scalp, probing the lump at the base of his skull. He winced and brought his hand away; the fingertips were moist and red. Blood trickled down the back of his neck. It felt like sweat. Kit's stomach flip-flopped, and he almost heaved. But he fought the feeling and won, though the victory left him gasping for breath.

He staggered toward the broad leather pouch that had almost cost him his life by dragging him under the wind-churned waves of the night before. He bent over, grasped the leather strap, and the world tilted on its axis and he fell over. Shards of broken seashells dug into his knees. His skull felt as if it were coming apart. A groan of agony escaped his lips as he rolled onto his side.

"Damn," he cursed softly. He needed help. So did Tibbs. Where did the children go? He began to crawl on his hands and knees toward the fringe of beach grass that the children had vanished behind, while the gulls overhead kept up a merry chorus of jeers. Kit pulled himself along; he didn't know how far he had come because he wouldn't let himself look back. He concentrated on moving one leg after another, one arm after another.

At last he gained enough confidence to try to stand again. After all, he hadn't thrown up in all of five minutes. He balanced on his wobbly legs like a one-year-old taking his first steps, and he lasted about as long. He pitched forward and never remembered hitting the ground.

Men can always find ways to get themselves killed. The crew of the *Trenton* did. The Baltimore clipper had battled the gale-force winds to within two miles of shore when Captain Horatio Clay tried to "thread the needle" between two reefs and brought his ship and crew to ruin. Kit McQueen, having fought his way to the wildly pitching deck, had tried to lend a hand as best he could under the worst of circumstances. In his dream, he watched once more, relived again, the waves crashing over the deck and the valiant effort of the crew to trim the sails in direct disobeyance of the captain's orders. Clay had been a man so sure of his skill that he could not imagine failure, not even when the bow reared up with a great grinding and splintering of wood and the whole ship shuddered like a mortally wounded beast. The mizzenmast came down in a tangle of canvas, timber, and rope that buried the captain and several of the crew. The rest were pitched into the storm-tossed sea as the *Trenton* capsized.

Kit could feel the cold embrace of the water. Something cracked him across the back of his skull. He choked as the turbulent waters carried him under, borne down by the weight of the treasure pouch. And to his horror, the pouch flap had torn loose and gold bracelets, rings, and necklaces spilled into the depths. Clutching the bag, he fought the ocean's grip, refusing to release his hold on the treasure pouch as he clawed at the black water. He managed by sheer chance to catch hold of a rope lashed around a section of mast. Hand over hand he pulled himself to the surface, thrusting his head out of the ashen sea to gulp air and cling to life. Where was the *Trenton*? Surely not that shapeless mass of timber coming to pieces on the submerged reef. Seawater stung his eyes. Waves lifted him and carried him toward the distant shore. God, how much of al-Jezzar's gold had the sea reclaimed? There was no time to look. Despite his pain-blurred vision he glimpsed a johnboat riding the crests of the storm-swept surface. The boat leaped like a dolphin and crashed with a thud against the section of mast Kit had found. He reached for the side of the boat, stretched his trembling fingers. In another couple of seconds it would be too late.

Reach. Reach, damn you, or drown.

Kit opened his eyes and found himself groping toward a wall of mud and coquina shells. He rolled on his back and stared up at a cedar-plank ceiling. Sunlight spilled into the room through an open doorway and the unshuttered windows that were opposite one another, permitting a gentle cross breeze through to freshen the hut's interior. A crucifix hung above the door sill. Kit was lying on a hard but not uncomfortable cot set in one corner of the coquina-walled hut. He noted at a glance he was not alone in the room. Long-legged Bill Tibbs was stretched out on a second cot, his bootheels dangling just inches above the floor. A comely Creek Indian woman in the late months of her pregnancy sat on a stool alongside Tibbs, who was not only conscious but propped up to receive the broth she was spooning into his mouth. His upper torso was naked, and his shoulder was bandaged. If Tibbs was in pain it didn't show. He obviously enjoyed the attention he was receiving from the woman. The rope and wood frame of the cot creaked as Kit shifted his weight. The woman turned at the sound, and on seeing the second Yankee was awake, she set the bowl of broth on the floor within Tibb's reach and hurried from the room.

"Well, you sure spoiled that." Tibbs scowled at his friend.

"From the look of her, she was spoken for," Kit replied. He sat back against the wall and felt a sharp, stabbing pain lance through his skull. He brought a hand to his head and touched a cloth bandage. Across the room, within view of both men, the large leather pouch had been securely fastened and left on a narrow but solid-looking table crafted from the dark wood of a young loblolly pine. An oil lantern, a worn leatherbound bible, and a quill and ink had been left on the table, no doubt by the room's owner, but shoved to one side to make room for the treasure pack.

"Spoken for, indeed . . . but talking was the farthest thing from my mind." Tibbs sighed, a wicked grin on his face.

"Half drowned and still as horny as a goat." Kit chuckled and then sucked in his breath as his wound sent a sharp protest from his head to his shoulder blades.

"Goats? Yes, we have goats," a brown-robed priest said from the doorway. He had brought another bowl of soup.

Father Ramone Saucedo at sixty moved with the grace and energy of a man twenty years younger. His skin was as dark as that of the Creek Indians he served, the color of old bark. Indeed, the lines and wrinkles that creased his features gave his skin not only a barklike color but the texture of some aged forest monarch that had survived wind and rain and fire. His hair was stringy, silver, and unkempt, but his mustache and goatee, also silver, were neatly trimmed. And if he had lost the beauty of his youth (once women had called him handsome and contested with one another to catch his eye . . . ah, memories) he had replaced such a transitory appeal with an air of wisdom and dignity that shone from his features as brightly as the Florida sunlight.

"Good morning, my friends," the Franciscan padre said. His sandals shuffled softly over the packed earth floor of the single-room cabin. "It has been a while since I have spoken English. I am Father Ramone Saucedo. You understand me, yes?" He handed the bowl of soup to Kit, who nodded his thanks and chanced a sip. It was salty, and chunks of fish and scallops floated in the broth. Kit found the sample to his liking. Father Ramone pulled over a three-legged stool and sat down. "You washed ashore on the island. Barely a strip of sand and beach grass. I go there to cast my nets. Maria and Esteban found you and brought me to you. Which was fortunate for you both." The padre toyed with the wooden cross dangling from a leather string he wore around his neck. "My humble house is a palace compared to the prison Sergeant Morales would offer you at the garrison in St. Augustine."

"Prison?" Kit said. He set the wooden bowl aside, introduced himself and Bill Tibbs, and then continued with his initial question. "Why prison?"

"There has been much trouble of late. Yankees from the north have come across the border and declared all of Florida a republic, free of Spanish rule. But the mission Indians have been well treated. Our colonists are of Spanish descent. We do not wish to break ties with our mother country, so we fight. The soldiers have hunted these Yankees down and killed or imprisoned most of them."

"Be we are . . . uh, traders," Tibbs blurted out. "We've nothing to do with any of this. A storm wrecked our ship, or we would never have troubled you."

"I believe you," the padre said, leaning forward. "But then my heart is filled with peace toward all men." Father Ramone kissed the cross he wore. "Sergeant Morales is a soldier, a man of war. If he discovers you, then . . ." The padre shook his head and sighed. The implication was quite clear: Their fates would be sealed.

"Do not worry," the padre spoke reassuringly. "I am no friend of Sergeant Morales. You are safe here. He seldom comes to visit. I have promised him the wrath of God if he touches one of my flock again." The priest seemed momentarily lost in thought, and he looked back to the barefoot Indian woman standing in the doorway. In a matter of weeks Sara would be having Morales's child. The woman disappeared into the sunlight; she was none of his guests' concern. The padre returned his attention to the matter at hand. "I will not reveal your presence here. But you cannot remain long. You will be in danger until you cross the border."

"How far away are we from Georgia?" Tibbs asked.

"Two days by horse."

"Good," Tibbs exclaimed. "We can make it. We'll rest up and then tomorrow or the next day borrow a couple of your horses and ride out. This Sergeant Morales will never know a thing."

"No," Father Ramone said.

"We will pay you for the animals, of course. Probably more than what they are worth," Kit said, thinking of the gold trinkets that had almost drowned him, the treasure of Bashara al-Jezzar.

"Of that I have little doubt," the padre conceded drolly. He glanced knowingly over his shoulder at the leather pouch behind him on the table. "Maria and Esteban spoke of the treasure. And I must admit I, too, examined the beautiful things you rescued from the sea."

"Our treasure," Tibbs emphasized. Just because a man donned a brown robe, sandals, and a cross didn't mean Tibbs felt obliged to trust him. He began to eat while scrutinizing the priest.

"Yes. Of course," the padre said, ignoring the man's suspicious gaze. "It is yours alone."

"So you see we can offer you much more than what a couple of your horses are worth," Kit explained. He was worried that Tibbs would antagonize the old padre. Kit recognized they owed the priest their lives. Father Ramone could easily have turned them over to the authorities. Kit didn't want the old padre to regret his decision. "Surely a portion of our wealth might prove useful for a church or a school outside St. Augustine.

Tibbs all but choked on a mouthful of fish. They hadn't even divided the spoils taken during the Derna raid, and already Kit was giving some away.

"It is impossible," Father Ramone replied.

"Why?" Kit asked.

"Because I have no horses,"the priest replied. "I sent Esteban for help. Four Creek men carried you here upon the very pallets on which you rest."

"Damn!" Tibbs muttered. Father Ramone gave him a pained look. "Sorry," he added.

"But across the St. John's river," the padre continued, "back in the woods, is the cabin of Alsino Escovar, the trapper. He has boats, horses, and a thirst for the shiny metal. He will sell you anything."

"How far past the river is his cabin?" Kit asked. Even with the pain hammering in his head he had begun to plan, to set his options, and to gather all the information necessary should the situation become desperate and the Yankees need to escape with this Sergeant Morales in hot pursuit.

"An hour, if a man is running," the priest said. "But much longer for these old bones." The Franciscan sighed and shook his head. "Enjoy your youth, my friends. Savor your days like rare wine. For the glass is soon drained. Ah, too soon." Father Ramone clapped his knees and stood. "How I prattle on when you need your rest. We will talk later. Sleep, compadres. You are safe for now. Heal yourselves. I shall pray for the return of your strength. And my prayers are always answered." The padre winked and vanished through the front door into the yellow glare.

Kit sat upright and watched the brown-robed figure through the window. Father Ramone had barely stepped past the corner of the cabin when he was immediately surrounded by a gaggle of excited children and a half dozen Creek braves. The men were dressed in breeches and worn, patched linsey-woolsey shirts. They might have been Spanish settlers save for the reddish-brown luster of their skin and their long, shiny, shoulder-length black hair that hung straight and framed their flat, dark faces.

The cluster of mud-walled cabins that comprised this settlement appeared to be set well back from the shore and nestled in a clearing of live oaks and black willows draped with Spanish moss.

"What do you think?" Tibbs said. He managed to stand and shuffled across the floor to the table, where he began to painstakingly unfasten the torn flap of the large leather pouch. The jewel-hilted scimitar that contained the Eye of Alexander fell into his hand. He sighed with relief. But his humor quickly faded on further inspection of the bag. All that remained of the stolen wealth was a handful of trinkets—a few solid gold bracelets, a couple of necklaces of pounded gold set with emeralds, and a golden goblet inlaid with pearls and lapis lazuli.

This was wealth, to be sure, but only a fraction of what they had taken from al-Jezzar's treasure room.

Tibbs's face became livid as he slowly turned to show Kit how they had been robbed.

"Damn their souls, they've taken it all. Robbed us blind, by my oath. Blood will flow for this!" Tibbs pounded the tabletop with his fist.

"They took nothing," Kit spoke up from the cot. He propped himself against the wall. "The pouch ripped open when the *Trenton* dumped me into the sea. I saved what I could."

Tibbs glared at his companion. Somehow he managed to calm himself. There was nothing to be said. He stared at the pouch as if willing the return of what had been lost. But he was no conjurer. At least something had been salvaged. A man could make a good life for himself on what remained. Tibbs returned the Eye of Alexander and lowered the flap.

"You did well, my friend," he said in a gentler, calmer tone of voice. "Best we heal up and quit this place as quickly as we can." He gingerly stretched out upon the cot.

"At least we're among friends," Kit added, trying to make the best of the situation.

"Sure. Friends," Tibbs echoed, unconvinced. Then he added, "Only where are our guns?"

Kit swept the room at a glance. A knot of fear reformed in the pit of his stomach. Tibbs was right about one thing. Their weapons were gone. *If Sergeant Morales and his soldiers came,* Kit thought, *we're completely defenseless.*

"You think we can trust the priest?" Tibbs muttered, eyeing the open doorway and the empty sunlight that had suddenly lost its warmth.

Kit looked from his friend to the window and the brown-skinned men and women of the village who had grouped together to keep the Yankees' cabin under observation.

"I don't think we have a choice," he said.

The next day dawned with a rumble of distant thunder. Kit had rested fitfully, dozing for a while, then lying awake. For the past hour he'd lain motionless, staring at the ceiling and listening to the patter of the summer shower. One by one he had counted the beads of sweat that rolled off his neck and soaked into the cot beneath his head. As dawn's gray light seeped into the hut Kit rose from his bed and managed to stand, swaying in the center of the room. After a few moments he gained his sea legs. A dull ache lingered in his skull, but the pain had lessened enough overnight to convince him he had suffered no permanent damage. He'd been willing to debate the matter earlier. But for now, as long as he could see and walk and he hadn't been clapped in irons by the Spanish, Kit was satisfied.

A loud snore erupted from the opposite side of the room. Bill Tibbs mumbled something in his sleep and then curled over on his side. Kit padded across the room, leaned over his partner, and caught a whiff of Jamaican rum about the same time as his bare toe nudged the cool, brown glass bottle Tibbs had left by his bed. The bottle toppled over, rolled beneath the cot, and clattered off the wall.

"Helped yourself, did you?" Kit accused. "And not so much as a drop for your friend. Ah, Bill Tibbs, you can be a selfish son of a bitch sometimes. Still, we've pulled each other out of tight scrapes and saved one another's neck, so I guess I can pardon your oversight."

Tibbs snored, then smacked his lips, and his long fingers fluttered as if he were clawing at the earth. Kit never considered attempting to rouse his friend. Tibbs had drunk himself into this stupor and time, not man, would have to drag him out of it. Kit left his besotted companion and walked across the room to the table. He started to reach for the treasure pouch, then changed his mind and turned back to his cot, where he retrieved his belt from the foot of his humble bed. He was happy to note his knife was still in its sheath. He slid the six-inch blade from its scabbard. Back at the table Kit discovered half a dozen hollow reeds of varying thickness that Father Ramone had intended to convert into writing pens. Kit selected one, and with knife in hand, he settled himself in the doorway and watched the overcast sky lighten in hue as somewhere beyond the clouds the sun rose above the horizon. Kit worked the blade point into the reed and dug out a series of four evenly spaced holes. From time to time he paused to stare out at the rain-spattered earth, the gray clouds reflected in the puddles, the dull green sheen of the willows and loblolly pines that screened the village from the coast. A couple of Creek braves hurried toward a partly completed coquina brick structure in the center of the village. Kit guessed it to be the mission church.

The Creek men were about Kit's height, and like the seafarer, they were well muscled and moved with quiet, quick steps. Between them, the two braves carried a load of timber into the church structure, with only the merest glance in Kit's direction. They kept their heads bowed to the rain. Kit resumed carving the reed, adding the appropriate air holes and shaving and tapering the mouthpiece. He put the crudely honed instrument to his lips and played a couple of trilling notes. One of the holes needed enlarging, and he went to work on it. He finished, blew away the debris, and tried the flute again. This time the sound came clear and piping and sweet upon the rain-washed air. Kit smiled with satisfaction, then looked up and was surprised to find he was no longer alone.

Maria, the little girl from the beach, and two more of her friends, both boys, peered around the corner at the red-haired stranger in the doorway. One of the boys, a chubby, sweet-faced child with rust-colored eyes, held a makeshift cage in which a seaside sparrow hopped from perch to perch and eyed the world through a cage made of twigs and bound together with strips of cloth. The sparrow's brown plumage was streaked with ashen gray feathers. The feathers on its breast were tinged yellow, and nature had placed a spot like a sunburst between its eyes and gray beak. It sang high-pitched notes to match the flute.

"I am called Kit," Kit managed to say in his fractured Spanish.

"I am Maria," the little girl said. "I found you," she added proudly, as if the Yankee were her very own prize.

"I'm glad you did," Kit told her.

"And this is Mateo and Juan." Kit noted that Mateo held the bird cage while Juan, who seemed a trifle more reticent, stared longingly at the flute. Mateo held up the bird cage for Kit to examine. He proudly described how he had rigged the snare and captured the bird all by himself. Kit understood only snatches of the lad's account, but he nodded approvingly and gave the appearance of being most impressed. All the while Juan scrutinized the man from the sea.

"He does not speak," Maria said, indicating the long-faced boy to her right. "Even after Father Ramone baptized him, he still did not speak," she added, incredulous that no miracle had occurred to give the mute child his voice. She shrugged and took a step toward Kit. "I am not afraid of you."

"Bueno." Kit smiled and placed the flute to his lips. He blew softly, and his fingers danced over the holes to produce a merry tune of his own composing. The music danced upon the rain; the children grinned with delight, and Maria began to dance in little circles. Mateo held his bird cage out so its occupant might sing along with the carefree melody. Only Juan seemed unaffected. However, appearances were deceiving. His appreciation was far more subtle in its display. He remained perfectly still, as one transfixed by the red-headed piper and the tune he played while sitting in the doorway.

Kit finished his song, much to Maria's chagrin.

"Play it again," Mateo said.

"Not me," Kit replied. He pointed the flute at Juan. "Him." He held the flute out to the silent boy. Time seemed to hang still as the child summoned his courage. Then, slowly, he outstretched his arm and opened his fingers. Kit placed the flute in the boy's palm. "Now you have a voice," Kit said. The boy closed his hand and dashed off into the rain, with Maria and Mateo clamoring at his heels. The silent boy was halfway to his parent's jacal when he skidded to a halt in the mud and turned back toward the man in the doorway. He raised the reed flute to his lips and piped a chorus of notes with such wild abandon that his whole body shuddered with the joyous sound. Then he turned and scampered off into the rain.

"You're welcome," Kit said. His head started to throb. The dizziness had returned, though less severe now. Kit decided to weather his discomfort lying down. A thundercrack startled him as he stood in the doorway and braced himself against the wall of the house. Overhead, the storm tracked to the north and loosed a torrential downpour that all but obscured most of the village behind its watery gray sheets. Kit glanced over at Tibbs's still slumbering form. A hurricane could spring up and blow them all away and Tibbs wouldn't stir. Kit had to admire the potency of the padre's rum.

The cot creaked and groaned as Kit stretched out, folded his hands behind his head, and closed his eyes. With nothing but the droning downpour to relax him, Kit's thoughts turned to home, the Hound and Hare Inn on the Trenton Road. His father, Daniel McQueen, a veteran of the War for Independence, had cared little for the bickering between political factions that oftentimes divided the populace. He had retired to the life of a blacksmith—honest labor, he called it. Kate

McQueen, Kit's mother, took care of the inn. She had a daughter to help her, while Kit labored alongside his father at the forge, working iron and learning to shape steel to his will. Kit heard once more his father's strong, truthful voice speak in his soul, touching young Kit with words of caution and encouragement. Captured like some living portrait in his mind, Kit watched the embers of a forge glow with life. He saw himself, a twelve-year-old boy, working the bellows. He cried out with glee as he sent a column of sparks like a whirlwind of miniature suns coruscating up into the black iron chimney.

These were good memories, the kind that anchored a man when he might be feeling hurt or lost and alone. They carried Kit into a place of rest and healing. The sound of the rain faded. Asleep, he did not even hear the storm slacken, the downpour lessen until it became no more than a fine, settling mist. Asleep, he did not hear the patter of footsteps across the puddled ground, nor could he be aware yet of the giggles and whispered asides of the children, all ten of them who had followed Juan and Mateo and Maria back to the hut. There the children crowded around the door to wait in respectful silence for the red-haired flutemaker to awaken—ten children with hollow reeds in their hands and hearts full of expectation.

"Why do the young die?" Father Ramone muttered softly with a sigh. "Why does anyone die?" He stared down at the two-week-old grave of a young man who had been bitten by a cottonmouth and succumbed to the poison before reaching the village. "Joseph was my first altar boy. I myself taught him to read and write. He wanted very much to be a priest." Father Ramone glanced at the Yankee standing at his side. It was late afternoon and Kit had been looking for the Franciscan for the better part of an hour. He'd misinterpreted little

Maria's directions and been forced to retrace his steps after becoming lost on the edge of the very same swamps that had claimed Joseph's life. It was only by sheer chance Kit had stumbled onto the Creek burial ground where the priest was wont to visit and read from the worn, leatherbound bible he carried.

"Answering that question is your job, padre. Not mine," McQueen replied.

"Perhaps you are right, my young friend," the priest conceded. "Then again, I have often suspected there is no answer. Only the search for it, as we seek the truth of our lives." Ramone placed his hand over the crucifix he wore. A gentle breeze tousled his thin, silvery hair and rustled the voluminous sleeves and hem of his coarse brown robe. "The cross is the only truth I know," Father Ramone added and he snapped his bible shut. He folded his arms across his bony chest and studied the Yankee he had rescued from the rising tide. "What truth do you know?"

Kit shrugged. Like most young men he intended to live forever. Thoughts of the hereafter were the farthest things from his mind. He believed in his quickness, in his strength and daring. He believed in the power of dreams and what a man might accomplish if he remained watchful and resolute.

"I believe, my friend, that I will leave tomorrow," Kit said. "We have been hiding for three days. We dare not stay longer."

Kit noted the padre did not try to hide his relief. He couldn't blame the priest, having the Yankees in the village threatened the very survival of the mission settlement. For three days, McQueen and Tibbs had remained in hiding, allowing their wounds to heal until both men felt well enough to travel. Oh, the two adventurers were still sore and hardly up to their full strength but Tibbs had declared he was confident of their ability to make the journey home. And Kit had agreed. Anyway, they were bound to find a settlement along the Georgia coast in which to heal the last of their hurts. What mattered now was getting underway. Everyday they remained in the village heightened the risk of discovery.

"I will have my people prepare food for your journey," Father Ramone told him.

"My thanks, padre. And while you are at it, why don't you have them return our guns?" Kit matter of factly added. He carefully watched the priest's expression, searching his features for any sign of duplicity.

Father Ramone did glance up rather sharply and he started to protest. But lies had no place on his lips. "Guns. I suppose I must." He sighed and hooked a thumb in the rope belt circling his waist. "I thought it best to keep them until you were ready to leave. Creeks have learned the ways of peace unlike most white men. I took your guns in hopes of protecting them." Father Ramone glanced up at the black willows and oak trees in the cemetery that were alive with the antics of the gray squirrels, chattering and scolding one another while dark winged birds darted among the branches and multicolored butterflies fluttered lazy spirals in the warm summer air.

"Do you know," the priest continued. "Saint Francis of Assisi could call the birds from the treetops and the animals from the depths of the forest. He would sing to them, talk to them, and tell them of the love of their creator." Father Ramone looked at Kit. "I have walked this clearing day after day in prayer and have yet to summon so much as a bee from a flower." The old man in the brown robe made a soft, sibilant sound as he exhaled. Father Ramone spoke like a man questioning his belief, Kit thought to himself, yet Kit doubted the padre had even begun to tap the depths of his faith.

"You've made your mark, Padre. I wouldn't worry about whether or not you can charm the birds from the treetops," Kit said.

"My mark...." Father Ramone muttered ruefully. "Is that what a man should live for? Is that what you think?"

"That or for gold. And the power it can bring," Kit said.

"I do not think you know yourself as well as you think you do," Father Ramone replied. "I have seen you, carving flutes for the children as they gathered at your door. The heart speaks that which lips often deny. I trust a man's heart." With a gesture of his hand he led the way back to the path that wound through the woods to the village. Kit started to follow, then paused, noticing the grave marker of Augustus LaFarge. Memories of the coarse, good-humored sailor returned. Poor LaFarge, he deserved better than to drown so close to home. But there were worse places to await the unfolding of eternity than here amid the willows and oaks and pines, here where the play of the distant tide lingered on the wind, here where flowers bloomed and an old priest came to pray and consider the meaning of life. At least LaFarge had a marker, which was more than could be said for the rest of the Trenton's crew.

"Augustus, sleep well. You know the truth of it now, I warrant." Kit turned and started after the padre. Father Ramone waited for him near a fallen log that had rotted away from the inside. A swarm of bees had chosen to build a hive within that brittle cover of bark.

"He lies in sanctified ground," the priest said, nodding toward LaFarge's grave.

Kit had to laugh. "Padre, old Augustus had a lot of attributes. But sanctified wasn't one of them."

"It is now," Father Ramone retorted, nonplussed. He stroked his silver goatee and smiled. "I am glad I did not hand you over to Sergeant Morales." He had begun to like this young man. Where Bill Tibbs was guarded and suspicious of every overture, Kit McQueen had ventured among the people of the village and treated the Creek with respect.

"But you won't be sorry to see me leave, either," Kit reminded him.

"No," the priest conceded. "But one day, perhaps, you will return and—"

"Father Ramone!" the priest straightened, a look of concern on his face. The voice that had called him with such urgency belonged to little Maria.

The girl appeared, breathless, out of the green gloom at the east end of the path where the tall grass grew in patches and sunlight struggled through the moss-draped trees to illuminate the woods' shadowy interior.

Father Ramone hurried as best he could toward the girl. Maria spied the familiar figure in the brown robe and ran to him as fast as her little brown legs could carry her.

"What is it now, my child?" the priest said, exasperated, as the girl ran to his open arms. Kit felt the goose bumps rise on the back of his neck. An image of the village beset by a detachment of Spanish troops from St. Augustine flashed through his mind. But the danger this afternoon came from a different source, one Kit knew only too well. The girl blurted out her message in a mixture of Spanish and Creek. Kit was unable to follow her. He waited patiently for Father Ramone to translate for him.

"It is her brother, Esteban. She fears for his safety," the priest reported worriedly. He glared up at the patch of blue sky. *Madre de Dios*," he muttered. "Esteban has been watching and waiting for you and Senor Tibbs to leave your hut. He told Maria he intended to help himself to one of your yellow metal bracelets."

"He better hope Bill Tibbs doesn't discover him," Kit said. His friend hadn't been the same since Derna. And the disastrous shipwreck, with the loss of so much of their treasure, certainly hadn't helped. Perhaps when they were safely out of Florida and strolling the streets of Charleston, dressed in finery, Tibbs would see things in a more favorable light. Part of the treasure was better than none at all.

"Come, my young friend," Father Ramone said. "Perhaps we will be in time to stop trouble before it begins."

By the time the priest and Kit reached the clearing and the circle of huts that made up the Creek village, things had already gone from bad to worse. The braves of the village, those who were not down by the beach tending their nets, were gathered outside the hut where Kit and Tibbs had recuperated. The men and several of the women clustered by the door of the hut were visibly angry. The men were armed with wicked-looking war clubs inlaid with jagged pieces of shell that could deliver a nasty wound when wielded by an irate warrior. Word spread among the villagers that Father Ramone had returned. The priest and Kit quickly became the center of attention. Father Ramone stopped to talk to the first braves he met in order to find out for himself what had happened. Kit continued through the crowd that grudgingly parted before him until he was almost to the hut. Then a broad-shouldered Creek warrior blocked the white man's path. The brave looked to be several years older than Kit. He wore a headdress of shells and plumage woven together. His war club sported not only a ragged line of razor-sharp shells but a wicked row of shark teeth inlaid in the wood where it curved to form a wicked crook.

Kit was unarmed save for the knife in his boot sheath, but he wasn't about to back away. He had the distinct impression that any show of weakness on his part might bring him a crushed skull. He met the warrior's stare and waited for the man to make his move. To his surprise and relief the brave stepped aside. Kit moved past the man and halted a couple of yards from the door.

"Come ahead, Kit," Tibbs shouted from within. "I found our guns in the padre's hut. I've got them loaded and primed."

Shadows had begun to steal across the land as the sun sank beyond the trees and disappeared into a pool of incandescent orange and vermilion clouds.

"Bill, come out here!"

"Like hell."

"Bill, come out and tell me what happened."

Movement in the doorway, a shift of shadows, then Tibbs materialized in the doorway, guns dangling at the ends of his long arms. Another brace of pistols was tucked in his belt. His dark eyes surveyed the crowd. His nostrils flared as he readied himself to fight. "All right! You satisfied? I searched the priest's quarters and found our guns. When I arrived back here I caught one of these little heathens trying to rob us. I gave him the back of my hand and chased him out. The next thing I know, the whole damn village is standing outside the door clamoring for my head. I showed them my guns, though, and none of them wanted to be the first to taste lead."

Kit closed his eyes a moment and shook his lowered head. Tibbs was going to get them both killed. Somehow he had to defuse the situation. How?

"The man who blocked your path is Esteban's father," Father Ramone said, moving up on Kit's left. The Franciscan priest folded his arms across his chest.

"It is an unheard-of thing for an adult to strike a child among these people." The padre began to stroke his goatee. "Unheard of," he repeated absently. "Now Esteban has run off, and I don't—"

But Kit had already begun to act. He headed straight for the hut and forced Tibbs to retreat as he entered. Tibbs misread his intentions, thinking his friend had come to help in the defense of the hut.

"Good," Tibbs said. "If we charge them together they'll probably give way." He tried to pass a pair of the flintlocks to Kit.

"Don't be ridiculous," Kit said. He untied the leather pouch on the table and dug into its contents. Gold bracelets and jeweled necklaces clinked and rattled off one another.

"What are you doing?" Tibbs asked, a scowl on his face. His features began to pale. "Oh, no...."

"Saving our lives," Kit replied. He selected a broad band of pounded gold and retraced his steps outside before Tibbs could even sputter a protest. Kit headed straight for the brave with whom he had almost come to blows. The warrior kept a tight grip on his war club. He suspected the white man of treachery, despite the fact that Father Ramone spoke soothingly in the man's ear, keeping his voice soft as he asked the warrior to give Kit a chance to prove himself.

Kit stopped directly in front of the warrior. He glanced at the padre. "What is his name?"

"He is called Isaiah. That is his Christian name."

"Tell Isaiah that my friend is not well. That his hurt inside caused him to harm the boy. Say that we wish to offer Isaiah a gift to honor him and his family." Kit waited for the priest to translate, and when Father Ramone stopped talking Kit held out the golden bracelet. It gleamed in the light of the setting sun. The band of precious metal was etched with winged serpentlike creatures the likes of which could only be found in myth.

The brave accepted the golden band and reverently slipped it onto his wrist. Then he held up his right arm so that all the men and women around him might see. Everyone was suitably impressed. The warrior turned back to Kit. He nodded and placed the war club at Kit's feet. Kit, relying on instinct, picked the war club off the ground and returned the weapon to the brave. Isaiah grunted his approval, then swung around and started back through the crowd that had already begun to disperse.

Father Ramone remained behind. "You did well, my son." He looked past Kit to Tibbs, who remained in the doorway, glowering. "I will find Esteban. Then I will see to food and water for your journey. Rest now. You will need your strength tomorrow." The old priest turned and joined those he called his "savage children" as cook fires were lit and life in the village returned to normal.

Kit started back toward the hut, where Tibbs waited, speechless and flushed with anger. Before he could vent his rage, Kit went after him.

"Let it be, Bill. Just let it be. This gold means as much to me as it does to you. But one trinket isn't worth our lives." Kit crossed to the table and poured himself a drink from the water jug that had been left for them along with a platter of smoked bluefish and fry bread. "You've changed, my friend. For the worse. It will bring you ruin."

Kit sat on the edge of his cot and waited for the inevitable outburst. To his surprise, it never came. Instead, Tibbs slumped on the cot across from him and leaned forward on his elbows.

"Hell, you're right, Kit," Tibbs said. He wiped a hand across his face, breathed in deep, and exhaled slow and easy. "I'm sorry." His darkly handsome face suddenly split with a grin. "Maybe it's because I had so many dreams and now we're back where we started, after almost two years, with nothing to show for it."

"Nothing?" Kit said. He stood, walked over to the table, and held up the jeweled scimitar that had once belonged to Alexander the Great. A golden shaft of sunlight poured into the hut as the setting sun seemed to hang suspended between a gap in the trees. A beam of light washed over Tibbs and made it seem as if he were afire, as if he had become one with the precious wealth he had hungered for and would kill to protect.

"Like I said, Kit. You're right," Tibbs repeated. He held out his hand and stood so he towered over Kit. "Friends?"

Kit clasped Tibbs's offered hand. "We've never been anything else, you hardheaded, quick-tempered bastard," he said with a grin. The sunlight faded. Then darkness began to creep into the room.

TERRY C. JOHNSTON

Winner of the prestigious Western Writer's award, Terry C. Johnston brings you his award-winning saga of mountain men Josiah Paddock and Titus Bass who strive together to meet the challenges of the western wilderness in the 1830's.

☐ 25572 **CARRY THE WIND–Vol. I** $4.95

☐ 26224 **BORDERLORDS–Vol. II** $4.95

☐ 28139 **ONE-EYED DREAM–Vol. III** $4.95

The final volume in the trilogy begun with *Carry the Wind* and *Borderlords*, ONE-EYED DREAM is a rich, textured tale of an 1830's trapper and his protegé, told at the height of the American fur trade.

Following a harrowing pursuit by vengeful Arapaho warriors, mountain man Titus "Scratch" Bass and his apprentice Josiah Paddock must travel south to old Taos. But their journey is cut short when they learn they must return to St. Louis…and old enemies.

Look for these books wherever Bantam books are sold, or use this handy coupon for ordering:

In The Tradition of *Wagons West* and *The Spanish Bit Saga* Comes:

RIVERS WEST

- ☐ 27401 **The Yellowstone #1**
  Winfred Blevins $3.95
- ☐ 28012 **Smokey Hill #2**
  Don Coldsmith $3.95
- ☐ 28451 **The Colorado #3**
  Gary McCarthy $3.95
- ☐ 28538 **The Powder River #4**
  Winfred Blevins $3.95
- ☐ 28844 **The Russian River #5**
  Gary McCarthy $4.50

Buy them at your local bookstore or use this handy page for ordering:

Bantam Books, Dept. RW, 414 East Golf Road, Des Plaines, IL 60016

Please send me the items I have checked above. I am enclosing $_____
(please add $2.50 to cover postage and handling). Send check or money
order, no cash or C.O.D.s please.

Mr/Ms _____

Address _____

City/State _____ Zip _____

RW–2/91

Please allow four to six weeks for delivery.
Prices and availability subject to change without notice.

A Proud People In a Beautiful Land

THE SPANISH BIT SAGA

Set on the Great Plains of North America in the 16th through 18th centuries, Don Coldsmith's acclaimed series recreates a time, a place and a people that have been nearly lost to history. Here is history in the making through the eyes of the proud Native Americans who lived it.

☐	BOOK 1: TRAIL OF THE SPANISH BIT	26397-8	$3.50
☐	BOOK 2: THE ELK-DOG HERITAGE	26412-5	$2.95
☐	BOOK 3: FOLLOW THE WIND	26806-6	$2.95
☐	BOOK 4: BUFFALO MEDICINE	26938-0	$2.95
☐	BOOK 5: MAN OF THE SHADOWS	27067-2	$2.95
☐	BOOK 6: DAUGHTER OF THE EAGLE	27209-8	$2.95
☐	BOOK 7: MOON OF THUNDER	27344-2	$2.95
☐	BOOK 8: THE SACRED HILLS	27460-0	$2.95
☐	BOOK 9: PALE STAR	27604-2	$2.95
☐	BOOK 10: RIVER OF SWANS	27708-1	$2.95
☐	BOOK 11: RETURN TO THE RIVER	28163-1	$2.95
☐	BOOK 12: THE MEDICINE KNIFE	28318-9	$3.50
☐	BOOK 13: THE FLOWER IN THE MOUNTAINS	28538-6	$3.50
☐	BOOK 14: TRAIL FROM TAOS	28760-5	$3.50
☐	SUPER: THE CHANGING WIND	28334-0	$3.95
☐	SUPER: THE TRAVELER	28868-7	$4.50